Seek the Living

Seek the Living

A NOVEL

Ashley Warlick

Houghton Mifflin Company

BOSTON   NEW YORK   2005

For information about permission to reproduce
selections from this book, write to Permissions,
Houghton Mifflin Company, 215 Park Avenue South,
New York, New York 10003.

Visit our Web site: www.houghtonmifflinbooks.com.

Library of Congress Cataloging-in-Publication Data
Warlick, Ashley.
Seek the living / by Ashley Warlick.
    p.   cm.
ISBN 0-618-34148-X
1. Young women — Fiction. 2. Women archivists — Fiction.
3. Brothers and sisters — Fiction. 4. Cemetery managers —
Fiction. 5. Southern states — Fiction. I. Title.
PS3573.A7617S44 2005
813'.54 — dc22   2004058830

Book design by Melissa Lotfy

Printed in the United States of America

QUM 10 9 8 7 6 5 4 3 2 1

For my brother, his wife, and their child

She thought to herself, "This is now."
She was glad that the cosy house, and
Pa and Ma and the firelight and the music,
were now. They could not be forgotten,
she thought, because now is now. It can
never be a long time ago.

— LAURA INGALLS WILDER,
Little House in the Big Woods

Seek the Living

1

WHEN THE SUN goes down, my brother and Hedy sit on the front porch and look out over the gravestones, through the bony November trees and beyond the road. The air is not warm with late fall, and they clutch sweaters around their shoulders, wear blue jeans and work boots, and from where they sit, throughout the cemetery, there are piles of leaves.

They have worked all day and now they rest, a fire barrel blazing full, cold bottles of beer in their hands. When I drive up the lane, I see Hedy has just lit a smoke. The flare of her lighter comes up out of the rising night, and she hands the cigarette to Den.

He's seen me coming too.

He lopes off the porch, a horse in man's clothing, all rolling, handsome motion. He rests his elbows on the open window of my car and hands me Hedy's cigarette, which I rub in the pinch of my fingers.

"Boo," he says.

"Oh. You got me."

"Yeah. Later, we'll tell stories, and I'll hold a flashlight to my chin. You'll likely wet your pants."

Even in this lazy light, his chin looks as if he took a file to it. There's a bruise on his cheek, a stitched place above his eye, welted and red. He grins at me, but then his gaze slips past my face and through the churchyard to the highway, as if he expects someone is to follow.

"Where's Marshall?" he says.

I flip my palm over and leave it open. This is to mean Missouri or New York or Apalachicola—who knows. Marshall tracks disasters for a big insurance company; he goes wherever something horrible has happened and measures the loss. The insurance company trained him out of college, when he might have been a doctor or an architect, and his understanding of buildings and what brings them down is still tied to the lines of a blueprint. He says you can tell as much about a structure from its pieces as you can from its whole. When he compliments a woman, it's on her carriage, or her bones.

He is never home, but I knew this when I married him and loved him so much I thought I wouldn't mind. It has not proved to be the truth, but I hold myself responsible. There was a time when I thought whatever I could get would be enough.

What I've got right now is Denny. A week ago, he got pulled through the window of his car by a bunch of guys he did not know. Hedy was driving, it was night, they'd had a few beers and were stopped at the light in town. A man stuck his face in the window and asked Den if he had a problem. Den and Hedy just laughed, and then there were six more guys holding him down and Den was looking at Hedy, then the pavement, and then the inside of a concussion. He yelled at Hedy to drive off, but she was busy rolling up her window on some man's arm come in to get her, and did not have the chance.

They went to the hospital and got stitches in Den's eye, some questions from the cops, but there's not much to be done. Denny says he never got a good look at the guys, and he acts as if he doesn't care.

"Does it hurt?" I say.

He shrugs, toes his boot at the door of my car. "Is that what brought you down here?"

"It's not so far to come."

"So I shouldn't get a big head about it."

"Oh, no. Don't do that."

His face is close, and I reach out to brush my free hand across his stitches. He doesn't flinch, but that's never been a measure of things with Denny.

I ask him again if it hurts, this time softly, to have an answer. The smoke from the cigarette laces the air between us.

"It's a small town," he says. "Half of it is husbands."

This is the most I know about the cause of such a thing, because Den is quiet and keeps his own counsel, most of it with women he should know better first. Hedy is the latest, and she lives here with him, probably has for some time. She hangs back on the porch, standing, brushing the seat of her jeans, a long whisk of blond braid at her back. Den tells me she's in the habit of erasing other women's messages she gets off the machine, so he was not expecting me today.

"I'm sorry," I say.

He shrugs it off: not my fault, not my problem.

"When I call, I should first say I'm your sister?"

"Oh." He looks back to the porch, to Hedy's arms crossed over her chest. "I imagine that's been done before."

"Right. So what, then?"

"So stay." He grins. "My sheets are clean."

This is a kind of joke, because before he got beat up, he had a job at the laundry for the university and his days were all clean sheets. It had been a decent job, a matter of flat iron and delivery truck, the heavy, even pressure of heat. He worked beside old ladies and black men and students in hock, and I think he liked being one of them, his time laid out in plain terms: what was dirty to be cleaned, what was wrinkled to be pressed, what was not his to be delivered to whomever it belonged. There was an exchange student from India who once told Den he should come back to Delhi and open a laundry there because, cleanliness being next to godliness, he said Den would be a king.

"All that gone by, Denny. Think of what you're giving up."

He takes the cigarette back, as I'm just wasting it.

"What's a boy to do," he says.

He unfolds himself from the door of the car and pops the latch for me to get out. I would have stayed anyway, even without his offer, because I've made the hour's drive down here to talk to him and we are not the sort of family that requires invitations. Too, I know how men are about the giving and receiving of pain, which is to say generous, and women seem to be their favorite solace. For men like Den, sisters are the safer place to look for such.

I have always felt this way about my brother, like I am the last, best place he comes, and so, sometimes, I come to him. So now, he reaches out and takes me in his arms for a long hug, rubs my back with it, and I feel special to him, as though he wants me here and has missed me, and I know that's all part of his trouble with women, the trouble he's in right now, that he can make that feeling even for his sister. I whisper into his shoulder that I am glad he's okay. He says, *Me too,* and it's like he means it, all of it, and now we can go back to the task at hand.

It's things like this, moments between us that make small sense in small ways, that make me think Den will be himself again for me.

When our father called about Den getting beat up, he'd decided it was a good lesson for a son to learn.

"In the paper, just last week," he said, "some family drives down the wrong street and the daughter gets shot—*blam.* Right out of the back seat. I'm telling you, Joanie, a man's got to have thick skin—"

"Yeah, but Daddy, all that family did was drive their car. Den was driving his car."

"That's not true. Some girl was driving his car."

"So what are you saying, drive your own car?"

He sighed. "No, kitten. I'm saying when I grew up, I could walk into a crowd of twelve drunk niggers and call them niggers and be fine, but nowadays, such will get your face beat."

"As well it should."

"Yes," he said. "I am too old for drunks anymore."

Our father, in his college office. He calls a spade a spade, or

4

whatever else suits his purpose at the time, all stories being flexible, biblical in relation to the truth. He says Den is digging a hole for himself and not coming out, that he wants to make whatever he might need to live on through the mail. He says Den hasn't licked a stamp in thirty years, that he might not even know how to use a mailbox, let alone get money from one, and what's the boy think, money comes in envelopes? He told me to get over here and straighten Denny out, as if it were something I could do with five minutes and a pair of pliers. And that's the thing about our father: he hasn't fixed anything that required more care than pliers in quite a while.

"Den's gone sour," Daddy said. "And that little lady he's shacked up with is jailbait city."

This is the first I've met Hedy. She is soft-looking, a sigh of a girl. She asks me how my trip was, shakes my hand and kisses my cheek at the same time. She does seem younger than I expected, but of the same sort Denny is always fond of, as though he's always had the same girlfriend, only under different light, at different times in her life.

She holds my hand as if we are still meeting, her palm hard in the spots that hold things, and already I'm trying to guess what work she might do to so mistreat her skin. It's a bad habit, and later I'll have trouble reconciling what is really her and what I have made up. I pull away, brush my hair from my face and keep it behind my ear with my fingers, as if the time I have for hand-holding is over.

"So," I say. "You're at the university?"

Yes. She's been in and out, most recently in mortuary studies, but that was not for her. I think of the damp, greenish basement rooms in Long Hall, the cadavers stored in tanks, like underwatered fish. Something must cross my face, because she tells me, really, she's a very happy person.

"I often feel like blue sky over the ocean," she says, and she smiles so I am given to believe her.

She pulls out the neck of her T-shirt and shows me the bruise on her shoulder from when they got jumped, and it's still blue and green and shaped like fingertips. I tell her that must have hurt and she says she's just worried for Den. This is sweet, and I want to say something in kind. Instead, I tell her what our father said about lesson-learning.

"And just think," she says. "That man's blood is in your body."

She looks squarely at me when she says this and there comes a pause in our hospitalities, the way we have been extending ourselves, one to the other. Something about her gaze, so fair and steady, I have to wonder what else Den's been telling her about our family.

The house squats on a rise above the cemetery, and it's Denny's free of charge if he keeps the grounds, opens the Old Stone Church for holidays. In the kitchen, the stove needs rewiring and Den has its innards spread over the floor such that we have to pick our way through to the bourbon, then back to the porch where there's more room and a view. We sit in rocking chairs, drink from jelly jars, watch the sun finish its set. We listen to Al Green, before he was Reverend Al, get next to us from the old Philco radio at Denny's feet. There is the sense the night could pass just this peacefully.

Den touches at his face from time to time, and I can see where his skin stretches tight across his brow bones. He has the look of a proto-man, fresh from the ice or the lava rock or the peat bog. When the phone rings inside the house, he and Hedy both just let it go.

"So, what'd the doctor say?" I ask him.

"He said it could have been worse. He said, 'Son, a man who is not with a woman is a dead man.'"

"In this situation, perhaps."

"I got the idea he was speaking generally."

"I've seen *Grand Hotel* too, Denny. You can find a doctor who'll say anything."

He shrugs. "So what?"

"Den's just upset because he has enemies," I say.

He says, "If I got upset over something like this," but then he trails off, and I wonder what he thinks upset looks like, if this is not it.

We stare out into the churchyard and cemetery, the white stones caught in the slow light. We try to pretend we are alone, each with another but not all three of us together, and this takes concentration. We can hear the cars passing on the highway, the call of dogs from another yard. When something moves, we all turn to it at once: Den's black cat, snaking her way out of a crack in the floor of the porch, a trapdoor leading to the hard pack root cellar below.

"What in God's name do you keep down there?" I say.

"Nothing."

"It's creepy, an open hole like that."

"It came with the house."

"An open hole in a graveyard."

He blocks his words carefully. "It came with the house."

"In the paper, just last week," I say, "there was an article about this guy whose hot tub came with his house. He started a kind of neighborhood spa, just for something to do with it. He called it a spa, at least. He's being arraigned on pandering charges. I don't think you're using your space here as profitably as you might be, Denny."

"Oh, you're smart."

"And you're sulking, for chrissakes."

He gets up to start a new fire in the barrel.

"Denny."

But the screen door slams behind him, and I can see the fat strokes of heat on his wrists and forearms, the yellow of his bruised face gone masklike in the firelight. The fire does not need him, but he keeps at it anyway, to keep away from me, and I feel this small, self-inflicted ache open in my chest. Sometimes I just want to be next to him, want it way down inside me like I would live with him if I could, be his sister for always and always in his home, his good graces, his closest confidence.

Hedy stares out after Denny into the night. She watches him

like a cat watching a pond. I wonder if he knows this, or if I will have to bring it up too.

"Be careful, Denny," she says, "with the fire."

He doesn't answer her either.

She turns to look at me, and I make that small open gesture with my hand, a kind of shrug, a kind of there-you-have-it. She just keeps looking at me, level and water blue, until I feel completely adrift.

I say, "I get nervous around fires," although this is not particularly the case.

She tells me a story about a woman who died up in Seneca because of a broken air conditioner in the middle of July. It was between a hundred and twenty and a hundred and thirty degrees in her house. Plastic melted in her kitchen. Hedy handled the body in mortuary school, and it's the reason she quit.

"I'd fucking sue," Den says, folding himself back into his chair, but Hedy just smiles, and it's as if he never left.

"I rebuilt her face to look like Loretta Lynn," she tells me. "It was an exercise from a photograph, and, I swear, I nailed it. But if you use the embalming fluid in black people that you've made up for white people, it turns black people green."

"How green?" I say.

"Greener than green. And there's nothing you can do to turn them black again."

"So what do you do then?"

"Drop out of mortuary school."

Currently, she keeps a chicken coop on the edge of the property, cochins and leghorns and some kind of fancy chickens with blue feathers in their crests whose name she can't recall. She's taking husbandry classes at the university and she's come across our father there, says he's a hardass with no appreciation for sustainable management, which is something we already knew.

But that brings up the subject of our father.

"I'm supposed to tell you you've got to do something, Denny. Get off your duff."

"And go where?"

"I was told to remind you of your age, your education foundering away in your head, your slim chances of—I believe it was finding a corner in this town you haven't already pissed in. There's quite a bit to say on the subject of geography, and horses, and—"

"Gift horses or dead horses?"

"He's worried, Denny, he really is," I say.

"Worried?"

"Yes." And then, "In his way."

Denny takes a sip from his glass, studies the laces on his boots. His face becomes as plain as a clock's.

"Right," he says. "All kinds of horses."

This is not a good answer, not an answer that will get us anywhere tonight, or tomorrow, not anything I haven't heard before, and I swallow to press against the creeping in my guts. I feel as though I've let him down and not the other way around, but it's just a feeling. I would like to bear more weight here than I do.

The truth is, this standoff is between Denny and our father, and it's talked about in terms of horses, of chickens hatching and with their heads cut off, in terms of wild geese and wild oats and wild hares up asses, but it's about the farm. We grew up on seventy-five acres north of here, which our father sold last winter, a decision he kept to himself so long that the sale became a sleight of hand; Den thought the farm would always be there, and now it's not. That's the pearl of it, anyway, and I've come to think it's the hard thing way down inside most boys, such unlikely disappearances, something as solid as land vanished before their very eyes.

A year ago, Denny had a cell phone, a sports car, a speed boat, and a day job where wealthy people depended on his services. He lived in a sprawling southern city that lit up at night, right off the rim of his balcony, and there were dates and dinners and sports teams he kept tabs on, all kinds of honest efforts he made. He was a charming man. But when the farm was sold, something snapped, the kind of deep, compound snapping that changes lives, and Denny left all that. He came home to where his home was sold, and most of what's gone wrong extends from there.

Daddy made the arrangements for the house in the cemetery, as though the problem was one of shelter. So Denny started up a thing with a dean's wife, which Daddy ignored, he wrecked a few cars, which Daddy ignored, and then he quit his laundry job, without notice. They quit speaking to each other, then Denny got the shit beat out of him. It's a gesture that thankfully lacks our father's sense of fair play, although I have to confess, up until I saw the bruises on Hedy's shoulder, the thought had crossed my mind.

I am here now because I'm worried. Not just for Denny, but for myself, our family, how this rift has gone unchecked so long that it's infected everything it's touched, and even before our father called there were nights I wanted to drive down here and have it out with Denny, pester and beg, whatever it took. All I know is, this is how you stop speaking to your father, to your son. There are families that completely come apart over less.

Den looks up from his boots, his eyes as melted sweet as I ever remember, and I let out a heavy breath.

"I don't know," I say. "You could run around here with your shoelaces untied. Refuse to zip your jacket in the wind. He might come chew you out himself."

"Kiss my ass, Joanie."

We laugh as if it's another country heard from, but I'd really thought my being here might make a difference to him, the way the right light can make a difference, a good night's rest and everything looks different in the morning. I drain my bourbon to the ice. I wish I could say it's just too soon to tell.

There's a banging at the back door and Denny jumps to it, Hedy close behind. I follow through the kitchen, and blue lights drill the hunks of things left sharp and broken in the otherwise darkness. It's a cop, with papers or a blackjack, a bench warrant for something I haven't even thought of yet: harassment, stalking, alienation of affection. Den opens the door, his thumb beating nervous time on the stile. Hedy stands nearby so she can listen.

She sees me watching her.

She crosses the room as if we are finally alone and have been waiting to be alone all night, and maybe it's the bourbon we've been drinking that makes her seem so urgent. I fix on the floor, the elements and wiring from the stove cast around our feet, so close together. She bends my ear to her lips and whispers.

"There's a woman who comes here," she says. "She walks from town and finds her way inside. I lock the doors and windows, but we wake up or we get home, and she's waiting, or she's been here. I know Den won't turn her out into the cemetery. I try to understand."

"What for?" I say, and I mean it all the way around.

"I don't know—maybe it's not so bad as it seems. A man calls for her, and he doesn't sound angry. He talks about her like she's lost. I would put my foot down, but then I think how she's just lost, and ended up here, like a dog or something. All that way from town. Again and again."

There is not a trace of guile in Hedy's face to say this, just the smooth coolness she seems to own the rights to, and I feel as if I'm stepping through a hole in their lives and falling.

"We've just begun this thing," she says. "I imagine it will take some getting used to."

For a moment, I think she is talking about herself and me, something we've begun here in the kitchen, but she's not. She goes to Denny, puts her hand over his and pushes the door flush against the wall. Her arm slides down around his hips. She leans her cheek to his shoulder and I have to turn away.

The kitchen is a mess, dishes piled in the drainboard, fruit softening on the countertops. I bend down and look into the blackness of the oven. When you get involved in other people's business, something you have no right to do anyhow, you have to be prepared to handle what you find without their help. I feel unsuited to my present task and I want to pull in my hands and feet, to be careful with myself and let that get me through.

I listen to them talking in the doorway. The cop asks Den if anybody hit him with a weapon, a pipe, a piece of the car, but he says he can't remember, he couldn't be sure. Really, they were all over him. The cop rattles something hard against his teeth, like a bottle cap or a piece of candy. Den scuffs his toe on the jamb; Hedy laughs. I walk out to where they stand and cross my arms over my chest. I recognize the cop; I dated him in high school.

"Hey, Stewart," I say. "How you been?"

"Well. Joan Patee, queeny bee."

"It's Mackie, now."

"Yeah?" He takes the sucker out of his jaw and smiles. "I got two kids. You beat that?"

"I don't believe I can, Stewart."

We all raise our hands as he rolls his cruiser down the drive.

Den seems chipper now. We decide we are hungry and take my car into the night, Den driving and too fast, through peach orchards and mill towns and long flat stretches of pasture. This is the country we grew up in, the same orchards and towns and pastures that have been here for a hundred years. We round another turn and I am struck by Denny on this same road when we were kids, the windows down or the top thrown back, and it's night and it's cold and we are going just as fast, but to make it somewhere on time, to make it home.

I ask him what Stewart had to say, but he just tells me everything is slick, and then he swerves across the center line to avoid something in his lane. Hedy says for him to slow down, for goodness' sakes, but he doesn't. I'm clutching the strap above the window and I can see in the sideview mirror, she's got her head back on the seat and her hand in her shirt, underneath her shirt, on her skin, against her heart. In the light of a coming car, I see her belly is flat and hard, the center line traced with a filigree tattoo.

I don't know what would bring a woman down a highway from her nice warm house in town, night after night after night, but there's something to admire in any kind of determination. Women are made to carry, to keep, to raise, and any talent can be ill spent. I can guess one thing about her though, this woman who appears in Denny's house; she and that man who calls for her don't have children of their own. I've come to think it's those loves you are born to, the ones you bear out, that keep you tethered, rather than the ones you pick yourself. And it's not that I don't love my husband, but here I am, in this dark, hurtling car with Denny at the wheel. Here I am, still hunting for the right thing to say, when it's long been clear that words are just a waste of time.

"I want to ask you something, Denny."

He leans over the seat as if I could whisper in his ear.

"The woman Hedy was telling me about. You invite her to the house, or you just don't want to be rude?"

He's staring at me with that look he has that could burn through paper, but I won't give him anything. In the sideview mirror, Hedy's lips are moving: *please slow down, please slow down, please.*

Nobody speaks out loud, the rest of the drive.

We go to a fish camp for supper and the lights are bright and greenish on our skin. We order perch and catfish, vinegar slaw and pickles and hushpuppies and quart-size glasses of sweet tea. The waitress is soft and loose in her uniform. She knows our father, but she doesn't recognize us without him. He always takes her by the waist and tells us they dated when he was in high school, but that can't be true as she looks about fifty years older than him. By the register there are scatters of children set upon the candy racks, as if Sugar Daddies are as necessary to life as water.

Walking to the table, Den put his hand to Hedy's waist but she stepped out of it. She sits next to me in the booth, stares into the restaurant as if her body is just left behind.

"What'd you get last time?" Den says, and she doesn't answer.

"I remember you liked it, didn't you? Hey. Didn't you."

I stay out of it, and study the calendar on the paper place mat, every day described in red. Today is the twenty-eighth, the new moon, a good time to go for bass. Den talks louder at her, trimming his words closely. By the fourth time around, he's yelling, how all they've got here is goddamn fish anyhow, so speak up.

Hedy takes a breath and then doesn't say anything, lets out that breath and lights a cigarette. The way she's treating Denny is strange to me and seems born of some theory long obsolete; it's like watching someone leech a wound. I want to tell her there are shrewder, better ways to save herself, but even I can see such advice would not be welcome.

The waitress comes with our food and there's a fierce ticking in Den's right eye, a vein pulsing in his temple. The waitress is quick and then away, and I want to follow her. I say as much, which is stupid, I know that.

"Go right ahead."

"I'm just saying, for chrissakes, Denny, relax."

"Fine." He whisks his fingers over his plate. "Fine, then."

He stands, leans across the table to Hedy's face, bending close as though to kiss her, taking her chin in the tips of his fingers, slowly, gently, the way you would handle something fragile or thorny, of which she is neither. The bottom edge of his coat rests in his food.

"I can play cold shoulders," he says. "I can play cold shoulders till the cows come home, till I'm fucking dead and in the grave. I haven't asked you for a thing here but a simple yes or no."

She bites her lips dryly. "What's the question again?"

There is a long, silent moment when they stare at each other. Then he bends down and licks her cheek, below her eye, as mean as he can be.

The whole restaurant is watching now, and as I look around everyone is still, quiet, hovering over their plates like to protect themselves. I look at all these people and I wonder how it can be, when it comes to Denny, I am so slow to raise my guard.

He drops a stack of money on our plates and heads out the door, palming a bag of M&M's as he goes.

Hedy lifts her hand to wipe her face and then doesn't, pockets her cigarettes, gathers herself up to follow Denny to the parking lot. She waits for me, her eyes cutting to the door and back, but I just wave her on.

I remember coming to this fish camp a long time ago, on our way to and from the farm and the lake, the crack of a jawbreaker and my brother and me stretched out in the back of the station wagon, full up and ready to go home. There has been the day, the warm fall day when we all went out to check the pumpkins, the late grapes, high piled on their stake beds like some haul of polished stones. Mom and I have sunbathed on a quilt with our shirts off. There used to be a picture of this day somewhere at home, the high pumpkins, Mom and me with our tan, long backs, the bend of my brother at the stake bed or the tractor.

There has been this day and now the night, all of us full of salt and pepper fish, full of candy and Sun Drop and now stretched out in the back of the station wagon, the night blue and coming on black and the lot outside the fish camp strung with winks of lights, coming through our reflections in the car windows and then our faces themselves, so the lights seem dripped across us, in our hair, and, if we opened our mouths, across our tongues.

This would have been when we were children, before our father sold the farm and moved to teach full-time at the university, before our sister was born, our mother dead. This would have been before Denny moved to the cemetery, before Hedy, before any women, just girls and mothers and people on TV. Such thoughts make me smile.

I wonder what they do for Den.

2

THE NEXT MORNING I walk into the kitchen for a cup of coffee and find Den and Hedy twined around each other on the floor, their heads in the open pantry, their feet amongst the parts of stove. They are naked and asleep, and I feel as if I've just come across a litter of puppies or a nest of birds; if I disturb them, they'll be left to fend for themselves. I go back to my bed, stare at the ceiling tiles, and wait.

I have loved a man the way Hedy loves Den, which is to say without knowing any better. It was years ago, before I was married, and that man was not able to love me back, so I can see how Hedy got herself in this spot. I believed for the longest time that if you loved someone truly, they would love you back, and other women, past and present, all that was just provenance. It came not to be a matter of that. It came to be a matter of getting on a plane without him at a point when it made all the difference, a particular day and time, a place where everything hinged. But maybe there's no moment like that with Den. He was not always the way he is now.

I pick up the phone to call our sister in the mountains. She is still in school and so removed from this, someone to call when I am wishing to be removed myself.

"What are you doing there?" she says, as if it's dangerous for me and I should leave at once.

"Oh, come on. Daddy said so."

She laughs.

"Really," I say. "I think Denny's down to his last chance."

"Let me talk to him."

I would, but from the kitchen I hear the scrape of linoleum, the quiet that is trying to be quiet.

"He's occupied. I think. Oh, hell."

"Where's Marshall?"

"Not here."

"You poor thing."

"I have to go home."

"What about Daddy?"

"Daddy can come see all this for himself."

And I mean that for an instant, that I've done my duty and now washed my hands. For an instant, I can feel the looseness of not caring anymore, and it's as soft and available as sleep.

I ask what she's up to, and she lets go a rabble of information —what she is doing in school and how long it takes her to do it, what she likes and does not like about it—and I am grateful for the noise but cannot offer much. She has a job in the afternoons at the campus daycare center, and someday she will be wonderful with other people's children; the last time I was in the car with her, she kept saying things like *Ooh, Joanie, look at the cows*. When I hang up the phone, I feel like a four-year-old, like she has worn me out.

I wake again to the sound of water in the pipes and pretend it is the first time, make my way to the kitchen to say good morning. Hedy wears a shirt of Den's that hangs to her knees, and she is filling a percolator for the hot plate. She has a purple mark on her neck; a bruise or a love bite, how to tell?

"Sleep well?" she says, and I tell her I did, quite well and it is so quiet here. It stands to reason, being a cemetery and all.

"Where's Den?" I ask.

"Shower." She squeezes my hand as though we have not seen each other in the longest time.

I take a seat at the table and watch her at the sink. She rinses some dishes, wipes at the back of her thigh and leaves a trail of soap. She hums. I can tell how it would be if the two of them were here alone: Den sitting in my place, watching her, neglecting the paper she's left on the chair. If he told her to leave the dishes for another day, I bet she would. We are all different with no one else around.

Den comes in from his shower and he has shaved, wears a blue shirt with the cuffs turned back at his wrists. He doesn't look half as pleasant as Hedy, and I have the thought how that might be my fault.

"Sleep well?" I ask, and nudge him with my knee.

He gives me a fake smile and unsnaps the paper between us. He doesn't read it, and, after a while, doesn't even pretend to. He stares out the window at some cars circling up around the church, women getting out and opening their trunks. He sighs.

"What's going on?" I ask.

"The Junior League," he says. "Come for Christmas."

"They stay until Christmas?" Den just stares at me.

"Go down," Hedy says. "See if they need anything."

"Okay," he says, but he doesn't move from the table or from looking out the window, and after a time it's as if he's gone and come back already, almost without our knowing it.

We have coffee and wax honey on sourdough bread, cherry pie for breakfast, and we watch the women carry poinsettias and garlands, candles and spotlights and brooms and vats of polish into the church from their cars. These women have fixed hair and they wear blue jeans and cute sweaters, and some wear sneakers, some boots with high stacked heels. They call and laugh. We hear them carry on in the crisp air, and from time to time they look back up at the house as if they are expecting something. It's a small town. They know Den, know he is here.

"Whatcha doing for the morning?" he asks, still watching out the window.

"I'll probably get going."

"Not yet," Hedy says. "Oh, don't."

"I've got work to do, really, and you all have your day."

I trail off, lamely, not sure of what's expected. Denny seems far off this morning, and maybe it would be best if I just let him lie.

"I know," Hedy says. "I'll take Joan out to meet the chickens."

Denny laughs, not altogether nicely. He pops the back of my arm with his fingers.

"Doesn't that sound fun," he says.

I will do whatever is asked of me here, but I have no desire to meet any chickens, outgrew my love for farm animals with the sudden and complete shift it takes for one of them to do something horrible to another. For Easter we used to get those little colored chicks that lived about a week. I tell Hedy how we'd get so jacked up on candy, it was like the room was palpitating, and then after lunch we'd tear out to the barn just to watch them peck around. The year we were six and ten, we found Denny's shepherd dog instead, sitting in a shaft of sunlight from the hayloft. That dog was never still, would not sit if you tied him down, and he did not like the horses, but there he was in that Easter Sunday light, like some kind of drawing in the Bible of when God made dogs and it was good.

Denny called him, but he wouldn't come. We could tell something was not right, and then this little pink feather floated out of his mouth, just one pink feather, the only thing he hadn't eaten.

"Joan," Denny says.

"It was your dog."

"Oh, God," Hedy says, trying to get a breath from laughing. "He ate it."

"Hedy." He turns the same face on her, and she sticks her tongue out.

"You better watch it, girl."

He takes her pursed lips between his thumb and forefinger and she catches his wrist, turns it, kisses the heel of his hand.

I have noticed some things about Hedy and Den. She touches him more often than he touches her. She sits beside him, one hand on the table at a time, and feeds him bites from her plate. Looking at him the way she does, she seems young enough to be his baby sister, or his little girl.

He goes into his wallet for a twenty-dollar bill.

"Why don't you all get us some Sunday beers?" he says. "While you're out that way."

"From Body and them?" Hedy says.

He nods and then opens the paper again. He is back to watching the women out the window, coming and going from the church, and Hedy busies herself at the sink. I clear my place and go to the bedroom, pull on my sweater from the day before, and in my purse there is a letter from Marshall I have not opened yet. I slip the envelope in the waistband of my jeans next to my skin, brush my teeth, splash my face. I take a long time in the mirror doing very little, as though what I need to know was once written on the glass in steam.

When I come back to the kitchen, Hedy is chopping up a cabbage for the chickens and Den is pretending to read. She leans over and gives him a long kiss, the length of his throat laid open to her hand, and I am embarrassed, for myself, for Hedy, for the way Denny is trying to get rid of us for the day. But Hedy just finishes her kiss, picks up her egg basket, and breezes out the door.

In the cemetery, the ground is soft like cake, because you know there are things beneath the ground, and because to walk atop these things is to wonder at their substance, their state of repair. The ground is soft because you think what's in the ground is soft.

In the time Denny's lived out here, I haven't taken stock of the cemetery, and I haven't really walked it since I was a girl. That was always in the thick of summer and quietly, lagging behind Denny and his friends enough to not be noticed until we'd gone too far to send me back alone. We'd come down the berm of the highway, the same path from town that woman takes to Denny now, and I feel the eerie folding of time for a moment, so much of our lives lived in the same spaces, over the same footsteps as before.

There was a night in the cemetery when Lewis had his father's car, a '79 Cadillac with red leather seats, and he drove it right in amongst the graves to meet us and talked like he was going to take us somewhere, if we could just make up our minds where to. You could see the stripes of his last beating on the backs of his legs underneath his cutoff jeans, but he said his father had given him the keys, and that was probably true. His father would give a beating, give a car, give an evening with a Bible and a handful of NoDoz. Lewis always took advantage of a situation when he could.

There were seven of us, too many for the Cadillac anyway, Charlie Beeder and his brother Lem, who'd walked the highway with Denny and me, and Lewis. There was Boyd Henderson, who'd been waiting in the cemetery since sundown with his father's deer knife and a half-dozen field-dressed chipmunks, another boy with a pet snake he passed around, draping it across people's shoulders. I don't remember ever seeing that boy again after that night, don't remember his name, or the kind of snake he passed around, but it moved like a slow, pretty woman and I could not keep my eyes off it.

Somebody had matches. Somebody had spray paint, a can of gasoline, a Ouija board. There was a rusty little pistol under the seat of Lewis's father's Cadillac, and it was loaded. Somebody had a sack of fireworks, and somebody else had matches too.

Then there was Bannon. He was late to meet us. He stepped into the lights of Lewis's father's Cadillac and Denny perched up on the door frame and whistled at him, and Boyd Henderson stood up from his carcasses and wiped his knife on his pantleg, and the boy with the snake grabbed the snake by the tail and pulled it off Lem Beeder's neck. We watched Bannon weave a path between the headlights and the stones. He had a bamboo rod on his shoulder, a jar of worms tucked beneath his arm, and because of that, we all went fishing.

I wonder who lived in the caretaker's house that night, just a spare summer night a couple dozen years ago, and if they saw us in the cemetery, if they thought they'd have some trouble, and if they were surprised when they did not. I remember being surprised. I remember the threats of that night gliding away from me, and how cool it felt when I hit that pond water for a swim. It's the same cool way I have felt relief ever since.

Hedy and I stick to the shadeless paths and read the weather-worn sayings on the gravestones, words about lambs and sleep and peacefulness. We come across the psalm about how God will not suffer his foot to be moved, and I think how this is a good, stubborn God, the God I want. Maybe that's what I believe in most, the virtue of being stubborn. But then, I bet that's what Denny believes in too, and our father. I am left to wondering which side God's stubbornness would come down on, if he had to choose.

Then, too, there is Hedy, and how she has yet to put her foot down about the woman who comes to Denny from town. Maybe stubbornness is a thing like love, a thing that takes time and trouble to reach its fullness, to reach the point where even your feet are involved.

"So," Hedy says. "Do you think you'll be buried here?"

"We don't have family here that I know of."

"I just thought, with Denny." Her hand brushes over her shoulder toward the house, but she doesn't turn, doesn't look behind.

"I hadn't thought he'd be here as long as he has, really."

"Oh," she says. "Right."

She is quiet and I get the feeling I've turned the conversation to sensitive ground. I say how we have never been a burying kind of family, that our mother was cremated, and, if I could pick, I wouldn't do either. I'd drown.

"Go with the waves," I say, "like a cradle. And then there's no closing a casket, no graveside weeping, none of that."

Hedy nods. "More people are buried alive than you'd think."

"Not anymore, surely."

"I don't know," she says. "You'd be surprised how long some people can fake it."

From the way she says it, I get the idea she's done as much, and that's how she comes by her opinions, by doing for herself. Maybe she is not so young as she looks, out here in the open, away from Denny. She has the kind of long blond prettiness that will always seem cheerful, always seem untouched, no matter what she goes through. I watch my own face temper in the mirror every day.

She swings the egg basket to indicate a path into the trees, and we shuffle through the deadfall until I can no longer see the cemetery behind us. A chill comes off the ground, as though winter is already happening in these woods, as though it might begin here, and I wish I'd worn a jacket. I fold my arms against my skin and feel Marshall's letter inside the body of my sweater, the paper thin against the cold.

Hedy's chicken coop has a tin roof and inside, bamboo poles for roosting and a laying house filled with straw, but she says the chickens will lay anywhere. She has to dig around for her eggs, which will rot if she does not find them, something she thinks would be upsetting to the chickens. She makes little calls to them as she unlatches the coop, sweet words, like you would for any animal with fur. They are all named for the royalty of England.

She likes the chickens, the idea of raising something that makes food rather than is food, although she says she's not opposed to wringing necks either. Her grandmother taught her how when she was a little girl. She scatters the cabbage on the ground and the chickens peck and bluster. The smell is of hay and bird, leaf mold and wood smoke. When she comes out of the coop, she has thirteen eggs in her basket, smaller and rounder than you might expect.

This has not taken very long, the meeting of the chickens, and I'm wondering if we're welcome back at the house just yet. I sit down on a tree stump so as to leave the progress of the morning up to Hedy.

She puts her basket in my lap and stands behind me, her hands going to my hair. There is the surprise again of her touch, a current that passes from her to me. Her fingers smell faintly sulfurous, of feathers and eggs, and she works quickly, with strength, as if

I'm a garden in need of weeding. I let the breath out of my chest, let her work her braiding, her easy touches, so comfortable with strangers.

"You have Denny's hair," she says.

"I didn't know that."

"Longer, but it's the same. When I was a teenager, I went to beauty school."

"How long ago could that have been?" I ask.

"I never finished."

What have you finished, I think, but I don't say it. It would not come out right, and I don't want to be mean. I think of last night at the fish camp, and how she held Denny at arm's length when he was so angry. There must be something very capable about her, a strength for when things don't play out in her favor, and I imagine sometimes that means the strength to say she's had enough.

Like she's heard me, she says, "I'm not afraid to quit, that's for sure."

Her hands are fast, her pull even, and my eyes close like a petted dog's.

I realize how much I don't want to go back to the house and find Denny not there. I see those Junior League women in their stacked heels, their high-lit hair, and I feel Hedy's hands at my head, her breath in my ear the night before. I have low hopes for Den, no expectations at all. The way he sent us on an errand. The way he kissed her goodbye.

"Have you thought about quitting Denny?" I say.

"Lately?"

"Sure."

"Oh, goodness." She lets go of my hair, flips the tail across my shoulder. She does not answer fast enough for what she says to come easily.

"I'm sorry," I say. "It's not my business."

"No, it's okay. Sure. I mean, don't you always have a plan?"

I'd guessed as much, and I cannot help but like her more for saying so, the way you like whole wheat, bright children, anything so willing to be honest. She hardly knows me, and we're talking about my brother.

"Yes," she says again. "I keep a full tank of gas in my car."

"A hundred dollars in a cookie jar."

"That would be nice just to have, wouldn't it?"

We laugh. But I have never thought about leaving Marshall, about not being there when he comes home. I feel his letter against my ribs, and then it's as if his hand is there, the steady, gentle pressure of his hand, and in my mind it's five days ago and I am cast across his lap in the front seat of his car, and we are nearly laughing with this goodbye, as if we have no other choice now but to think it's funny, how he goes and I stay. He runs his hands beneath my sweater, sighs, and kisses both my cheeks. I stand. His hands are pulled from underneath my clothing with the motion, the last light touch at my waist, and then he closes the car door and is gone.

I miss him, and even though we have been together nearly five years, I pine, I linger, I lose my way around him like we have newly met. He will be home again next Friday; I think of it and the base of my neck flushes hot into my shoulders. It is not a feeling that lasts into most marriages, not something many people can afford.

Hedy asks me if I feel like a beer, and even as I don't, we set off for Red Hill, farther through the woods, then a stand of cedar trees, then across the highway, because it's what Denny asked of us. My braid unravels as we walk.

Hedy's steps are light, her expression cloudless. I know she must hurt for the things Denny has done, for the ways he's let her down, but sometimes there's nothing more to say about it than that. I think of my message erased on Denny's answering machine, how the silences Hedy makes are eloquent, whether she means them to be or not.

At the bottom of Red Hill is a cement block machine shop. Here you can get Bondo for your car, parts for your lawn mower, and black market beer on Sunday from a four-year-old. Denny spends more time over here than is good for him.

When we get to the shop, they wonder where he is.

"Hain't seen that boy," Body says. "Junebug, you seen our Denny?"

"Not in a month of Sundays."

Body laughs. "Not in a blue moon either."

"Hoo. Not since the cows come home, I swear it."

The place is strong with fumes, rife with metal. There's an industrial-size mayonnaise jar on the counter, filled to the shoulder with dimes. I can see the shoes of a man asleep on a cot in the back room, most likely Russell, who is often sleeping on Sundays.

"You all need to open a window," Hedy says. "Denny was down here last weekend."

"Now that's right," Body says. "He's a good boy, Denny."

"Good as gold," Junebug says.

"Right as the blessed rain." They are laughing again, and this time it seems less friendly, Denny just the crazy white boy across the road.

We buy a sack of beer. The four-year-old counts the cans into a bag, counts our change. Body and Junebug, they laugh and pat his head, how smart, how smart. We walk the shoulder of the highway back to the cemetery and I think we're headed home, but Hedy parks herself against a mausoleum and breaks open the sack.

"The truth is," she says, "the good he's done outweighs the bad."

"I love Denny," I say. "He's right as rain."

But she's serious. "I guess I mean, half the rest? Well, that's my fault."

"Hedy." I say it like she should know better, but maybe not. Maybe I should know better.

She drinks from her beer and she does not look at me, but into the can. "Those guys, the other night. I might have egged them on a bit. I might have said some things that made it worse."

"Like what?"

"Oh." Her cheeks color. "Ugly things. About their wives and mothers. And I believe Denny was trying to defend me when those guys pulled him through the window."

"I'm sure he was," I say.

"I feel really good about that, that he would let himself get hurt for me. I know I shouldn't. It probably says something bad about my self-esteem or something."

"Oh. If it's bad, then it's been that way since skirts were invented."

But what I don't say is how the opposite is true, how she let herself get hurt for something Den had done, in this town of half-husbands, and what that might say about her self-esteem. The bruise on her shoulder could have been a broken bone, worse. I take a sip of my beer, tinny and warming in my hand.

"I'm just tired of waiting for the other shoe to drop," she says.

She looks up at me, her eyes wide and clear and blue, a ring of gold around the centers. The morning's eggs are still in her basket on her lap; not a single one is broken. She is a careful woman, a smart woman, I imagine. She understands even with the pile now at Denny's feet, something else is always coming down.

When we get back to the house, he is in the kitchen. There's a long bone, a leg bone, crusted with dirt and cast across the table with the breakfast dishes and empty glasses, and he sits with his chin tucked into his palms, his work between his elbows, and the busted, bent pieces of a shovel, a pick, and finally a garden trowel at his feet. He looks up as I walk in, looks back to the bone, and I realize then how hopeless this is, this saving of Denny. He has the dirt of the graveyard on him, the debris of a morning's anger around him, and there is just more to come, mornings of broken dishes, of busted cars, fires and pestilence. I think how there are fault lines in men as old and uncharted as the earth itself, made known just before the ground starts separating, and by then it's too late. For Denny, it is just too late.

Behind me, Hedy is laughing.

She goes to him and crawls into his lap, and he lets his hands come around her waist, pushing back from the table and the bone, and he's laughing too. They talk in low voices, the sound of mice in the walls. It's exhausting just to try to make out what they're saying, and I close my eyes to make it dark, to make myself alone. Then there's a crash and Hedy's voice cuts the air, shrill as a bird's, calling for Denny even as we are all right here together, and I snap to it, a ball at the end of a rubber band.

There's blood.

It's on the floor, in the sink, in a dishtowel Den has wrapped around his hand. He's tipped back over his chair, cut himself on a piece of the metal, and now he holds the hand to his chest as if to hold it together. Hedy watches as the blood stains the dishtowel in pulses, her own hands going to herself, touching at her belly, as if she too is holding something in and together.

The fly of her jeans is unzipped.

I think how many places on our bodies we have to hurt ourselves, and how fast we are to do it, whenever we get the chance.

Hedy goes to the refrigerator and fills a fresh dishtowel with ice, and Denny holds it in his good hand until she reaches down and presses the two of them together. She disappears and comes back with a kit. Inside there are needles and envelopes of catgut and nylon for suturing, scissors and gloves and other vaguely medical things I don't recognize.

"I don't have any Novocain," she says. "They never gave us anything so useful."

Because what tools she has, they're for dead people.

Den is watching his hand as she unfolds it onto the table. It's his palm that's cut and it pumps steadily; as soon as she wipes it clean, it's flowing again, and I can see the flash of new bone he hit and blood spilling over ice, like something meant to be there. She ties off his wrist and washes her own hands, and then she's got bits of steel and thread in him and Den's face is starched white. I think he might pass out, hit the floor, and cut himself again, and then again, and then again, like a strip of film snagged on its advancing teeth.

I have not moved, not spoken. And then Hedy's saying, *We can do this, Den, we're fine,* and Denny's head is nodding, up and down.

In the night, Hedy and I sit on the porch and drink our Sunday beers. It's cold and I figure the fall is over. I tell her I'll be leaving tomorrow and she doesn't say anything, just smiles and tips her head to show that she has heard me.

Den is in the church, sweeping up. It seems the cat has dragged all kinds of prey in there since Easter and the last round of decorating and left the scraps to rot. It cleared the place out pretty good, Denny said. But the women will be back throughout the holidays, giving tours and showing off their handiwork. This is the oldest church in the county, or the state, I can't remember.

It was digging a hole for what the cat left behind that Denny found the bone. He was back in the woods behind the house and there was no coffin, but Hedy says she can tell it's a human bone and not a dog's, as it turns out she's taken her share of anthropology classes too. I told Denny he ought to check the conveyance and plot maps; he might find that the cemetery has migrated over the hundreds of years it's been here. I wonder if this will be enough to tell our father, that Denny's off his duff and robbing graves.

Hedy and I sip our beers on the front porch, and from inside the church comes music of the prayerful sort, sweet and pining, where Denny plays the pump organ, an old hymn about dust and blood and the crosses we have to bear. In the darkness next to me, Hedy is smiling. The music comes in the air and it's gentle and pleasing, and, after all, she is a happy person. She whispers, half sings, how she's the host, how she's the way and the light, and I imagine she is thinking about Denny and herself, this thing they have begun that will take some getting used to.

The night is such, so deep and cold and dark, I can only hope she's right.

3

THE DRIVE HOME is long, not by distance, but by choice. I have no obligation to be here or there, and so consider the drive to the mountains to see Piper, the drive to our father's house on the lake. I end up in the parking lot of a brightly lit bookstore, well off the interstate, reading the life of Queen Elizabeth the First.

We have a dog at home, Luther, who hardly knows me. Gail is keeping him across the street while I'm gone, and neither she nor the dog seemed to mind overly. Luther is Marshall's dog. His father got him from the pound when Marshall was younger, and we brought him home from Thanksgiving dinner because Marshall said that he belonged with us.

Marshall is adopted. He just found that out, but he should have guessed for himself long ago, as he's very tall and smart in a family of short, dim people. For example, when he was ten, his parents consulted a child psychiatrist to see how they should tell him he was adopted. The psychiatrist told them to take the boy to the pound, let him pick out a dog, and then say how, even though the dog wasn't born in their family, they would still love it and feed it and take care of it until it died. Then they should tell the boy he was adopted. Like the dog.

So on his birthday, Marshall's dad took him to the pound, let him pick out a pretty speckled puppy, and then chickened out. When they got home with the puppy, his mother asked how it went, and his dad said fine. That was it, for eight years. That dog died, and Marshall and his father went back to the pound to pick another one. Then at Thanksgiving, we're all gathered around the table, and Marshall's Aunt Liddy says, *Well, thank God Boo-Boo here's adopted,* sort of shaking his shoulders, and Marshall says, *What adopted?* Aunt Liddy and his mother look at each other. Then they look at the dad. Then everybody looks at the dog.

So Marshall took the dog home with us and he became our dog. Marshall says it's as if Luther is his true family, but I am not sure where it leaves me and Luther. He's a nice dog, but still.

What I want is a baby of our own.

I start my car and get back on the interstate, headed home. I live not ten miles from the farm where we grew up, north from Denny's and the university, along the little chain of mill towns and pastures that threads the upstate. I bought my house before I met Marshall, when my mother was sick and I needed to be close. It's a house a girl would choose, a pale blue front-gabled cottage with a wraparound porch, a fenced-in yard, a white pea-gravel drive. The stark bare limbs of the crape myrtles show almost white against the sky.

I walk across the street for Luther. I hear him banging around in Gail's house, the scratching of his nails on hardwood. Last week, Gail swore he recognized the sound of my car, started thumping his tail as soon as I turned down the street, and I trust there are many things that dog knows that I can't account for telling him, so I just clicked my tongue. Gail was to marry Bannon eight years ago this past April, but he's gone now, and Gail lives in his house alone. I've come to understand that's the way things sometimes go.

The front door opens and Luther noses his way through the screen. He's a stocky dog, tiger-striped and slick coated, and when he puts his paws on my knees to lick my face, I feel like he is glad to see me.

"How is your brother?" Gail asks.

She is leaning against the doorjamb in a cowl-necked sweater and a pair of cigarette pants, her red hair piled up and wrapped around a pencil. She works at home, something with computer software I do not understand, and I've never seen her wear something so comfortable as a sweatshirt and jeans.

I tell her he's okay, a few stitches in his face, but nothing a big boy like him can't handle.

"You know Denny," I say, even though she doesn't really, has met him only once or twice at our house, maybe a Christmas party or a barbecue, but she laughs because even with the little she's seen him, she's seen enough.

"Have you had dinner?" I ask.

"No, but I'm on deadline. Thanks anyway, Joan. Maybe later in the week?"

"Yes. Later in the week."

She goes back inside her house and I hug myself against the cold, walk Luther across the street. We are the only women alone on this block, maybe for blocks around. It's a situation neither of us is comfortable with, mostly for the way it hangs between us, an invitation to be friends that we've declined.

My newspapers are piled on our doorstep as if someone has raked them there or intends to start a fire. I step over them, and in our front hallway there's mail strewn across the rug from the slot in the door. I push at the envelopes with my shoe to see if any are worth collecting and find an express pouch: inside, another letter from Marshall.

He has a cell phone. I've called him on it only once, and we were disconnected twice in three minutes. He sounded so far away, we had to yell and repeat ourselves, and I felt worse afterward than before. But he writes letters that are like making love on paper, and that paper is solid, a thing passed from his hands to mine, or wherever I choose to hold it, and so we manage that way. It's never news he's sending me, so I read the same letter until I have it nearly memorized before I move on to the next. It seems a thing between us that happens outside of time, because I can read and tuck away and read again, because he could have written me this way a hundred years ago, if we'd been lovers then. Like any true love, it feels as though we've known each other all our lives.

I take the letter I've been carrying out of my purse and replace it with the new one to keep, sit down in the hall amongst my bills and catalogs to read.

He calls me sweetheart. He says it is dusty where he is and he wishes I would be there when he returned to the hotel, to take him to the shower, to turn the water hot and put his back beneath the spray. The soap here, he says, smells like sandalwood and warming oil. He loves it; he has bars and bars stashed in his suitcase. When he's clean, he tells me, he'll take that soap and take me by the waist, me and whatever I am wearing, and depending on my strength, it could go either way.

He says it would be my legs he washes best, my ankles, the backs of my knees, the tuck beneath my ass, and then the inside, the between. *Your legs,* he says, *for running and for wrapping and for stretching long.* He wants to know if I can picture it, and I can; I spend so much time picturing the two of us together it's like we live as much inside my head as out. *Your legs,* he says. *What do you do with them when I am not around?*

We have made love in this hallway, in most all of this house. My eyes are closed; I cannot keep my hands from myself, but I know they are my hands, not his, and all I get is sad.

So I tuck the letter in my pocket and make some food to eat, some toast and jam and tea, like in a children's book. Luther is hungry and pacing by his bowl, and I make some toast for him as well. He looks at me, his head tipped impossibly sideways. I was not raised with house dogs, but I am trying, and I bring his bowl into the dining room with me so we will not eat alone. I sit at the table with Saturday's paper, but it's too hard to concentrate for wanting.

Saturday was the twenty-eighth, the new moon, a day already happened on the red-lined calendar at the fish camp. In the kitchen, by the phone, I keep another calendar marked with appointments and dinner parties, another in my office, another in the bedside table drawer, with a thermometer, and a pen. I am not ashamed to say that I get lonesome and cannot think of better company than carrying a child. To that end, I study the dailiness of my body, its fertility and lack, the particular passing of the smallest, oldest kind of time.

It is another way I count on Marshall's letters, to distract me from myself, my ticks and tocks, stops and start agains. I miss him terribly, and someday it will make me something other than wistful. Not yet, but someday, I will miss him too much to be nice about it anymore.

I drop my cheek onto my knitted fingers. On the dining room walls are the pieces of blue and white pottery Marshall brings me from every place he goes, bowls and platters and plates I've hung chair rail to picture molding. There are distinctions of pattern, china alongside stoneware alongside an olive dish from Talavera, but all in blue, all in white, as if that's what we eat from all across the world.

I splash some water into my teacup and take it to the den, curl up in the leather chair and pull a quilt across my lap. Across the house, Luther heaves himself onto the bed, digging at the sheets, trying to make himself a place to sleep. His indifference to me is touching, as if he's being stoic for us both. I take Marshall's letter from my pocket once again.

There is a code. Sometimes he talks on and on about a dress he's passed in a shop window on the street that would look beautiful on me, and those are the worst, when there is nothing of his day he wants to tell me about. Sometimes he has been to a good restaurant, or better, someone he has met with feeds him, or walks him through their property, and he will tell me about Jersey cows and trout fishing, about the martinis they serve at the Brown Hotel in Denver and a joke he overheard at the bar. I can draw up the rest from what I see on TV.

There are the people he runs into everywhere, the FEMA people, the coroners, the salvage men who travel the country in caravan, like carnies. There's a routine they all perform, step and shuffle, pick and roll, and sooner or later it begins to feel like chasing ambulances. There are days he spends in mud, in ash, days he wears a mask to breathe. And there are mornings he wakes up and thinks about his job when he started it, behind a desk in a tall glass building with a calculator. He misses that calculator, the passage of numbers into checks into envelopes someone would open far away from that tall glass building and that desk, someone he would never have to see.

But he doesn't talk about these things in his letters; he talks about the drape of fabric and late-night cocktails, about making love and missing me, and in this way he is like his dog, his true family, trying to make himself comfortable for my sake. And I appreciate the effort. I just want him to come home.

I wake in the chair hours later, every light in the house still burning. I'm cold. I should get up, wash my face and brush my teeth, go to my own bed and stretch out, but it seems too cold for that, and I pull the quilt higher to my shoulders. I feel a sinking in my stomach, and the end of the week suddenly seems very far away.

Some nights, I think he'll die. It's a fast descent, a what if this, then what if that, because I know he spends his time on ground that's crumbling, or burning, or being swept away, and what small thing holds him to it? Maybe they'd call me in time to take his hand in some hospital, but maybe we'd just miss each other, and then I'd be alone in our house for good. Like Gail. When I go that far, it's hard to sleep at all.

So now I want to go to our bed, curl up atop the sheets, and sleep with what's left of Marshall on the pillowcases, but everything's been laundered in the week since he's been gone. I think about that over the washing machine, the detergent blue in its cup, but I do the laundry anyway, to measure swords.

I find the clock. It's five long hours until daylight. I pick up the phone and call Lewis, because sleep to him is just so many pills in the palm of his hand.

He answers from the shower, his phone with him all the time.

"Joanie, dear. You still down here?"

His voice is too large, not so much loud as enormous, deep, wide. His house is always full of people, and someone is always sleeping and someone else awake, so quiet seems to lose its point. He heads circulation over at the university library, and even as you'd think quiet was inherent to the job, he's not much better there.

I tell him I've slipped away and gone back home, and he plays cross with me.

"For shame," he says. "Without even a la-ti-da to your old Lewis."

"Things at Denny's were worse off than I'd expected." I draw a deep breath. "Where to start? He's got a girl up at the house with him, and there's some other girl that girl is worried about, all kinds of women coming to the church—"

"Now, you must have expected that."

And he's right; I had. But I'd thought I might be able to clear the girls away for a moment and really talk, but it all got away from me so quickly, and then there was Denny bleeding in his kitchen and Hedy stitching up his hand.

"I thought you were going to jerk a knot in that man's tail," Lewis says. "I thought I was to see his smiling face in the Sunday crowd, dreaming the dream of fried chicken."

"Right." I can hear the water sluicing over his face. "What would you know about the Sunday crowd?"

"Nothing?"

"I don't know, Lewis. I think I ended up just one more girl, causing one more headache."

"Oh, poor Joanie."

"I swear, you're laughing at me."

"That would be my guests."

I hear a toilet flush. "There's somebody in there with you?"

"Not anymore."

"For God's sake, Lewis."

"No, not *in here*, in here. But this is it, dear. The upstairs bath is still torn up, and far be it from me to keep the women from their natures."

I hear a tiny bell laugh and Lewis shuts off the water, asks the woman in the bathroom with him for a towel.

"I'll call you back," I say.

"Now, don't be like that."

"Christ, Lewis, you're busy."

"I am here for you, Joanie," he says. "Why don't you come on down to the library? I've got a stack of queries on my desk you can have."

When I was in grad school in Columbia, I worked in special collections, and I got to be the liaison for a prominent historian with a quiz show on the radio. It was Sunday nights, all state history and trivia, and I was good at digging up little charms of information. The next thing I knew, I was working for several of the historian's friends: journalists, colleagues, sometimes even people from TV. Lewis used to needle me about it, how I was librarian to the stars.

"I don't know, Lewis," I say. "I don't really have the time." As if I've called at three a.m. just because I'm so busy. He sees right through me. He asks when Marshall's coming home and I start to come apart.

I finish things quickly and hang up the phone so I won't have to explain, but then I am alone again and I give over to it, as if to have to listen to myself crying might shame me into stopping. Luther comes from the bedroom and sits by my feet, cocking his head this way and that. I scratch his neck, under his chin, and he leans into my touch. It passes.

It's times like this I wish most that my mother were still alive. She was a smart woman, and loved to give advice. She would tell me the story about how it was when she got pregnant with Denny, how she and our father tried and tried, for two whole years. She'd tell me about the time they were to dinner at some friends' house in Charlotte and the friends announced they were expecting and my mother locked herself in their bathroom for how sorry she felt. It got down to brass tacks; she'd had herself checked out, then it was Daddy's turn, and he hated doctors. Before she could turn around, she was due in June.

She would tell me I just needed to make Marshall a little more uncomfortable with the circumstances, and I know in some broad and elemental way, she'd be right, but it would make so much more sense with her arms around my waist, her chin resting on my shoulder. It would make so much more sense if she were here. And if she were, I bet Denny would still be in Atlanta, with a car and boat and phone of his own. She would not stand for this contention with our father, and there are things a boy just will not put his mother through. Maybe all of this goes back that far, to when Denny became a boy without a mother, without a woman over his shoulder to make him a little bit less comfortable with himself, a little less likely to do exactly as he pleased. I know I'm no good substitute, not in any way that matters.

I find the box of tissues stuffed under the couch and blow my nose. Luther jumps and skitters, like a springboard toy. I need to move, and if it were not the middle of the night, that dog would have just won himself a walk around the block.

As it is, I drag the quilt across the room, to the light beneath my office door.

The lamp is on above my desk, a pendulous frosted shade that swings in the draft as if someone ticked it with a finger on the way out. I cannot shake the feeling that there's someone else here, that there should be someone else here, someone to ask, to tell, to go for drinks with after work. I think I rely on it, the chance we just keep missing each other, as it's hard to understand how I've come to spend so many of my days and nights alone.

My office used to be a laundry room; if I stretch out my arms, I can touch each wall. It fills easily, like a warren or a can, and newspaper is everywhere, cut into ribbons, rolled and stacked, leafed across the desk and file drawers, the chair, the rug. I've strung a clothesline from the ceiling and clipped my notes to it, odd photographs, banner headlines, the ragged slips like so many prayer flags, wavering. I keep volumes of the archive's bound runs stacked against the walls; the *News and Courier*, the *News Gazette*, the *Star*, the *Sun*, the *State*, the *Times* of several different places, day next to day, month after month. The funniest thing is how I can sit here and lose track of time entirely.

There's a path to my chair, and I take it. I press my hands to my face, and I see my reflection in the strange half mirror of the window, my cheek already smeary with ink. Everything you touch in here leaves a ghost behind.

When I worked for the quiz show in Columbia, one of the historian's friends was a woman interviewing root doctors along the Edisto River basin. She talked about how oral history was such a textured artifact, and I'd drive down there with her to these shotgun houses on the water to take notes while she ran the interviews, little things I could look into later: what kind of animals they kept, what kind of gardens they grew, what they left in their garbage cans, their storage sheds, the back seats of their cars. That's how it started anyway, but these were people who said they knew how to poison you through your footprints, who read the future from a scattering of animal bones. I became a grounding wire for Audrey, corroboration. When one of the root doctors told her he'd walked to Georgia for a particular revenge, I was the one who checked the odometer in his Valiant and knew he was taking her for a ride.

One afternoon, we arrived at this man's house and sat in his driveway for an hour and a half, listening to his yellow dogs barking in the pen. It was late August, miserable even with the air running, but he'd promised to show Audrey some photographs and she was hoping to make copies. We'd driven several hours of back roads and had no intention of leaving empty-handed.

"It's hot," I said, but she was looking out the window. She had responsibilities here. I knew she was weighing what she ought to do against what she wanted.

"He's old," she said finally. "How old, would you say?"

"I don't know."

"Yeah," she said, and we got out to look around.

We found him laid out neatly in the bottom of a rotten skiff behind his house, hands folded at his waist, eyes kept closed with silver dollars. Audrey called the police from her cell phone, but when that phone snapped shut, it was like we'd dropped our last pebble on the path and the swamp rushed in to cover it. It was a locust year; they were blaring in the trees, the yellow dogs barking, mosquitoes biting, sweat running underneath our clothes. It became impossible to think, to move, to do anything but stand beside the skiff, its dead man, and wait. Shortly, the police arrived and ushered us back to our car.

All the way to Columbia, Audrey wished she'd given herself half an hour before she called the cops, just half an hour to pick through the root doctor's things, to see how a person like that plans to die, because she was coming to be convinced of all this stuff and she knew he would have seen his death foretold. She even went back down there and let herself into the house to see if she could find the photographs he was holding, but everything he might have left was gone: no books or papers, pots or jars; the rooms swept clean, just a few pieces of furniture and a broom. His were the sort of people that would do that. When they ran the autopsy, they found brackish water in his lungs, the kind from downriver, closer to the coast. They ruled the death accidental anyway, a drowning, and the case was shut.

Audrey tabled her project after that. I'd see her at the gym, running on the treadmill for hours at a time, and she'd wave and smile and say how we should go for drinks, but she never asked for my help again. It made me sad, to think of all the material she collected, the transcripts and tapes, the curiosities boxed away, and Audrey, running circles around herself.

I feel that same sadness now, thinking of Denny in the darkness, with his shovel and his bandaged hand. He needs something to do, other than regret and philander, and I'm not sure if I ought to encourage him or just wait for the cops to show up. The fact is, Audrey could have found a good bit that day on the banks of the river, with the half-hour she wished she had. Denny's got all the time in the world.

4

THE SUN RISES sour pink across my desk. Luther paws at my shin, and I leash him up for a walk around the neighborhood. I never run—I don't believe in it—and I hope he is prepared for this.

The streets are empty this early, all the cars still in the drives, but I see lights coming on in the windows, smoke rising from the chimneys, papers waiting on the doorsteps, single rolls instead of the dozens that come to my house. I feel a little omniscient, a little alpha and omega. Luther wakes every dog behind every fence, all along the block.

Gail is ahead of us on the sidewalk. She wears fluid black pants, a fleece nipped in at her waist, her ponytail nearly violet in the stretching light. Our pace is the same, and we get neither closer nor farther apart. I begin to feel silly with the blocks crossed in tandem, and call out to her.

She whips around, pulling earphones from her ears, the tiny kind that fit inside.

"Joan," she says. "You startled me."

"I'm sorry."

Luther strains at the end of his leash, and she crouches down to rub his muzzle. Her hands are gloved, her breath cottony on the air.

"Walk together?" I say, and she nods, and starts out.

This does not happen often, our pairing up unexpectedly, and so there's no choreography for it. I'm not certain how to fill the silence, if it even needs filling. The oaks arch and tangle overhead, and a breeze picks up to stir the leaves around our feet. I defer to Gail, and, after a time, she speaks.

"Bannon's sister is coming for Christmas."

"Alice or Corinne?"

"Alice. Both, maybe. They're bringing their sons. They want to stay at the house and go through some of his things. I was going to mention it yesterday, but I don't know. I didn't."

She catches an acorn with the sole of her shoe and tips into my shoulder. I can hear the music from the earphones draped around her neck, something dramatic, with strings. My head swims a little bit to think of Bannon, always does.

"If you want," I say, "one of them can stay with us."

"Thanks. That might be better. That might be more room. You're sure it wouldn't be a trouble, with the holidays?"

"No."

"Well, it's trouble for me."

And I think how this must be true, as I've never seen Gail entertaining company, not one strange car in the driveway the eight years she's been across the street. I've never been invited over, really, but always just intruding with my Christmas cookies and my invitations for dinner. There was a time the phone rang in that house and I picked it up as if it were my own.

Now Bannon's family is gone from here too, his parents passed away, and his sisters married, with families someplace up north that keep them busy. They grew up here, though. Everyone but Gail grew up here.

"I'll have to cook," she says. "I can't do that."

"You can get takeout. You can get Alice or Corinne to cook. I'm sure they make big dinners all the time."

"They're going to want to take things with them, Joan. That's why they're coming. And at Christmas, with children, when they know I can't turn them down."

"Really," I say. "You think?"

The thing of Bannon's I've always wanted is his knife. Not his chef's knife, which was ceramic and sharp and really expensive, but the knife he kept in his pocket. He used it to open boxes and peel fruit, to pick splinters from his palm. You could see the outline of it in his pants where they had faded to it, see him laughing, taking the knife from his pocket and throwing it open with his thumb, taking the peach from my hand and paring off a slice, wiping the blade on his shirtsleeve, laughing at something I had said to him. But I've never asked Gail for it, and never would.

When I bought my house, it had been a dozen years since I'd seen Bannon, and I had no idea he lived across the street. Denny was in Atlanta fetching cars, and he and Bannon had lost touch when they went off to school. We heard he'd married quickly, a very young girl, that the marriage had fallen apart. He didn't return Denny's phone calls.

I was back and forth to the farm then, as our mother had just come out of her first surgery. It was months before she could lift her arms above the break of her shoulders, and so I kept her company under the guise of opening jars, reaching the high, high shelf. I never saw a car across the street when I came home. The windows were only lit late at night, and I never found the time to stop and say hello.

It was summer, and I had some girlfriends over for drinks, just taking a Thursday night and throwing it to the dogs. We camped out on the front porch after the sun went down, the ceiling fan nudging a breeze out of the darkness. Eventually, the ice ran out, so we came to our tequila straight, with limes and salt, and it was getting very, very late when we saw a truck pull up across the street.

It backed into the yard. Whatever was in the bed was so rotten you could smell it from my porch, so much so that Laura Becking leaned over the azaleas and got sick. I came back from the kitchen with a wet washcloth, and Frankie Tam put her long hand on my arm. She said, *Would you look at this.*

Two guys stood in the bed of the truck, shoveling, and whatever it was hit the front porch across the street with a heavy, wet sound. It smelled like low tide. Frankie yelled, *Hey*, and the guys straightened up. Somehow, they'd missed us, or thought we'd missed them, and we could see the red bandannas tied around their faces, but not much else. They were big guys. They knew how to handle shovels.

What the hell are you doing? Frankie said, and started toward them.

One of the guys smacked the cab with the flat of his hand and the truck jounced over the curb and pulled away, the tailgate down so we couldn't catch the plate. Frankie picked her way up to the porch as if she were walking on eggshells, but she hauled it back, her hand over her face. There were oysters, she said, and seaweed and other muck, and none of it had seen the ocean since last month.

We waited up.

When Bannon's car pulled into the driveway, Frankie and I called out. I recognized him immediately. He looked just the same.

He hugged me, kissed my cheek. He'd been meaning to come by, but things were a little crazy for him right now, and he jerked a thumb over his shoulder at the seaweed on his porch. He ran a restaurant downtown, Lydie's, and it was always something. The guys in the truck were purveyors. There'd been a disagreement earlier in the week about quality, and purveyors were bastards in general. He'd have it cleaned up as soon as possible.

I insisted he couldn't sleep over there. I poured him a tequila, and Frankie put Esther Phillips on the stereo. I acted like it was fine he'd kept to himself until now, and before long, it hardly seemed strange. That was just Bannon. In the morning, he made all of us crepes with brown sugar and peaches, and he started taking Frankie out for a while. It was as if he'd never gone away.

We played poker at his house, ate food and drank wine. He set me up with friends of his, and he was right: purveyors are bastards in general. It got to where I'd excuse myself, go back into the kitchen, and refuse to return to my date. But Bannon loved the idea of a bad match as much as a good one, and he'd tie an apron over my dress and put me at the prep station to chiffonade, to julienne, while I told him all about his pinhead friends. He'd take any excuse for a meal, would make me breakfast at three a.m. and then again at noon. He'd come to Sunday dinner at the farm; he made my mother laugh into her hands.

We were friends, the best. I found out why he dropped off the face of the earth, all about the girl he ran off with and how it came apart. But I didn't meet Gail until Bannon had already asked her to marry him. And Alice and Corinne didn't meet her until Bannon was dead.

"What is it they want?" I ask Gail. "Things from the restaurant?"

"That all went with the building, to creditors. I don't know what all there is anymore, really. I just don't want it gone through. I don't want it parceled out, you know? Any of it."

"Sure."

She starts to say something else, then stops, swallowing, her voice gone liquid. We turn a corner and the wind rushes our ears, through our coats, and we hug ourselves like thin, sick people. Luther plays out his leash, nipping at the leaves, and then it's just me and Gail once again, with nothing good to say.

I talk about not being able to sleep, and working, about this paper and that article and what the weather is supposed to be this week. I know she's not really listening to me, but I sense it's the right thing to do, to leave her to more private thoughts.

That day eight years ago when Gail came home from Mexico, she came to my house first. I remember watching the car pull into the drive and no Bannon, my stomach climbing up my rib cage, and over and over thinking, *What has he done? What has he done now.*

I came out onto the front porch and waited with my hands pressed in the small of my back. Her face was red and swollen, her voice like a voice in the movies, floating over everything. The azaleas were out already, scarlet, and the new grass was up, bright green, and my porch rail needed painting, peels of it standing up in the breeze.

She said Bannon had an allergic reaction in a hospital in Mexico City, something they'd given him for something they didn't even have in this country, and now he was dead. He died the night before. He was still down there, somewhere, and she didn't know how she was ever going to get him back.

She walked back across the street, and she was crying now, went into Bannon's house, which was hers now, and she did not come out for the church service, or to see Bannon's sisters off, for food or work or fresh air, until summer. Then, she was so steely and thin I didn't think I recognized her, but I had not known her well to begin with. And so the Gail without Bannon became the Gail I know, and I've done the best I can by her ever since. It seems the least he would expect of me, were he still around.

When I get home, my father is rambling from the answering machine, not yet seven in the morning. He wants to know if I've heard from my brother. That's what he calls him, *your brother*, not Denny, and he's making something in his voice light and gossipy, as though he's only interested for sport. I reach for the receiver and then don't pick it up. I can always say that I was in the shower.

I bring in the morning's papers, snap the rubber bands off the rolls, and lay them flat on my desk, newsprint like chalk on my hands, still dry and tight from the cold. The front pages show people across the state lighting their Christmas trees in their town squares, arms linked, children lifted to their shoulders. These people might be the last I see today, these and Gail.

Up until last spring, I worked in archives at a girls' college in Spartanburg, and it seemed as though everyone was always giggling or playing tennis, meeting for tea, and I was organizing the papers of the late poet laureate, her beautiful handwriting penciled across the drafts. It was a good job, and I was happy with it. I missed Marshall, but there was always tennis in the morning.

Then this man called me. He represented a foundation of other men like himself, men with degrees and money and a little thought behind it, and he offered me application for a private grant. I asked where he got my name, and he said that was unimportant, so I hung up on him. There were stories in school knee deep in the aisles about this lawyer representing that famous, sad, or dying client, calling you up to their own personal paper chase, as if it's fun to watch, or maybe they need to feel their papers are important. But it's not the kind of thing I do.

Mr. Baulknight knew that already, and he's the sort of man who's probably never been hung up on. I think he liked me from the start. He showed up at the library the next morning with a big long car to take me out to lunch. Marshall was in New York — there were months he spent in New York — and I hadn't been out to lunch with a man in longer than I cared to think about. And Mr. Baulknight was charming and copper-skinned and somewhere past midlife, with a classically trained voice and a sharp linen suit. We went to the Poinsett Club in Greenville, with its fine oil paintings and ladies in hats, and he ordered champagne like it was going out of style.

"You know my father," I said.

He smiled. "We went to school together. Oh my, Joan. Nothing escapes you."

"There's no need to be flattering."

"So I should make my point. You have seen me through, and here I'm keeping you from a perfectly good day in the trenches, doing what-all important things — filing, shuffling, etcetera."

Etcetera had all its syllables. I made to push back from the table.

"This has been lovely, Mr. Baulknight. I'll tell my father that we spoke."

"Okay, okay. Here. We've bought a building in the northern part of the county, a venture in preservation, really. The tuberculosis hospital? I want to fill it."

"With?"

"Paper."

"And I thought you said filing was beneath me."

His hand swept over mine, patting, conciliatory. The least my father could have done was warn me.

"Joan. You're a funny girl. Let me tell you all about it."

He ordered another bottle of champagne, and when we were both quite drunk, he signed for the check, loaded us back into his big long car, and drove us up to Piney Mountain.

The tuberculosis hospital closed before I was born, in the late sixties, and it sat empty, developers advancing from all directions as the mountain gave way to golf course and country club, state park and gas station. The foundation outfoxed everyone, Mr. Baulknight said, with the keyword *preservation*. No one likes to see the old things torn down. So as we rounded the drive, the wide green lawn was filled with contractors' trucks and Mexican laborers, shoring up what had once been just a large brick hospital building, but now, because of its age, seemed elegant and expansive, its windows leaded glass, its porches columned and broad. Mr. Baulknight squinted over the steering wheel to see the clock tower, as if we were pressed for time.

"It's like a rabbit hole in there, Joan—you'll love it. If you unwound the hallways and stretched them end to end, you could walk to Florida."

And he was right. I loved the idea that you could walk and walk and walk and still might find some unexpected corner, some hidden bookcase, a passage to nowhere. I had the feeling then that this was a man who knew more about me than he had a right to, but he was decorous about it, and I tried to act in kind.

He took my elbow and led me inside, where the plaster was flaking like snow. It was loud. Somewhere, walls were coming down and going up, echoing with the regular fire of a pneumatic hammer and riffs of called-out Spanish, at turns frantic or angry, strange for how much meaning you could determine from tone.

Mr. Baulknight began to walk fast, and talk faster. Bound runs of upstate newspapers would be stored in climate-controlled vaults on site; the foundation was in the process of acquisition, and I wouldn't believe the paucity of avenues. The main floor would be reception and reading rooms, exhibits of an eclectic, historical nature. There would be docents and Oriental rugs, vast, searchable computer databases, perhaps a summer Chautauqua with lectures and music and picnics on the grounds. Mr. Baulknight got a spark in his eye at the mention of picnics, the kind another man might get over dry flies, or German sports cars. But I wasn't exactly sure what he was offering me, and was beginning not to care. I felt the wine thickening in my head. I began to think of home, and bed, a jar of olives in my fridge. I can't say Mr. Baulknight noticed; he had the pound of the work around us, like applause.

We walked a long, twisting hallway and turned a corner to find a clot of men, their thumbs hooked into their low-slung tool belts, peering into a wall they'd knocked through. Mr. Baulknight made way so we could see, and, inside, the floor joists had been hacked away, the ground dug out about six feet down, a hole the shape and size of a man. It was old work, the cuts in the boards gray from exposure.

"*Cucharas*," someone said. "*Allí abajo*."

He handed Mr. Baulknight two steel serving spoons. They were bent at their necks, scabbed with clay. He turned to the light, holding the spoons up as if to read their maker. Clinging to the dirt, long and black, I could see a strand of hair.

He drew a handkerchief from his pocket, wrapped the spoons, and asked if I could put them in my purse.

"I need some air," I said. "Badly."

He kept talking but put a hand to my back and led us to a service elevator with a pull-down metal door, and I stopped hearing him for the whine of mechanics in my ears. There are reasons not to drink champagne in the middle of the day with a man you do not know, and a ride in an elevator only serves as proving grounds. I felt that long streak in me turning over, physically, like an opening palm, that thing that got me into any trouble, that did not think, but turned, and said yes.

The elevator stopped, and Mr. Baulknight rolled up the door to the eager green afternoon.

"I don't read microfilm," I said. "It makes me sick."

"It's not necessary, Joan. I am giving you an oyster. You can stay at home, or we could make an office for you here, overlooking the grounds." He stretched a hand toward another wall gaping with steel, the mackerel sky beyond. "You know, they thought the mountain air was good for the lungs. That, and milk. An unwavering faith in the healing properties of milk."

"I don't read microfilm," I said. "It makes me sick."

"We have someone else to do that, I said."

I swayed a bit on my heels. "How many someone elses are there?"

"The scope of the preservation is grand, really, and eventually we see this building as a kind of daily-use repository. Not only newspapers, but physical things, spoons, for instance. But the newspapers, those are for you."

"I just seem like that sort of girl?"

"You seem, to me, the sort of girl who might see value here. Think. What else do we have to record our daily life, the quotidian dramas of eggs and bread, or school board meetings, political campaigns, so much who-shot-john?"

"Quotidian."

"Yes." He was serious.

"You were a preacher in your last life."

"No. No, I wasn't. I was Prometheus, Mary, Queen of Scots, and, I believe, once a German shepherd, but I have never preached. For money."

"Well, goodness, Mr. Baulknight. You don't want me to record the price of bread, do you?"

"Of course not."

"Well, then, what, exactly, would you be hiring me for?"

It's a complicated question. The foundation has invested in digital scanning and indexing software offered by the United States Newspaper Program, and so all of the bound runs are being photographed from their original hard copies—classifieds, obituaries, advertisements, and all—before they are stored in the vaults at the hospital. People will be able to sit at one of the foundation computers and search two hundred years of firsthand, small-town history by keyword. They will be able to go down into the vaults and look through the papers themselves, page by page, issue by issue. My job is to make them want to do that; most people just throw their newspapers away.

Mr. Baulknight is worried about the dispassionate quality of what is saved these days, what is discoverable about our neighbors and how little that might really tell us. The state of correspondence depresses him, the loss of telegrams and love letters and the labor of having to make words for your thoughts to make sense on a piece of paper. He believes there will come a day when we no longer know our own handwriting, and that day will be worse than the day all of our children have drug habits.

He sees a kind of correspondence to the newspaper like that with an elderly neighbor, the way it arrives on your doorstep every morning bearing information and gossip, predictions for the future. People who read nothing else in their lives read the paper; stories develop, mysteries are solved, things are bought and sold and mated, all in language that's trustworthy and direct. Efficient. Portable. And it happens every day. It might be crumpled, burned, wrapped around the crystal in the attic, because the next morning, it comes around again.

"That's where the rubber meets the road," Mr. Baulknight says. "We confuse regularity with disposability. What if we thought that way about our good night's sleep? Our marital affections?"

"What is it now, half of marriages end in divorce?"

"My point," he says, "exactly."

So I receive newspapers from all across the state, dailies, weeklies, little tiny rags and Sunday supplements, right to my front door. I read them and take notes, make sketches and schematics for possible exhibits. It's like painting a portrait from a family snapshot; the view of history is different when taken through the most disposable, everyday lens. I see an article on the overwhelming vote in Greenville to retain Sunday blue laws for liquor service, and I go into the archives and find how in 1927 four men were arrested in Abbeville for playing golf on Sunday. And then there's Prohibition, tallies for moonshiners arrested, stills busted, the number of people hospitalized, blinded, or dead from what they drank out of their bathtubs. And further back, liquor had a state dispensary with its own force of constables who could go into your home and search your shelves for what you ought not to have. The constables had guns, and if they shot you, most likely they'd be pardoned. In 1894, they shot a man in Darlington who had friends with guns; the papers called the resulting firefight "The Dispensary War." The governor ordered militia units from five counties before he could get anyone who felt strongly enough about the constables to come to their rescue.

All these articles go into a file, a daisy chain of paper. To go from one to the other to the next is to make a kind of laundry list of history, a kind of recipe or map. I feel as though what I'm doing is that simple, but also that essential. Everybody ought to know how to bake a cake.

I've had lunch with Mr. Baulknight three times in the nine months I've worked for the foundation, and when we meet now, it's in Charleston, amidst the church bells and piazzas, the patina of water, time, and decadence. We chat, about architecture and opera, mostly about him. In the new year, I will appear before a board of directors, and any questions I might have can be ironed out then, in person, issues of time and space and general progress. I have enough to occupy me, don't I? Now, let's enjoy the smoked duck.

And so I do.

The reason I took this job is simple. I can work at home, to my schedule, to a baby's schedule, and I make a thousand dollars a week. That's a good job, and every morning, there's the stack of papers waiting, tight rolls of narrow-minded editorials and bad recipes for soup, profiles on musicians and criminals and people who make cheese. The question of what to do with it all is pleasantly endless. And while I know my father probably pulled some strings behind my back, I can keep it going for myself.

In the Greenville paper this morning there's a story about two men from Columbia who robbed a Wal-Mart. They made off with what was in the safe but got only as far as a motel by the mall before they tucked in and started spending: twelve thousand on strippers, more for a pile of Wrangler jeans and embroidered shirts, snakeskin boots, every LeAnn Rimes CD ever recorded, two gallons of strawberry ice cream, and a pair of samurai swords with scabbards that could hang from a belt. They had a duffel bag of cash on the sofa when the cops came to the door, in plain view. They had five days, and this is what they did with it.

So Mr. Baulknight has a point; even bank robbers don't rob banks anymore. They rob Wal-Marts, because banks don't keep enough money in paper to pay the tab at the strip club. But how to account for the lack of imagination, of cleverness? One of the guys answered the door, like a knock-knock joke, like Clyde Barrow never existed.

I go into the archives, to find better bank robbers than that.

On Friday I call Denny and tell him I'm coming down to see Lewis, that we should have lunch. Then I call Lewis and tell him I'm coming down to have lunch with Denny, that we should see each other in the afternoon. They both act as if I'm running a racket on them, which I am. I don't want to see them both together because I want to talk to Denny, and Lewis's answers are almost always pharmaceutical.

We meet at a barbecue joint in Pendleton. We get sandwiches with slaw, beans, split an order of hash and rice, and the sun is warm so we sit outside at the picnic tables. I'm encouraged. He's left the house. His face is scrubbed and clear of bruises, and his hand, where Hedy stitched it, is already smooth and pink.

"It's like a miracle," I say.

He flexes his hand out in front of himself, as if he's just considered the possibility.

"You could have brought her with you," I say.

"She's got class."

"Every day?"

"Nine to five."

This is nothing to talk about, but I'm thinking how that leaves Denny so much time to get in trouble.

"So," I say. "What are you going to do, nine to five?"

He wipes his mouth on a paper napkin and shrugs. "Junebug says they'll take me back."

"But?"

"But no."

"Come on, Denny. I feel like a jerk."

"Look. The old man's always going to have a problem with me. If it's not this, it's something else. You don't have to broker for him."

"I know that. And it's not that."

"It is."

He reaches over and pinches my cheek so that it stings, and I smack his hand away. He's laughing.

"I got one for you," he says. "What goes in hard and dry and comes out soft and wet?"

"You're a sick man, Denny."

"Gum." He grins. "Russell's. He was pretty proud of it."

We finish our lunch. I'm quiet, but it's what Denny is asking for and I'm giving it to him, so there's a conversation even to that. And he's right; I've avoided calling our father since he left his message on my answering machine, and I feel bad about it. What I know is pretty much a punch line anyway: Denny digs up bones, Denny chases skirts, Denny and his girlfriend get in fights, but she seems nice and here's her phone number. Maybe she can help you with this straightening out.

The sun is warm, and I lie back on the picnic bench with my hands folded beneath my head. Across the table, Denny does the same.

"What do you think about something like this?" he says.

The something skips across the tabletop above my head, but I don't open my eyes. I sound like our mother, a little bit on purpose:

"I don't know, honey. Where'd you get it?"

"You know. The yard," he says.

"The graveyard."

"Would you look at it, for chrissakes, Joan?"

I sit up. It's a piece of a dinner plate.

He says, "Over where I found that first thing, there's all kinds of this stuff."

"The first thing?"

"We got the rest of him in the root cellar."

"Denny, I'm pretty sure there are laws you need to think about."

He's got his elbows on the table now, leaning into our talk. "Hedy says it was a guy from the shape of the eyes in the skull, and the length of certain bones. Are you headed to the library after this?"

He slides a slip of paper across the table. He wants books on forensics, bioarchaeology, the history of burial practice in the South.

"What are you thinking here, Denny, going back to school?"

"Might."

"Will not."

He looks away. "I was lying in bed last night and my head was just flying. I tried to remember all this old stuff, family names, soil makeup, where I could get in touch with the guy who had this job before me. Hours of this, and then I got up and just kicked around out there where we found him."

He takes the piece of china from me, runs a finger down the sharper edge.

"I got handfuls like this."

His face waxes in that moment, somnolent, opening in the way men's faces open in sleep, and I can see what he wants, and it doesn't seem as if we are talking about bones in a graveyard but rather legacy, heritage, what passes on. He's being honest with me.

I tell him I poked around online the other night and there are seven unsolved missing persons cases in Anderson County right now, five of which are men, and that's just what's run in the paper. And that's just right now. People have gone missing for centuries.

"So this could be anybody's dead guy," he says.

I shrug. Denny is thinking.

"I'll keep looking," I say. "If you want."

I try to sound casual. I do think it's crazy to dig in your yard for dead people. I do think it's crazy to collect the bones and store them in your cellar. But I can think of ten places to find out more about that land, who lived on it, who might have died there. The pull is very strong, to do what I am trained to do.

Denny laughs. "Not that you're interested, mind."

"Come on. It's practically my job."

"Yeah?"

I throw a balled-up napkin at him. "Smart-ass. And Hedy's helping you. It's not like you're out to Lone Ranger this thing altogether."

"That girl is smarter than you think. Hell, she's smarter than I think half the time, and I keep upping the bar, upping the bar, and there she comes around again."

"I like her, Denny. I wish you'd be good to her."

"I am," he says. "The best."

But it's a lie and he grins at me to tell it, and his face goes back inside its handsomeness. I half expect him to pinch my cheek again, if we were standing, to pinch my behind. Suddenly, I understand schoolground fights, how little boys end up with so many black eyes, football injuries, barstools to the head. It would be easier to pull Denny through the window of a car than talk to him across this table. At least then I could guarantee his attention.

I lie back down on the bench and pretend he has gone away entirely.

Leaving, we meet a woman in the parking lot he knows, coming in as we are going out.

"Oh, Denny," she says. "I'm glad I ran into you."

The whole time she's talking, something about the Junior League and its project with the welfare babies, she's taking off her bra, lacy and gold, through her shirtsleeves. She reaches under her skirt and shimmies out of a pair of matching panties, stepping out of her slides, one by one, to leave everything in a pile on the pavement at Denny's feet.

She leans close to him, goes to put a hand on his chest, but then seems to think better of it. Her face is full of the woman scorned.

"I believe these are yours," she says, and walks on toward the restaurant.

Denny stares at the lacy things, goes to pick them up and then just toes them with his boot. He looks after the woman and cusses under his breath, pulls his cigarettes out of his pocket.

"I bet they look sweet on you, Denny," I say.

"Leave it. Just leave it."

"Well, Jesus. How do you cross a room for the people with their feet stuck out? You're spending a lot of time flat on your face, Denny, a lot of your time."

He doesn't say anything, just lights his cigarette and wanders off toward his car, leaving the panties as if they're not his business, and leaving me, standing next to the panties, as if maybe they are mine. I have the want to push it, to make him really mad this time, just to see the works go off.

"Denny."

He doesn't stop, doesn't even turn around. I yell again, and there are people coming out of the restaurant behind me who have not seen what's happened, but they see me, and the panties, and Denny driving off. I launch a handful of gravel at his rear window, but he doesn't touch the brakes.

A small crowd has gathered in the parking lot. I see a man headed toward me with a cell phone as if to call for help, but I wave him off. What good would help do now.

5

To go from Pendleton to the university is to pass through time; from antique stores and the village green, to golf course, condos, fields of experimental corn, and I'm leaving Denny miles in the past. He would have done well in a time when fresher starts were possible.

I park by the office where our father works, the Strom Thurmond building, and run in to say hello. I knock on his door, but there's no answer, and across the hall I can hear the department secretary making his excuses to someone else. I leave a note on Beryl's desk, that I was by, and I love him, nothing more. It's Dean Schelling's wife who's waiting in a wingback chair, crossing and uncrossing her long legs, the impatient sound of pantyhose.

This too is about Denny. The last I heard about Dean Schelling's wife, she was getting all her laundry done on campus.

Beryl's pretending to be busy with the copier, rattling into her headset about toner cartridges. She acts about thirty years older than she is, and she's been known to bake cookies for Denny on his birthday, so it's clear to me that she wants no part of whatever's going on here. And I wouldn't put it past my father to lock his door and put out his lights and pretend he's elsewhere. That leaves the dean's wife waiting for a good long while, and there's a piece of me that feels for her and however she imagines things are discussed between rational people.

As I'm leaving, she catches my arm in the hallway, familiar as a preacher.

"Joan, right?" she says. Her thumb spins the diamond on her left hand.

"Yes?"

"I've been trying to get ahold of Dr. Patee for ages, and he just never seems to be around."

"I know what you mean. I had to leave a note for him myself."

She's smiling too hard, her face suddenly on the edge of fifty, which may be closer to its true home. I'm thinking of the time in junior high when Denny and I took the johnboat and a case of beer instead of the bus, and Denny hooked his forearm on a cast. We got caught on our way in the kitchen door, our father straddling a ladderback chair, the evidence still hanging out of Denny's shirtsleeve. Daddy wanted to know when the crappie started fishing back.

"Have you tried a note?" I say.

"He doesn't return my calls. I thought, if you see him, you might tell him the matter is urgent."

"Of course, Mrs. Schelling."

"Dianne."

"Of course," I say. "Dianne."

We cannot end the conversation fast enough, and, pushing out of the building into the late day, I'm winded, feverish. I check my watch. I wonder if Lewis needs a drink, and keep fast through the campus, to put distance between myself and Dianne Schelling, as though distance really does make time, like with Denny at lunch. Students lounge in the grass beneath the trees, jam the paths with their book bags and their mountain bikes. Their thoughts are as pressing as calculus, the history of art, nothing I could use now even if I remembered what I once learned in school.

When I get to the library, Lewis is in the middle of a transaction. I catch my breath in the stacks, but I can hear him. Everybody can hear him. He's talking to his assistant, Chuck, as clear as if from stage.

"Chuck," he says, "Spence here would like something on Valium. See what you can find in the card catalog."

"Goddammit, man," Chuck says, "shut up."

Lewis ignores him. "Are you wanting a real lot of information, Spence, or just what Chuck gets off the encyclopedia?"

I peek around the shelves at Spence, and he is one like all the others, a frat boy with low-slung jeans and a Braves cap, enough scruff to his cheek to look old enough to be here. Lewis looms over him. He pats Spence's hand, which only makes Spence more the boy and him the headmaster.

"Here's how it works," Lewis says, and his voice fairly echoes. "You put what you've got for me in your book—this one here, Dickens. Put it where the card goes."

He slides a copy of *The Pickwick Papers* across the counter, and Chuck rises out of the labyrinth of desks behind him, hunchbacked and sweating.

Lewis says, "Then Chuck here puts what you want in another book, *A History of the Federal Reserve System,* and you can check it out over there. It's beautiful, a beautiful system. You'll enjoy yourself."

He puts an arm around Chuck's shoulders, and Chuck flinches and slinks away again.

Lewis beams. "Easy as pie," he says.

I can smell Spence's nerves on him when he passes me, a deep-down orey smell, as if they've been exhumed from grade school. I wonder if he might not be able to get that Valium on his own, if he could be as anxious for a doctor as he was for Lewis.

I lean across the desk, give Lewis a kiss on the cheek. Chuck is on his hands and knees in the back, swaying like a metronome.

"Chuck's a mess," I say.

"He's an idiot, and a pig. You know and I know, pharmacology is the subtlest science. He thinks we're talking about jellybeans."

Chuck gives us both an "eat shit" look, or maybe he just feels sick.

60

I laugh. "You really ought to try a whisper, Lewis. Somebody could get you into trouble."

"Pooh. It's a farm school. Without me, they could shut the library down and it'd be twenty years before anybody tried the lock."

It's good to see him, and I feel a release in my shoulders and spine, the weight of what I'm holding as it shifts around.

"What's your poison, sweetie?" Lewis says. "Anything your heart desires, Chuckie here will fetch it for us."

We both watch as Chuck pitches forward onto his face in what seems to be a permanent way.

"Buy me a drink?" I say.

"Smooth-talking devil." Lewis takes my hand and leads me out the back of the reference desk, slipping his coat from the hall tree as we pass it.

He dresses like a king. Underneath his long felted ulster, he's got a cashmere T-shirt tucked into a pair of flat-fronted charcoal trousers, a wide silver belt buckle, and shoes that are awfully close to what you'd wear bowling, or to sing in a cocktail lounge, only somehow wonderful. They are red and black, and they did not come from anywhere around here.

"Lewis," I say. "The next time you go shopping, will you think of me?"

"Every time I ride an escalator," he says. "Or valet park, or straight-arm the girl with the perfume."

"I only meant to say I like your shoes."

"Then I'll only think of you the once."

We leave the library for campus, into a blustery quad with big oaks and hatches of path, cut in front of a large hall and the statue of the founder himself, squatting, and then the wide open green down to the street. Lewis still holds my hand, and he tucks it in his pocket with his own as the wind comes up. We are indulgent with each other, solicitous, such careful friends since Bannon died. I know that happens to people when they realize the ones they love don't live forever, and not everyone who dies is old enough for it, but with Lewis, our closeness seems more special. He has that way about him, to make what's near ordinary seem otherwise. And I know he's not really a nice man, that Spence's nervousness was justified, that Lewis is capricious and imposing and far from a practical friend to have. He generally operates outside of any regulations that might protect the consumer. But we grew up together, and sometimes you value a person for what they once were to you rather than who they are to others.

He takes me to Nick's, and we sit in a booth near the back and the kitchen. It's one of those bars that occasionally caters to men who like men, which is something I think Lewis does too. He orders me a whiskey sour, a tonic and lime for himself.

"Your dad was in the stacks this morning. He have lunch with you and Denny?"

I shake my head. "They're still on the outs, I guess. Neither one of them really says so, but they've got me in the middle like the telephone game."

"Poor baby."

"Yeah, yeah, yeah."

I take a long swallow of my drink, let the cold go to my head, let myself think I could drink ten more just like it. I have nothing to go home to tonight, and tonight unfolds itself from the table and stands taller than I would have guessed. I'd like to get a little drunk in a bar, behave a little foolishly, to make this night something other than the thing I have to get through. Lewis is the perfect partner for that. I lean across the table and kiss his cheek again.

"So what do you know about Denny these days?" I ask. "Because I think I'm at a loss."

Lewis wears his careful face. "He came by the library a couple weeks ago, but that was when he was out at the laundry, before the thing downtown. I don't know. I called up to the house to see if he needed anything, but I just got the machine. He never called me back."

"Do you know who beat him up?"

Lewis looks into his drink and shakes his head. He knows all the guys who would do this sort of thing for money, has hired them himself when he needed them. He either can't tell me, or he won't.

"I got the idea it was a personal matter," he says.

"I stopped by Daddy's office," I say. "Schelling's wife was waiting to talk to him."

"A-ha."

"It seems kind of bold on her part, don't you think? I mean, what could she have to say to my father, that Denny ought to be grounded?"

"What you want to worry about is what the dean himself might have to say, should he get wind of all this business."

"How's that?"

"Schelling's got a whole cardboard box of incriminating evidence. Hard stuff, or else really personal. He spends years hording it away, and then he'll trump you at the most poetic time. You remember Llelenwald, in physics? Twenty years ago, Llelenwald's wife leaves him one weekend while he's off on conference, takes half the furniture, half the record albums, all that. The thing is, Llelenwald remembers the car was in the shop and the bank account was empty. Something had fucked up with his paycheck and there was not a penny, and wouldn't be until Monday. They fought about it, how he was leaving her stranded for the weekend with three dollars in her pocket, and how she hated him for it, or whatever. Still, he comes home from conference and she's found some change in the sofa cushions or something, because she's gone. So two weeks ago, Llelenwald goes to his mailbox and there's a Xerox copy of a receipt from 1984, for a timing chain and a set of valves. Signed Albert Schelling."

"You're kidding."

"Hey. I saw it myself. And the thing is, he kept it for twenty years, a little piece of paper, just thinking when he'd slip it in Llelenwald's box."

Dean Schelling is, for all intents and purposes, my father's boss, and my father is not the sort of man who cleans up after himself. He is a clever man, a crafty man, but dismissive about whatever trouble he's already waded through. *What's past is past,* he says. *If it didn't kill you when it had the chance, it's missed the boat.* The fact is, men like him don't work at universities anymore.

"You don't think she'd get my father involved in this, though. Do you?"

"What I hear, she's living up in Greenville with her sister these days. Maybe she feels like she's owed a little something for her trouble."

"Yeah, but that's a thing to bring up with Denny. He was a big enough boy to take to bed."

Lewis laughs. "And what happened the last time you brought up something with Denny?"

"Point," I say. "Point taken."

I am embarrassed for Denny all of a sudden, like I would be if he'd been caught kicking dogs. It's pathetic for his girlfriend to go to his father with her grievances, not even his girlfriend, but some woman he was fucking. And maybe that's why Dianne Schelling feels she has to put something more at risk than her hurt feelings, because this is all so pathetic. I lift my glass again and Lewis and I drift into other talk, work talk and Marshall talk and dog talk, but my mind is still chewing at the bone.

Growing up, I was always wary of our father, like you would be of open flame. He never once laid a hand on me in anger, not even a smack on the wrist, but he knew what to say, how to say it, and when. It is an absolute way to raise your children, and more effective with daughters, it seems, than sons. I only know that now, I am thirty-three years old, married, in a bar on a night when I have nothing more urgent than the drink in my hand, and I'm worried about my father in Denny's stead. Foresight is no different from guilt if you can't do anything about it.

Lewis puts his chin in the air for another round, the waitress steps away from the bar, and there's Hedy, cross-legged on a high stool, her head thrown back, laughing with another woman I don't recognize. They have cigarettes burning in their ashtrays, beer bottle labels peeled off and blown over the bartop in front of them, and it's clear they're deep in their cups. I could go over, say hello. I'd even think Hedy might be glad to see me.

But they're talking about Den too.

Hedy says, "Really, it's not that big a deal."

"But what about the good doctor?"

"Oh, jeez." Hedy laughs. "The *doctor.*"

I get this high-wire feeling in my stomach, not for myself but for this cluster that is our family. It's slipping from me, from anything I can do to make it right again, and that seems to be the course of things; I only need allow for it. I think of a fall day in the woods, years ago, the four of us together, Mom and me and Denny and our father. Denny has shot ahead of us on the trail, scrambling up rocks, across roots, nothing but fast, scabby, bare ankles in the tanbark. Daddy yells at him to not be such a fool, and his voice is big and his own, even in these woods, but Den just keeps running and Daddy yelling like to raise the dead.

I am tired. I want to sit down or be carried, because I am only three years old, but before the thought is even mine, I'm swept up in my mother's arms to ride against her shoulders. My face is tucked into her shirt and she smells like the forest itself, damp and green and healthy, and I am so tired I could fall asleep, barely holding on around her neck. The last thing I hear is my mother's voice coming through the bones of her back, my mother calling out for those boys of hers, to wait, to wait, to wait.

I put my head down on the tabletop for a moment, for just enough contact with a hard surface to make it settle, like to still the swing of a rope. I am tired now, and my mother has not carried me in years.

"Lewis, honey," I say. "Let's go home."

"You okay?"

"Just let's go home."

I look up and he's already pulling bills from his wallet to leave for the check.

"I forgot," I say, and let out a long breath. "I have to get some books for Denny. I said I would."

"Denny doesn't read. What does he want?"

"If we knew the answer to that one . . ."

"Right. We could rule the world." Lewis drains his glass, rattles the ice. "Okay. Grab your purse, and let's make this a quickie."

And so we go back to the library and he doesn't even stop by the desk to check on Chuck or use the computer. He stares at the elevator ceiling as if that will make our progress faster.

"Your change is jingling," I say. "Nervous?"

He stops his leg. "Never."

And I don't think Lewis would even remember what nervous feels like, but he is a man who lives by his plans, and he had not planned on coming back to the library tonight. When the doors open, he sweeps me out ahead of him into the foyer, the people bent over their books like workers in a field, exam season fast upon them. And even though no one is watching, Lewis hits the room like a shift in climate. Whispers make our wake.

"I feel like we've arrived," I say.

"Hmm. Lookit, if we don't move, I will be here all night."

He throws a glance over his shoulder and there's a trail of people through the stacks, at a distance, but following. No one looks particularly needy or strung out, or even thin or pale or over the age of twenty, but they are dogged. Lewis puts a hand behind his back to shoo them and, like strays, they drop away.

"They'll be back?" I say.

"The young can be surprisingly determined."

"Oh, Lewis, fast cars, loose women, good highs. And you're no better. How did you spend college, when you weren't getting caught?"

"Like I said."

But I have no idea how Lewis spent college, or why he even bothered, as he had a hand in more lucrative work even then. And his master's in library science took two more years.

But I remember running into him at USC when I was still an undergrad. He had a corner in the library, tucked back and away in the upper floors, and he'd made a warren of books called up

from storage and special collections, obsolete histories and eso-
teric political theory from the fifties. He was working on a paper,
tome length, written on a dozen yellow legal pads, and I don't
think he'd slept in days by the time I saw him. I had just come
from an aerobics class and had a hangover. I saw what he was
doing and felt a flush of embarrassment for my own lack of re-
sponsibility, of bearings on the future. By the time I graduated, I
had a corner in that library for myself.

He pulls *The Archaeology of Death and Burial,* a skull and
crossbones on the cover. "What in God's name is Denny up to?"

I shrug. "Come see him with me."

"What, Joan? Nervous?"

"I guess, a little."

"Oh, my. One Patee making another nervous. We'll all read
about this over breakfast for sure."

His face is pure grandmother, and when I laugh, whispers rise
again.

Lewis drives me through the night streets of the campus, the
classrooms and dorms tall and darkened like office buildings of a
tiny city emptied for the dinner hour. Girls in car coats and long
striped scarves run the crosswalks, laughing, the bars spilling slick
light into the gutters, and then we're in the testing fields, then the
real country, and blackness.

When we get to the cemetery, Denny's car is in the lane, but he
doesn't answer his door. My guess is he's over at Red Hill with
Body and the boys. We could walk over there, but I'd rather leave
the books and go.

I lead Lewis around to the porch, and there's the root cellar.

A pull chain runs to a light bulb hanging from the floor joists,
and when it comes on, the cellar glows the dull red of the clay
walls, sore and moist to the touch. Lewis stops short, and even as I
expect to see what I am looking at, my stomach goes loose inside
me. We both sit back on our heels, on our places on the stairs, as if
we've been blown down.

The bones are laid out on a table made of sawhorses and plywood, and they are not white bones, but muddy red like the walls, and they are not arranged in the shape of their body, but paired: two femurs, clavicles, the rib cage, the pelvis, which is cracked. There are little bones, and little rocks that could be bones, a large plastic bottle of some clear fluid, Hedy's kit of instruments, a spiral notebook I do not have the courage to read. There are beer cans, a plate of food, an ashtray full of stubbed out cigarettes. At least half are marked with lipstick.

"Does Hedy wear lipstick?" I ask Lewis. I can't remember that she did.

"What?" His voice has gone soft, as if to soothe a child.

"Never mind."

I take a deep breath, and the air has the taste of earth in it. Den and Hedy have brought two kitchen chairs down here, and a pale pink angora sweater hangs by its shoulders across the back of one. I sneeze.

"You think he's okay?" I ask.

"Sure. Oh, sure."

He says it as though he means it, but I turn and look at him and it's clear that he just has a lot of practice at meaning bizarre things. He draws a pack of cigarettes out of his coat pocket and lights one for each of us.

"I didn't know you smoked."

He exhales, fixes on me from underneath his brows, drawn tight.

"Right," I say. "Kind of like a Boy Scout."

"Did you want the cigarette or not?"

"You don't like this, do you."

He shakes his head. "It has unfinished business written all over it."

"Lewis," I say. "Did you ever see that Letterman years ago, when they brought out the dentist to be a film critic?"

"No," he says. "What?"

"All he talked about was teeth."

"Yeah, okay. But I tell you, the last time I saw your brother in

Atlanta, he had just picked up a vintage XJE for a client who wasn't taking delivery until Monday. He was living with a girl and she was out of town for the weekend. He had two dugout seats for the Braves game, it was payday, late July, and Wilson Pickett was on the stereo. The fridge was full of cold beer. Can you imagine?" He's staring at the sawhorse table, the ruddy bones. I would think he's seen worse than this before, but the whole time he's talking, he pats his pockets for his pillbox. Lewis does not like open-ended questions, loose strings. It's a sensibility that's informed both his professional lives.

"He was like one of those gods in a small Polynesian country," Lewis says. "I don't know what the hell happened."

"Is this like an allegory, Lewis?"

"No. I tell you, it was just like that."

I look back to the sawhorses, the pink sweater, as if somebody just shrugged it off.

"I never got to Atlanta much," I say. "It must have been something to see."

There are footsteps on the floor above us, and I push past Lewis, calling to Denny that we are down here, not to shut us in. I am tripping over myself as I come from the trapdoor, balancing as much with my hands as my feet, embarrassed to be caught spying on him, a little girl with her big brother's friends, her big brother's toys, such as they are.

There's nobody on the porch. I yell again for Denny and try the back door, but it's still locked, the stack of books still on the mat. Denny's car is still parked in front of Lewis's in the lane. Nothing's changed.

But then, out in the cemetery, she hits the path of headlights from the highway and she's running, fast, as if she's been trained to run at some point in her life and takes some pleasure in it, her bare heels kicking high. Her long red coat unfurls behind her, and her hair is short and dark, or pulled back, but it's clear that she is who she is, a woman, beautiful, running back to town.

6

LEWIS DROPS ME at my car on campus, and I can see my father's lights in his office; now after midnight, he must think Dianne Schelling is safely home and tucked in bed. I gather up a handful of gravel and pitch rocks, one by one, at his window until he comes to the blinds. It has become a convenient way to communicate with these men in my family; perhaps in the future we will leave dolls at the crossroads, hatchmarks in the dirt, but for now, I throw rocks.

He opens the main door, his briefcase in his hand, and it's as if he's been expecting me to pick him up.

"Hey, kitten," he says. "How was school today?"

"Daddy." I kiss his cheek.

"What keeps you out so late?"

"Lewis DuRant and I had some drinks over at Nick's."

"You can't go home now." He puts an arm around my waist and leads me toward the parking lot. "Come out to the lake house with me. I get so old and lonesome."

"I don't believe that."

But he's tucking me behind the wheel and then himself into the passenger seat, his briefcase balanced on his knees. My father, taking so much more room than is made available.

"Where's your car?" I say.

He points the way through the maze of parking lots, with their medians and curbs, to a section for a dorm.

"It's that Schelling lady," he says. "She's giving me fits."

"I think she's serious, Daddy."

"If you buy her act, honey, I got some property in Arizona you got to take a look at. That woman has the tiniest goddamn teeth I've ever seen."

"Her teeth?"

"Yes. Never trust anybody with small features—small nose, small lips. Most of all, small teeth. Never trust anybody with small teeth."

"I ran into her at your office this afternoon, and she was pretty keyed up. I got the feeling you might be in trouble."

He slaps my thigh like I'm telling a joke. "Come on."

"What? Because she's a girl?"

"Now, honey. I haven't done anything to that woman." His hand still rests on my knee. He pats now, and I think of horses I have seen him quiet. "It'll all come out in the wash."

I give up. "Where on earth is your car?"

"Oh, phooey," he says, and unlatches the door while we're still rolling. "I'll see you at the house."

But I keep my lights on him as he passes behind a stand of wax myrtle and disappears. It's from the myrtles that the Avanti flares and sweeps, swings into the parking lot at its far edge, already out ahead of me on the road, like the escape is going according to plan. I follow him and he takes the curves fast, the straightaways faster, cannot get away fast enough. I have to run two red lights getting out of town.

After Mom died, Daddy moved down to the lake permanently. If he could have dropped the farm into the ground, I think he would have, buried pets and cattle and cleaning ladies and eyelet curtains all together, as they had best served my mother, as he best held her in his mind. Denny and I had houses of our own by then, and Daddy had Piper, who was only thirteen and devastated. For months, she went everywhere with him, to class, to conferences, and living at the lake house was a kind of new start for her. Still, Daddy slept on the floor next to her bed because she had nightmares and would wake in a panic and could not go back to sleep alone. It was easier to be there than to come running, he said, and in that light, the move to the lake seemed obvious.

He sold the farmhouse last winter: the house, the farm around it, and everything inside it. He didn't want to make a fuss, he said, and by the time he told us what he'd done, I was the only one close enough to pack a few boxes, to take a few things for each of us: my great-grandmother's marble-topped vanity for Piper, the heavy-legged queen bed for myself, our father's pigeonhole desk for Denny. I have the china, the crystal, the silver, a couple of portraits, a chaise longue, as much as I could gather in an afternoon. The rest went to the buyer.

The thing of it is, I was alone. There were heirlooms I couldn't find or didn't remember until it was too late, and there was no one to tell me where to look. Even now, I can still go through that house in my mind those last hours, always a little out of breath, always thinking in a three-pronged way: what was important now or in the past, what might come to be important someday, to my children, Denny's children. Piper's children, years from now.

I've forgiven our father what I could not take, and my sister supported the idea from the first, being a great fan of clean starts. But for Denny, it's become the thread to pick at, the snag that's unraveled the whole. When I tell him I have the desk in my garage whenever he wants it, he looks at me like frogs have fallen from my mouth.

He left Atlanta the day the sale went through. He pulled into my driveway with a U-Haul, one in the morning, the armpits of his suit coat ringed with sweat even as it was beginning to snow. We wrapped ourselves in blankets, sat on my front porch in the swing, and watched the lights go off in Bannon's house. We did not mention him, or Gail, whom Denny has never known well. We did not mention our father, and what he'd done, or why, or what Denny was going to do without a job or a place to live. We talked about baseball, when Denny used to play it, and his baseball cards, now gone, and I cried like a baby for how sad he was, but I doubt Denny even knew it for that. The sky spit snow all night, but there was nothing on the ground to speak of in the morning.

I follow my father's taillights up the drive. To my left, Lake Keowee climbs out of the darkness in a broad swath of moon between the trees, the water blacker than the night itself. Floodlights pitch across the gravel, the bed of the old farm truck, the rocking chairs tipped against the porch rail. We had rocking chairs at the farmhouse too, but they were punched-steel kind from the forties. Mom painted them a different color every spring, and when we sat on that front porch, all we watched was the open pasture to the road, the sun rising and not setting, the trees distant on the fence line instead of flocked against the house. The two have always been different worlds.

Inside, the lake house smells tannic like the lake water, and like coffee burned in the pot. My father's breakfast dishes sit on the table, the paper folded open to the sports page and tucked beneath the rim of the plate. He comes out of the kitchen with two peanut butter sandwiches, undoubtedly our dinner.

"Kitten," he says.

His smile is so big, I have no choice but to take it on. I think maybe he will talk for a while, tell me about some new scheme, some lobby for the statehouse, some timber deal up in the mountains. The teaching is his job, not his avocation. When we were children he told us he was a con man so often, we repeated it at school. So tonight I want to hear some story that rolls on awhile and makes me laugh, to have our sandwiches, and go to bed without tearing anything open. It's late. I started the day tired and have only ventured deeper into it.

He lays a fire and we settle into wide-backed club chairs before it. The fabric on the armrests is starting to wear through, a red toile with bird-of-paradise. Mom picked the chairs, but I know Daddy must have helped, because red is his favorite color and "bird-of-paradise" is the only decorating term he knows.

None of us has been okay since she died, and that's the truth.

"You want me to get these chairs recovered?" I ask, even though I know the answer.

Daddy bats the air with his big hand. "They're chairs."

"They're fading."

"Who notices but you? Your sister?"

"I'm sure she will."

"Well, you two go pick something out when she comes home. Something you all like." He goes to his pocket and pulls out a fat fold of money, starts peeling off bills.

"Daddy," I say. "Come on."

He shrugs, laughs, brushes crumbs from his thigh. He's fidgety; there is no story he's going to tell tonight, but I'll be damned if I'm going to bring Denny up. We sit in quiet, watching the fire lick the grate.

"So how'd you make out with your brother there?" he says.

I take a deep breath, but he's way out ahead of me.

"See, I heard about what he's up to already, out at the school. That little girlfriend of his asks some Joe in archaeology a question, who asks another guy a question in earth sciences, who wants to know what for, and after too long, it's all over everywhere."

He rubs his hand on the thigh of his pants.

"I believe they are on to something, I really do."

"You're serious."

"As a heart attack."

"Daddy, I just came from Denny's, and he's got those bones in his cellar—"

"All of them?"

"What?"

"Possession is what I'm talking about, possession and the law. He found those things and now they're going to have a helluva time getting them off him if he says they're his. I tell you what, I'm going to send a guy over there, not now, but after the holidays, casually. He works for the state, and I can guarantee he's going to be impressed by what's going on."

"You think he's going to give Denny a promotion?"

"Now don't be ugly, Joan. But I know what that boy is going to find next. I know it."

"What?"

"One of those cast-iron coffins, or two folks buried in there together, or some guy crosswise to the rest, and they're going to
come out of the woodwork over at the school to see it."

He sounds, I think, proud. As proud of Denny as he would be
of himself, if the idea had been his own to start with, like the
bones are some shell game or get-rich-quick scheme and he's
about to beat the house. The two of them are more allied now
than they've been in months, and Denny is his only son. The want
to be proud must be a strong one.

I am struck with sadness as full as an open hand to the face,
and it's in part the tiredness I feel now, the drinks I had hours ago.
But I see my father, delighted, and I don't know how to make this
turn with him. I thought we were down to last chances, but now
I see what's after that, and after that, the infinite between him
and Denny. What do they need me for, running back and forth,
wringing my hands? I feel my loyalties break and tide, the way
you feel your nerves when they get too far away from you. Daddy
doesn't even pretend to wonder what happened out at Denny's
when I said what he wanted me to say.

"So I guess you've got it all worked out."

"No," he says. "No."

There's a lift in his voice, as if he still holds reservation and I
might come to change his mind on some contingent matter or another, but it's just a cat's-paw. Denny is as good as famous.

He makes a big show of getting me something to drink, of
changing the subject, asking what I did today, but we have already
covered most of that, and so the quiet lodges between us. He
knows I'm disappointed, but he knows it the way a child would
know it, without acknowledging his own connection. He sits on
the edge of his chair, his elbow cocked, his hand gripping the arm
to push him up at first chance to change the space between us, any
change a difference.

"Here's the thing," I say finally. "Dianne Schelling told me she
needed to speak with you. Urgently, I think it was."

"Joan," he says, and he breaks the corner of a grin.

"That's exactly what she said. And Lewis tells me her husband keeps tabs on everybody at the university, that he holds on to stuff, sometimes for years, waiting for the right time to present itself."

He eases back in his chair, rubs his chin in the split of his fingers. He doesn't want to talk about this with me, I know, has never wanted to talk about this with me, and won't tonight.

"I'm just worried," I say. "I just wonder what Dean Schelling's holding on to of yours."

"Honey," he says, and he shakes his head at his shoes. I remember in high school telling both my parents that I was worried about how lightly they considered my privacy, and he got the same look on his face, the same tone in his voice, and he said, *Where'd you read that, Joan,* Seventeen *magazine?* He hasn't heard a word I've said.

"Now you need to just sit back," he says. "Let me tell you a thing or two I've learned about people."

He tells me how there are sour people in this world, and sorry people, and people who lie down when they ought to get up. He tells me there are people who will use what they can take, and there are people who will take anything that's not nailed down. There are bitter people and sneaky people, and people who will treat you one way to your face, and another way when your back is turned. He knows all these people, and I don't need to worry about him. He knows how to handle people like Dianne Schelling just fine.

"I'm a lot older than you, kitten," he says. "I have seen about all of it."

"Okay, Daddy."

"Really."

"Okay."

He looks at his watch, brushes his pant leg again. The fire is down to embers, and it's time to go to bed, but he is waiting on me to close the show, to say things look rosier than they did before.

"I am so tired," I say, and this is good enough.

"What time do you have to get going in the morning?" he says.

"I got eggs, and ham. I'll make you a good breakfast."

And I know he'll be up before dawn by habit from the farm, and he'll have coffee waiting for me when I come down, and he'll want to feed me, and follow me out to the highway, to see me safely on my way. I kiss his cheek and tell him I love him, thanks again.

I climb the stairs to the loft, the row of wrought-iron beds beneath the dormers. The sheets are clean, and I try to imagine my father changing linens on a bed, but I know better. He's had the same cleaning lady for years. I slip off my shoes and pull the covers to my chin, the blanket pink and unused, still creased from its time in the package.

I remember when I was a girl, getting dressed in the morning and then climbing back in bed to wait for Mom to call me for school. I don't know why I did it, maybe just that it was warm beneath the covers and I was not ready to get up. I feel like that now in reverse: the end of the day, still in my clothes, and reluctant to let go of where I've been, to move from one place to another. Maybe I could call on her to come down from wherever she is, to come to me, and hold my head in her lap, stroke my hair, and sing me off to sleep. I can't imagine it was once that easy.

I fumble beside the bed for my purse, the letter of Marshall's I have not read yet, have not needed until now. I unfold the paper and petals dust across the sheets in the lancing moonlight. They have stained the folds a deep, bright violet, and that's all he's telling me tonight.

I wish that my mother had known him. I wish she knew all of us as we are now; she would have done a better job of caretaking than I can. I cannot help such thoughts from time to time, the way I wish I were taller or prettier or smarter, or had said as much when it would've meant something to her. She must have known, though. She must have felt her strength when the chips were down.

About ten years ago, Mom and Daddy started screening their phone calls at home. It was my last year of school in Columbia, and I called home every weekend or so, and the first couple times I got the machine, Mom said she'd been running to catch the phone. Eventually I pinned her down. Daddy was in trouble at the university, had been suspended, in fact. There was some business about the sale of intellectual property, what he said was his and what they said was theirs, as if you could keep track of such things, who owned what was in somebody's head. It was silly. She was sure it would all blow over before the year was out. When I was home for Thanksgiving, I went to the laundry room for a bottle of Windex and found a grocery bag full of cash on the high shelf, mostly twenties, mostly bundled by the thousand. My head got light just looking at the money, but when I asked about it, Mom said it was for a rainy day.

I found out later, the university had filed a $3 million lawsuit against my father and they were trying to bring him up on criminal charges, so I'm not sure what rainy day she was talking about blowing over. She knew what was going on. I think Daddy told her everything and showed her everything. When we were kids, she used to hide candy on the high shelf in the laundry room, birthday presents behind the chimney in the attic, confiscated toys under her bed. I did not go looking any further, but I imagine there were grocery bags all over the house.

Then one morning after Christmas, they were having coffee in the kitchen and Mom crossed her arms over her chest and felt something hard that had not been hard the day before. No one has ever told me how, or why, what exactly was lost or gained, but I know when Mom got sick, Daddy needed his job and he got it back quick. Maybe he lost a few of those grocery bags in the bargain, but that's what it was, a bargain, a deal he settled, something by which everybody's back got rubbed. If he really changed his ways, I'd be surprised.

I get up on my knees and fold my elbows on the sill above the headboard. The lake throws so much light on a clear night, and it's been months since I've been here to see it. When I was little, Mom and Denny and I spent most all the summer on the lake with a speedboat and waterskis, with hammocks and lanterns and the deck boards warm beneath our backs when we stretched out to take the sun. Daddy would come down from the farm when he could, and Mom would sit in his lap with a glass of bourbon they were sharing, and they would cheer Denny on his jackknives, his backflips from the dock, how high the splash, how loud the smack of his back against the water. I was too young to dive like that and so would stretch out on the dock by their feet and try not to get sent to bed. Some nights, nobody got sent to bed, just blankets snapped out and settled over us against the breeze skimming off the water top.

After Piper was born, our father started teaching at the university. He spent a few nights a week at the lake house, as it was closer to the university than home, and I think that was the way he and Mom wanted it, to be apart and come together, as if it were summertime and they were sitting on laps and drinking bourbon from the same glass, only now at home with their little baby instead of on the lake.

And so the feeling of the lake bled over into everyday at the farm, into Denny and me, now cast out of the house when the baby was sleeping, or nursing, or fussy, which is to say nearly all the time. We ran a little wild, ran barefoot in the dry field grass, throwing ball, riding horses, and, later, driving the farm truck to the back pastures with the bed full of people, Bannon and his sisters, Lewis and girls he brought around, girls named Ginger or Shelley or Lois or Dawn, all of us out to drink Pabst Blue Ribbon from cans and smoke hand-rolled cigarettes, to play cards, to have fights and kiss the girls, all the girls but me.

That summer Piper was born, we did not go to the lake house but once or twice for the day, as she was too little for speedboats and waterskis, and the next summer it seemed as if the house was Daddy's office and we hardly went there at all.

I wonder if my father does get lonely as he says he does, although I think he is like me and allows it only so much room. But too, like me, he spent his marriage given over to the flux of leaving and return, the small thrills of anticipation, and I imagine all such is a hard thing to put down. Even as Mom has been dead for more than eight years, I bet there's a part of him that still has her waiting back at the farmhouse, still longing for her hand at the small of his back, her smart words in his ear. I would be.

I am.

7

MARSHALL COMES HOME at least a dozen times on Saturday.
I can't concentrate on work; I think I hear the door open, think I
hear his car in the drive, and the newsprint runs together before
my eyes. I take a shower and know I feel him in the house when I
get out, something shifted, tipped his way after all these days in
my balance. I walk through the den to the front hall, calling his
name, making puddles across the hardwood, and Luther laps the
floor behind me as if I'm providing a service.

There is nothing in my closet I want on my body, but I take
a bunch of stuff from the hangers before I admit as much. I call
Piper in the mountains, because she changes clothes at least five
times a day, and all her clothes are not her own; half of them
are mine, the Salvation Army's, a boyfriend's coat, a girlfriend's
boots. She makes dresses herself to sell in town for pocket
change, high-waisted, full-skirted dresses that brush the floor.
The woman who sells them for her says clothing is the key to
emotional stability, and I'm in need of a little of that right now.

"What are you wearing?" I ask.

"Well. Hello to you too."

"I need advice. Marshall's coming home tonight, and I want
things to go well."

"Wear nothing."

"I thought I might could do better than that."

"More baby-making, less streetwalker?"

"Exactly."

We discuss the virtues of red, of silk, of comfort. Piper is nearly twelve years younger than me, and her perspective somewhat lighter. We are closer than age might tell, and her distance away helps. She sees home as a fixed point behind her, beneath her, and unlike so many women her age, she appreciates the jaggedness of good intentions. She tells me about a boy in her department so cute she has to look at her shoes when she passes him in the hall. She wore a red turtleneck dress to class today, with black boots, and she'd say the effect was a good one, but how can she be sure? He's like looking at the sun.

My hair drips down my neck and gives me chills, so I lie back on the bed and pull the corner of the quilt over me. I used to nap this way when I was a child, the covers skinned up from the bottom of the bed, the barest commitment to sleep. And now, just the action seems enough to make me sleepy; I do not remember hanging up the phone.

Marshall wakes me with his mouth. He has the most beautiful mouth, a full mouth, full lips like a baby's, and I wake to his mouth on my shoulder, his beautiful lips, his teeth.

I turn toward him but he has stepped away, working the buttons of his jeans.

We spend what's left of the weekend like that, tangled and sleepy and just the two of us in our home, not going out, not even to the porch to get the papers, not even to the car for his suitcase. The answering machine takes our calls. The refrigerator is suddenly filled with what we want to eat. Luther makes sighs from one end of the house to the other, and we are happy.

Then it's four on Sunday afternoon and I sit in panties on our kitchen countertop, eating an apple as green and crisp as grass. I hate Sundays. They are empty days between what I want and what I've got, and eventually I know Marshall will tell me what time he'll be leaving tomorrow or, if I'm lucky, on the next day. I try to put that out of my head, but to know it's coming is to test the spring of an old step.

"I brought you something," he says.

He wears a towel wrapped around his hips, his hands behind him, hiding what he's got. His stare is like a flashbulb in my face; nothing I look at after him seems to hold still. I thread an ankle through the space between his elbow and his rib cage. He has showered, and the skin on his back is warm and wet beneath my foot sole.

"You sure did," I say.

"No. Something else."

"Animal or vegetable?"

"Neither."

"Mineral, then."

He lifts me off the counter by my waist, gently—he is always gentle—and then I am standing with my head tucked beneath his chin, the apple forgotten by my side. I use my body to touch him, not my hands, wrap one of my calves around the back of his, my hips to his, our bellies and chests, and there's his mouth again, the most beautiful mouth I've ever seen. I pull his mouth to mine, his lower lip to my teeth. And then it's like he's been letting me play and that's over. Someplace far off, there's the bruised sound of dropped fruit, rolling across the floor, and we are at each other again.

We curl up in the armchair in the den. We light the gas logs, and I think about dinner.

He says, "I really did bring you something."

"Should I close my eyes?"

He makes a pleased sound in his throat, and I drop my forehead against his.

"Baby, you keep bringing me the same thing," I say.

"Just don't move," he says.

He goes to the kitchen for a box that fits in the palm of my hand. Inside, there is the tiniest ring, intricate with gold and stone, tiny green and blue stones, the byzantine made small.

"I could wear it on a chain," I say.

"It's not for you."

It's a ring for a baby. And then he tells me that he doesn't have to go, not anywhere, not until after the holidays.

For a long moment, I can't make words. My face is breaking, my stomach full of wings. I feel time crack out in front of me like a whip, and everything ahead is changed, that fast, that instant. I throw my arms around his neck.

"This is wonderful." And then, "What happened?"

"Nothing."

"You're okay at work?"

"I don't think it's about work, Joanie."

"Hey." I take his face in my hands and make him look at me. "Hey."

When Marshall has been away on site and it's been bad, he does not sleep, and there are times when it's been worse than that, when he does not rest in his sleep but sweats and thrashes and walks the house and does not remember so in the morning. He's had pneumonia, third-degree burns, blood poisoning, trench foot, and I change the dressings, pick up the antibiotics, make the appointment with the dermatologist. But then there's what doesn't make him sick, and we don't talk about that. I try not to ask too many questions.

Now his eyes are yellowed at their edges like old cloth, all that smoke and ash, mud and dust, the other things that make for ruin.

"You got those wolf eyes," I say. "You look tired."

"Yeah?" He pulls his face from my hands. "I just don't feel like it tonight, Joan."

"Feel like what?"

"The fretting. Let's not do the fretting. I'll be here for weeks. Let's do the fretting, I don't know, next Tuesday."

He smiles, but it's like he's smiling from years away inside himself and it will take my lifetime for that smile to mean anything to me. I sit still, and we're in the same chair but separated, and for some reason I don't get up. Getting up would mean something. I have never been any good at leaving well enough alone.

Finally Marshall turns on the TV. Finally we talk, and it's about the old movie he's found with Tallulah Bankhead. Marshall loves old movies, loves Tallulah Bankhead because he's heard the story about the time she got a standing ovation from the crew on the set of *Lifeboat*. It had been because she spent most of the scene bent over the side of the boat and wasn't wearing any underwear. I let my head down onto his shoulder.

"I'm glad you're home," I say. "And I'm glad you'll stay awhile."

He kisses the top of my head. "You'll have to kick me out the door."

I look up at his face, his jaw line, his beautiful mouth, and I wish I could have that feeling of everything falling into place. But maybe next time, I think, the next time he goes away and I miss him and he comes home again, maybe then everything will fall into place and feel that way for days on end. I try hard to think so, that we have another chance, that chance turns on some great wheel and requires only patience to come around again. And maybe if we were together all the time, I wouldn't get that feeling as often as I do. I would miss it, and maybe worse than the things I miss now.

The first week is politeness and sex. When Marshall is in bed, I want to be with him, and the same for showers and eating and walks with the dog. We hover over each other, and it is untold pleasure to reach out and he's there, to hear him in the kitchen, sharpening knives, rinsing glass, burning toast. When I go into my office, he wants to know how long I'll be, and I say not long, no matter what I have to do. I shuffle papers, and I can hear him pouring coffee for himself, settling into his chair, can hear him sigh, and all I do is shuffle paper. After a while, he comes to the office door with the book he is reading and his cup of coffee and asks if I would mind. I say no, please, and clear a space for him. Every once in a while, I reach back and stroke his bare foot. I get things done that way.

"We're pitiful," he says.

"Starved."

"Want to go to bed?"

I laugh, and he twines his fingers with mine, brings my wrist to his mouth.

"Want to dance?" he says. "Blow in my ear, sit on my lap?"

He has my elbow now, my waist, gathering me in like rope.

I have missed him so much.

But sometimes I catch him staring into nothing and I wonder if a month away will be enough. Maybe he needs a vacation, a true clean break, a week someplace warm, to come back with a sunburn, a hangover, an appreciation for the habits of his days, such as they are. We have never been on a vacation together, not even in the most honkytonk sense, a trip to Vegas or Myrtle Beach. Marshall spends all his time traveling; it's a vacation for him to be at home.

Midnight, I turn, wake, and the bed is empty. Marshall has pulled a kitchen chair to my side, and he sits now, in his shorts, watching me.

"Hey," I say.

"Hey."

"Whatcha doing?"

But he doesn't answer. I reach out and the flat of his shin is slick with sweat.

"Marshall?"

"I'm just thinking."

"You're awake?"

"Yes."

And I believe him but would rather this were some dreamlike event, something that could be laughed away in the morning, the time he woke up in the bathtub, the time he broke a dozen eggs into my purse. But it's not. I can't see his face. I close my eyes, my brain slamming around my head for something to say.

"Hey."

"Hmm?" He gnaws at a fingernail, spits into the dark.

"You need sleep."

"Oh, yeah. Yeah, I do."

"So get over here."

"I will," he says, but I am to take that to mean later, to leave him be. I try closing my eyes again but I can feel him staring at me without seeing, and my face goes hot as if I am onstage.

I keep my eyes closed and he whispers my name. There is a lot in that whispering; we know each other well, and I hear him telling me that he has to slow down, and it takes time to slow down, and he is settling, not to worry. All he's got to offer people is how fast he can get a number, a piece of paper from one place that's wrecked to another place that's not, and being fast is not much, but he has gotten good at it. Now he has to practice being still again, and it's harder than he remembered, even to be still enough to sleep.

He says my name, says not to worry, and I keep my eyes closed the whole time as if I'm just half listening, half asleep.

And in the morning, he has some kind of flu. Nothing stays down except ginger ale and crackers, and he sweats through two sets of sheets. By afternoon, he feels better, and by dinner he's grilling steaks in his overcoat, his gloves with the fingers snipped away, whistling. He has the constitution of an oil drum, the ability to flush what's wrong with him out quickly.

And I have work. There's an article in the *Independent Mail* about a man who dresses up like a weasel for Christmas, and the connection between the holiday and the animal is one of his own invention, something about the lowly laid lower before God. He quotes from Genesis, Adam and Eve being cast from the garden, and you can go to his home in Honea Path and see the light display in his yard, the glowing manger scene with weasels, the shepherds keeping watch over the weasels, the weasel angels come to earth. The whole thing culminates in a shed on the back of his property, where he will tell the story of the Christmas weasel, dressed as such himself.

I should go to Honea Path to see this, but also to see the mill there where deputies opened fire on the strikers during the Depression, to Gaffney, where the machine guns were bunkered at the mills, to Union, where the eight-year-olds slept on racks of bobbins between shifts. Here in my own neighborhood, the mill whistle could be heard for fifteen miles, whether you had to make a shift or not.

There's no sound like that anymore. We keep to our computer screens rather than front porches and shift schedules. Our bells and whistles come from our pockets. At the zoo in Greenville there're these monkeys from Southeast Asia that get going extraordinarily loud a dozen times a day; you can hear them howling from the verandas on McDaniel Avenue as clear as you can from Nicholtown, but there's no regularity to it. It doesn't mean anything to us, to anybody but the monkeys.

That zoo is on land where the old public swimming pool used to be. When the state ordered the pool integrated, the city just filled it in and made a park, integration made more palatable the more clothing was involved. There is a history of problems with swimming pools in this part of the state; a judge in Saluda County once declared them instruments of the devil. He blamed the boll weevil, the lack of rain, and the labor unrest of the 1930s on the fact that South Carolina had allowed people to be half-dressed and wet inside her borders.

My thoughts drive loops like this all day. I keep charts and diagrams, where to look for more information, whom to ask, what might best represent this feature to the public. I'm constantly amazed by how broad and shallow my knowledge is, the bone-stupid things I've never considered: how slaves buried their dead at night, how time was only standardized with train schedules, how all the cows you see, all along the side of the road, are female, and if they are old enough, mothers.

When Marshall asks, my desk seems something to get up and walk away from rather than something to explain, and I imagine he feels the same about what he does. But I keep the letters he writes to me in the drawer beside our bed, and I think about who might read them someday, and what they'll tell about us. I keep his letters for that very reason.

Evening, I go to the fridge, pull out red peppers, Parmesan, a bag of arborio rice. It makes a pile on the countertop.

"Maybe we should go out to eat," I say.

Marshall has just hung up the phone. He's staring at it now, his hand bent back across his mouth.

"That was your brother," he says, and then he looks at me.

"Oh, yes. That."

"That."

I take a seat next to him. I don't know what he's thinking, but he has always liked Denny, always been generous about him, and I meant to tell him what was going on out at the cemetery.

"He has a backhoe?" he says.

"Those guys over in Red Hill do, I guess. They have all kinds of equipment."

He lets out a breath against his hand, and then he looks at me.

"I might go over there tomorrow, check it out."

"Are you serious?"

"Yeah. Why not."

"Because it's crazy, that's why not. You're encouraging him to be crazy."

"You remember me telling you about Leonard Lopey?"

"No."

"Sure. I met him in Mississippi a few years ago: tall guy, would eat off your plate when you weren't looking? He's on that federal disaster mortuary unit from time to time. He was in Noble, Georgia. I could call him, see what he does in a case like this."

"This is not a case, Marshall."

He looks at me. "I know. It's something to do."

"You're bored?" I slide my foot up his leg.

"No. I mean for Denny. He quit his job, right?"

"Yeah. He did."

But I catch the moment before he collects himself, his face

slack, his bones wearing at his skin. We're not talking about Denny, what Denny does or doesn't do for a living.

"It's harmless," he says. "Rather, the harm's already been done, in the past. It's just some old bones."

"Yeah," I say. "But."

He joggles my elbow. "Come on. You've dug around for him too, I bet."

"A little."

"A little more than that."

"You know, depending on a bunch of things, that guy doesn't have to be dead for natural reasons. South Carolina had more murders than Chicago around the turn of the century, and Lewis seemed to think the whole thing looked suspicious."

"A *murder*." Marshall puts on his voice of grave suspicion, wringing his hands.

"Stop that."

"A *mystery*." He begins to loom over me, paw and clutch.

"Quit it. Oh, quit that."

He doesn't.

We go into Spartanburg and eat downtown, the first time out of the house since he's been home. Marshall shows me how Leonard Lopey steals from your plate when you're not looking, and I show him how Hedy sits so close to Den, one hand on the table at a time. He sings into my ear, an old song about a chansoness, a cigarette, two hands slyly meeting beneath a serviette. I laugh. We drink wine. It is a lovely evening.

8

MONDAY, THE SUNRISE runs full-bore through the knotting clouds above the cemetery, cherry-red on steel, on stone, a car wreck of a day breaking. It will rain later, but now the light seeps off the markers as if it needs to be wiped up with a sponge. I walk the paths Hedy and I walked, the names a rhythm in my head: *jeremiah, jacob, jessamine, jane.* I see my own name, first and middle, but not on the same grave, and Marshall's name, and my mother's, Valerie, a name I would use for a girl child if I were to have one. The wind whips up, and I have to tuck my hair behind my ears to keep it from my face.

It's been only a few weeks since I was here last, but people have brought fresh offerings, new flowers, a pack of cigarettes, a can of Coke, open, with a straw. There is a picture postcard of Waikiki tucked between the dry grass and the stone, a long view up the beach to Diamond Head. The writing on the card is faded already, but signed with love, stamped as if to mail. I fix it back exactly as it was.

Up at the house, the boys are gathered in the lane, as Hedy is still sleeping and Denny's kitchen is still in shambles. Leonard Lopey has made the drive from Norcross, Georgia, he was so intrigued with Marshall's call, and he and Marshall lean against the trunk of Leonard's Gran Torino, sipping from Styrofoam cups of coffee that even at this distance you can tell tastes awful. They are waiting for somebody from the archaeology department.

About which Denny is pissed.

As I come out of the cemetery, he's got Marshall pulled aside, his voice snapping and tight. He's trying to reel it in, because he likes Marshall and to have a fight with your brother-in-law is a waste of time, but reeling in comes hard for Denny.

"Goddammit, though," he says. "I am not interested in the university being out here. They've got my ass already."

"I thought you quit that job."

"Jesus, man. The job's just the half of it."

This occurs to me too: Dianne Schelling, her long legs crossing and uncrossing outside our father's door. "Marshall," I say.

He sighs. His brow is knitted. "Okay, okay, already."

He turns to Leonard Lopey.

"It's kosher, boys and girls. One hundred percent." Leonard stands from the fender, all pointed joints, tissue thin, like a wire hanger. "This lady owes me several major favors. Plus, she's not even tenor track."

"Tenure," I say, before I can stop myself.

Leonard smiles greasily. "Right you are."

"So she's a friend," Marshall says, "who just happens to work there."

"She can be made to understand that, sure."

Marshall turns to Denny. "Why don't you wait here, and make her understand."

"Come on, man."

"She's on her way. Tell her whatever you want. Tell her she's got the wrong house, I don't care. We'll take Leonard back in the woods, and the rest is up to you."

Denny scuffs his boot in the dirt. "Fine."

"Okay. Fine."

Leonard and Marshall pour the rest of their coffee out on the ground and Leonard pops the trunk for his gear. Denny lights a cigarette, and you can tell he's still angry but needs for his anger to dry up, for the sake of fair concession. These rational battles of his are sluggish and difficult to watch. I tuck an arm through Marshall's and turn him toward the church.

"Is this okay?" I say.

We look back to where Leonard is bent over a toolbox balanced on the car fender. He slings a Polaroid camera around his neck and goes into the trunk for something else.

"I don't know," Marshall says. "I thought this was just a busman's holiday, but your brother's being weird. And Leonard's got his toolbox out."

"What's he keep in there?"

"Serious stuff. Forensic stuff."

"Ooey."

"You're not kidding."

"We don't have to do this," I say, but I know we do. Leonard's come all the way from Georgia, everything already set in motion, and Marshall doesn't answer me.

Leonard slams his trunk and Denny waves us straight ahead, beyond the church, into the woods. We can't miss it, he says. Still, we push through snarls of brush and summer vine peeled bare, the path long overgrown. It's hard going, and Marshall walks too fast.

There's a meter to his breathing, his long strides and quick eye. I get the idea this is how a runner runs in place, a swimmer snaps his suit or toes the block before the start: necessary, anxious habits, but ones I've never seen before. I catch his sleeve but his face is closed to me; I realize how this is all like work for him, how a day at work must go.

The first hole could bury a sports car.

It's cut through the strata of soil to rock like the ground has been bitten into. There are maybe a half-dozen more holes in the near woods, some shallow, some deep, the red-turned clay piled up beside them. Leonard comes from behind us with his Polaroid snapping.

"What the hell is this?" he says.

And he's right; I look into a couple of the holes and there's something strange about them, something missing, perhaps a sense that someone was actually looking for something. Under a blue tarp is a backhoe, Body and Russell's, and it looks as though most of the holes have been dug with it. It's as if Denny couldn't be bothered to take his time, to be careful or concentrated, or maybe that he couldn't resist the big machines. I think how he can't even be crazy right, and it's enough to make me laugh out loud.

I am alone in this. Marshall stands with his hands jammed in his pockets and watches Leonard climb out of one hole and into another.

"What you got, Leonard," he says.

Leonard squints in our direction. "It looks to me like they were testing equipment."

"Yeah. This is crap."

"I don't know. Dig anywhere you like, I say. You're bound to turn up something."

Leonard throws a leg over the lip of the hole and hoists himself out. He scoops soil into a little vial and pockets it, takes a compass reading and notes it down. When he lowers himself into another hole, Marshall checks his watch.

"What's the call, Leonard?" he says.

"No call." Leonard has gone back to the view through his Polaroid. "Unless you like to see the way other people dig their holes."

"Christ," Marshall says, and then he walks away.

"Hey," I say, but he doesn't turn around, or wait.

I don't understand. This was his idea, the busman's holiday and the harm already done, but now he seems bothered by Denny's lack of professionalism. I think again how similar this day must feel to the ones he spends at work, how he's not going to work this month, and how I might have just seen a little of the reason why.

Leonard's still got his camera to his eye, snapping one plate after another, falling into the dirt at his feet. He turns to me.

"Smile," he says, and the film advances once again.

Denny's smoking on the porch when I get back to the house, the trapdoor propped open with a fire log. There's a woman in the root cellar, talking into a tape recorder. Denny just rolls his eyes, sweeps his hand like I should help myself.

"The archaeology department?"

"They don't make them like they used to."

"Is Marshall down there too?"

"No. He said he had to make a phone call. Went off that-a-way."

"Oh."

That-a-way is not inside. He went somewhere to use his cell phone, which I didn't even know he brought. I tell Denny what happened in the woods, how Marshall seemed to have had enough and cut out, but I don't really know how to end what I am saying. I don't want to start a fight between them, but I don't want to consider what else might be bothering Marshall either.

"He's all right, Joan," Denny says. "Don't worry about it."

I shrug. "And Leonard Lopey. What do you suppose he's going to do with all his pictures once he gets them home?"

"I don't guess I like to think what Leonard Lopey does on his own time."

"You didn't tell him about the pieces of china you found."

He grins, shakes his finger at me, as if I have been a sly girl.

"I'm not giving anything away here I don't have to." He takes my arm, draws me closer. "Look."

He reaches into his coat pocket and pulls out a handful of dirty things: a bronzed coin marked with a horseshoe on one side, a swastika on the other, a heart-shaped lock and key, an old wishbone dipped in ink, a blue-eyed marble. I pluck the marble between my thumb and forefinger, rolling it back and forth, red clay dusting Denny's open palm. I know from my days with the root doctors, these are all for luck.

He says, "Hedy found out what those china pieces are all about too."

"Yeah?"

"You were right. Dinner plates."

He tells me the custom was to break the dishes of the last meal over the grave, a slave custom, even further back to West Africa, and he thinks they might have found some kind of potter's field or lesser cemetery, antebellum, maybe. He's pleased with himself. He needs to go slowly, he says, to think about what he's doing, which strikes me as the understatement of the year. The ground is so torn up out there, you couldn't find another body if it was holding on to your ankle with one hand.

"Oh, that," he says. "I dug that up last night."

The real spot, he tells me, is off behind the house, toward the railroad tracks. He and Hedy are mapping it now, and they've marked out plots and grades, plan to dig in one-inch layers, all of which sounds very learned and practical. They figure they've got pretty good marks for more bones if the plates mean what they think they mean. Marshall's back there looking at it now.

"But you're not going to show it to Leonard," I say.

"No. And not his little friend from the archaeology department either. If they can get a date on those bones, that's enough to go on, right?"

I nod, but it's as if he's talking about cold fusion, something so far beyond my needs I don't even have to pretend to understand him. That word, *antebellum*, keeps going through my head, the corroded, floral sound of it. It's one of those words that stands out for me when I'm reading at my desk. It's a word that's very interesting to Mr. Baulknight and his board.

"Is there anyone you can think of," I ask, "who might actually know something about all this?"

Denny smiles his hail-mary smile, and starts walking.

When we get to the shop at Red Hill, the service bay is open and the laundry truck pulled up as though Body and Junebug are working on it. Denny bangs his fist on the broadside and calls out for them, but there's no answer.

Russell's feet hang out the back of the truck. He's sprawled over a nest of laundry bags, out cold. Denny takes the toe of his sock and shakes it, but nothing. From behind us, we hear Body laughing.

"Boy is sleeping. You see that?"

"Hey, Body," Denny says. "You remember my sister?"

"Hey, little lady."

Body has a row of men's shoes laid out on the counter, lace-ups and work boots and canvas sneakers, even a pair of bedroom shoes, and he's shaking an industrial-size can of pepper into their throats. He's pretty set on what he's doing and does not stop for us.

Denny says, "I came by to see if we could talk to Miss Mary Soomes."

"Who talk?"

"Me and Joan here. We want to ask her about that property her family worked across the way. Russell said—"

"Russell say, Russell say." Body seems put off, and he sets the can of pepper down. "Russell drink too much, that's what I say. I doubt his mama want to talk about that."

"Why not?" I ask.

"She talk to you about politics, and relations between the races, and why there ain't no God. She talk to you about the football game, over at the university. She goes to all of those. She talk to you about the time she took ole Sam Cooke by the scruff of his neck and made his eyes pop out of his head, but the one thing she don't ever want to talk about is her daddy the sharecropper."

"She's a proud woman?" I ask.

"That don't take the top off it," Body says.

"I know that kind," Denny says.

"Shoo." Body gives him a look like he doesn't know squat.

He takes the bedroom shoes off the counter and slides into them, lurches over to where Russell is sleeping. He grabs Russell's feet, just as Denny did, and shakes them, just like Denny.

"Russell, man. Get up. We got to call on Miss Mary Soomes."

Russell is up in seconds, tucking in his shirt.

"She here?" he says. "She here?"

"Nah, Russell. Denny want to call on her. Denny want to ask her questions."

"Jesus." Russell sits down on the fender of the truck with enough force to rock it. "For good God's sake."

"I'm sorry, man," Denny says. "If you just want to give me her phone number, I'll call her."

"Nah." Russell's got his fists pressing into his eyes. "You can't. I'll call her. I'll set it up. I'll let you know for when."

Body chuckles under his breath, like we are in for something we have no idea about.

"Yeah, boy," he says. "You call her. You see how much she want to talk to some whitey and his sister from the university. You just go on and try."

Body is shuffling away now to the back room and their tools and solvents, their spare men sleeping barefoot on the cots. He's still mumbling to himself about how far we think we'll get with a woman as sharp as Miss Mary Soomes. We look at Russell, dazed on the fender of the laundry truck.

"I believe he's always been a little sweet on her," he says.

The skies open up and Denny and I run the whole way back to the house, stopping only long enough to throw a tarp over the chickens, which I think is considerate on his part. When he spoke before of the bones and the digging, he spoke of both himself and Hedy, *we*. I can't recall hearing him do that before.

Marshall is waiting on the porch, with towels. He folds me up, kisses the top of my head, and he seems improved from before in the woods. He's been listening to Leonard and the archaeologist.

"Have they come up with anything?" Denny asks.

"Not since I've been sitting here," Marshall says.

"How in God's name do you work with him?" I say.

Marshall is in a funny mood. He leans against the porch rail and keeps me against him, wrapped in the towel, but his hands won't be still on my arms, sliding up and down, up and down

98

again. He looks out over the cemetery and the rain slanting through it.

He says, "I once saw Leonard sort two handfuls of skull material out of a corn crib after a kid was hit with a sixteen-penny nail during a tornado."

He's still rubbing my arms, still watching the rain. Denny and I don't say anything, and Marshall doesn't say anything else, not for a long time. From downstairs, we can hear the light tones of the archaeologist turn impatient, the click of her machine, off and on again, recording whatever thoughts she's come to, and Leonard asking questions. I catch Denny's eye, but it's hard to gauge what his concern would look like, and his concern over Marshall is not really the point. My concern is the point: my husband, my life.

"Anyway," Marshall says finally, "I run into him from time to time when I'm in Alabama and Georgia. He's not such a bad guy."

"No," Denny says. "He's not a bad guy at all."

The trapdoor flings open and up comes the archaeologist, Shirley Temple on a pout.

"This has been real sweet," she says to Denny, "but I can't really work this way, in the goddamn ground, without a hood, in the rain. In the ever-loving rain. I do not do fieldwork, do not, do not, do not."

"Well," Denny says. "I appreciate your coming anyhow."

Her posture toward him shifts. She runs a hand through her curls, her cheeks impossibly pink and pretty.

"If I had to guess," she says, "you've got somebody down there who's been dead about a hundred years, give or take. This isn't a Confederate soldier or anything. Sorry."

"Well, that's all right," Denny says.

"It might still be interesting. Here's my home number." She digs in her bag for a pen and slip of paper. "If you find anything else."

"Thank you, Elodie," Denny reads. "Thank you very much."

Out of the corner of my eye, I see the curtains on the kitchen door fall shut. Things start banging around inside the house, heavy things, and Hedy gives over to a little cussing herself. Perhaps she is putting her foot down finally, and hard. I give the two of them a month before she moves out.

The faintest veil of concern settles over Denny's face.

"Let me get you an umbrella," he says, and he disappears inside.

I give Elodie a look that lets her know she does not need to wait.

There are handshakes and goodbyes in the drive, but I just wave from the porch. Inside, I can hear the raised voices of Denny and Hedy in argument, an argument that was bound to happen sooner or later and will probably continue to happen as long as they live here together. The Gran Torino pulls down the lane and Marshall stands to watch it go, rain dark on the back of his shirt. The door behind me opens a crack and slams shut just as fast. I feel unwelcome in the break of someone else's misfortune, and I call to Marshall from the porch for us to get the hell out of here and fast.

I laugh, as if to shake off the dark turn this day has taken. He opens his arms for me to run, and I do, still laughing, Denny's towel still wrapped around my shoulders, the both of us laughing as if it can get no worse and we will not be touched by it.

But in the car, on the way home, we are quiet. Whatever we think to talk about, the prospect of dry clothes, of dinner, a movie for the evening, hangs limply in the air between us. Marshall turns the heat too high. I watch the interstate slip past in rivulets of gray, and we stay quiet, to ourselves.

9

LEWIS HAS LEFT a message on our answering machine. He's having a Christmas party and we must come. I suddenly remember that Christmas will pass by without us if we don't go to parties, if we don't bake cookies and string lights.

"Marshall," I say. "We have to bake cookies and string lights."

"Oh, right," he says. "Of course."

He goes and gets the ladder from the garage. All week, he moves the ladder around the house, leaning it in the coat closet, tucking it in bed, inside the shower after I have turned the water on. He buys boxes of lights at the drugstore and stacks them on the kitchen counter, bringing a new box home every time he goes out. By the end of the week, I can't make a cup of coffee for the amount of lights we have not strung.

Friday night, I stand in my closet, panties and bare feet, trying to decide what to wear. Marshall sits on the corner of the bed.

"This?" I say. "Or the red one?"

"The red," he says. "Jesus."

He gives up on the cuff he's working and just lets his hands hang between his knees, as if I've overwhelmed him from the fingers up.

I paint my mouth, pull back my hair, and Marshall wears a tie. He smells like lime leaves and sandalwood, and before we leave the house he makes himself a go cup of whiskey for the car. He does not offer me a drink and I don't make one for myself.

It's a small show, like the ring he brought me, a wish on the candles of a cake, but there could be a thousand of these small shows between us and I'd still catch myself happy every time.

I drive, and take the back ways off the interstate. Marshall rests his hand on my thigh, his head on the back of the seat, his eyes lolling shut and the sway of the road fast beneath us.

"It is so nice," he says, "to sleep while you are driving."

And it's nice to give him sleep, to give him time and warmth and company. I remind myself again how we have all month to be together, and I feel chance thrown wide in front of us again.

The houses we pass are lit up for Christmas, front lawns full of glowing angels and snowmen, mangers, messages spelled out in twinkle lights. Lewis lives in the country, amongst farms, and soon even the barns are decorated, their broadsides hung with stars. We park on the road with the other cars, next to a giant inflatable Santa Claus, and walk up to the house.

The driveway is long and cut deep into woods, and Lewis has lined it with paper-bag luminarias. I hold Marshall's hand, and music staggers out to us, Nina Simone and her bowls of sugar.

"We don't have to stay," he whispers.

"All that dancing we might do. The expensive food, the lovely scotch."

"The lovely bed we have at home we haven't made in weeks."

But this is just a game.

We step into the house lights, and at the door there's a total stranger to take our coats. The foyer is round with a sweep of floating staircase, the banister wrapped with garlands, lit with candles, the whole room waxy with the scent of pine. There's a ball of mistletoe hanging from the chandelier by a red ribbon, someone passing trays of drinks, Manhattans, and trays of food, oysters. It all looks opulent and good-mannered, even more so for the way we've driven through the country to be here.

Marshall flags a passing waiter and I'm attacked.

It's Chuck, and it's my own fault, as I'm standing nearish to the mistletoe. He has cleaned himself up, wears a velvet smoking jacket over a stand-collared shirt, his hair slicked back into a ponytail. He is strong and fast and some recovered from the last time I saw him at the library.

He dips me back over his arm and kisses me, all lips and hard. Marshall taps his shoulder.

"Oh," Chuck says.

"Yes," Marshall says.

"Here, then."

And Chuck passes me off like something he had not examined well before purchase. Perhaps I have lost my touch with kisses from strangers.

Marshall takes my arm and we lean against the chair rail. As more guests arrive, Chuck gets two kisses and a knee to the groin. Marshall claps for the woman with the reflexes.

"Maybe I should be concerned," he says. "You seemed too overtaken to defend yourself."

"Yes. Well."

"Your mouth," he says. "Here."

He takes my purse and pulls the lipstick from it, puts a hand beneath my chin. He strokes the color back on, his own mouth parted in concentration, his empty cocktail glass tucked beneath his arm. I feel his knee against my thigh and rest my hand on it, and when he runs his thumb beneath my lip to make a clean line, he licks his own.

"How is it," I say, "in a room full of people, I am still alone with you?"

"Shhh," he says. "Be still."

There's a fire roaring in the fireplace off the foyer, and women are beginning to remove their clothes to it. People treat it as a feature of the evening, that one in five of them is topless, but it's still a lot of skin if you haven't had a Manhattan or two. I tell Marshall we might have to stay to see the show come midnight when it gets really hot in here and all the pills are gone, but he doesn't think the pills will ever be gone from these parts. He goes off to find another drink, a little something for me, and I promise not to let myself be ravaged until he gets back.

The man behind me is telling someone the same story for the fifth time, exactly the same, word for blessed word. I turn around and recognize him from the newspaper, a candidate for office two towns over. Lewis knows, and is good to, everyone. From where I'm standing, I see members of the school board, and the Junior League, high-ups from the university, also table dancers, library workers, and college students. I do not see Lewis, and it's impossible to tell his voice from all the others. Everyone is yelling.

And it's not just speaking loudly — they seem to be yelling at each other, making their points, but every statement is a point. I hear the woman tell the candidate behind me that she is *going to get a drink* and expect to hear a slap across the face to go with her leaving, but there's only the candidate, telling his same story once again to someone else.

There's a leap of static at my shoulder and I whip around to Hedy. She is hugging me, her lit cigarette close to my ear. Denny stands behind her, one hand shoved in the pocket of his jeans. He's holding a bottle of beer and looking at my shoes.

"Nice shoes," he says.

"They are nice," I say. They are slender-heeled and blunt-toed, red like my dress.

Hedy still has her arm around my neck, and she reaches across my body to switch her cigarette to her free hand. She too is dressed up, a strappy, sparkly dress with a ruffled hem, her blond hair bone straight down her back. She bumps my hip with hers in time to what she's hearing, and we face Denny as if we want something from him, like call girls, or a firing squad.

He sighs. "Where's Marshall?" he asks, but not as though he really wants to know.

"He went off in search of the bar. Quite a while ago, actually. I have no idea what's keeping him."

Hedy wipes at her nose.

"I'll go find him," Denny says.

"I'll go," Hedy says.

Den chuffs his breath. "You don't have the slightest idea what he looks like."

"Kiss my ass, Denny," she says, and she's smiling. She squeezes my shoulder and passes into the crowd.

Denny stares after her, and I can't tell if this is a real argument between them. He must know so many of the women at this party, and so many of those without their shirts. I'd be surprised if that is not a problem.

I say how I had not thought I'd see him here, and he remembers himself, remembers me.

"Yeah," he says. "I thought I wanted to stretch my legs a little bit, but I think a lot of stupid shit lately."

"It's quite a party."

"Ole Lewis." He gets a thought, levels it at me. "He offered me a job."

"Really. Doing what?"

"You know. Doing what he does."

And I don't know, don't want to know, have only come across Chuck and another handful of road-worn men leaving Lewis's house as I am coming in, their suitcases distended, their cars running in the drive. I know what I read in the paper, this or that lab overturned, pharmacy robbed, what assault remains unsolved, what charges remain unpressed, but how close Lewis might be to such things is not a question I ask myself. Regardless, the sympathies are few in his circles, and dangerously far between.

"Jesus, Joanie," Denny says. "You'd think I'd said I'd been offered cancer."

"No. Just surprised. What you tell him?"

"I'd think about it, I guess."

"Would you know what you were doing? I mean, doesn't that kind of thing take some practice?"

"No more than anything else." He grins at me, turns up his bottle of beer.

I'm scrambling. "What's Hedy say?"

"Nothing."

He looks off in the direction she disappeared, and if I have ever wished to read his thoughts, I wish to now, to know if I have hit ground or something softer.

"I went to see Miss Mary Soomes the other day," he says.

"How'd it go?"

"She's a funny lady. What she wanted to talk about and what I wanted to know couldn't have been more different. I guess she ran with some artistic types in Harlem back in the day, and then she was in Paris before the war. She practically whispered what to do in Rosa Parks's ear, you get the feeling. But then I ask her about the land behind the cemetery, and suddenly she doesn't remember anything."

"Body said she was a proud woman."

"Yeah, but you know. She said she left home at fifteen and didn't come back until the seventies. I figure something must have pushed her out the door."

"What year would that have been?"

"Nineteen twenty-seven, summer. That's what I was thinking too; maybe something happened out there. Would you check in your papers?"

Of course. And I'm happy to look, even as the panic I feel for Denny only deepens to think about it. I weigh the two against each other: grave robber, drug runner. I cannot find the upper hand.

Denny has gone back to staring after Hedy and sipping his beer. He's so preoccupied, and I want him here with me. There's a band playing in the other room, and I take his hand from his pocket and pull.

"Nah," he says.

"Come on, Denny. Please."

He looks, for an instant, like a shy boy. If he won't dance with me, I don't think I can forgive him for it. I realize, suddenly, how much I mean that. What could it cost him, this small thing, for me? Years ago, we used to dance whenever we were drunk enough. It was a way to mark the evening's progress, right before driving somebody's truck through the pasture or passing out, and it was never a sweet thing, but more like having the breath slung out of you in time to music. Someone would eventually fall down, laughing, and we would move on in the course of the night to something more destructive.

But in Lewis's dining room, it's even less than that. A group of college girls in overalls and heavy wool cardigans are spinning, not nearly in time to the music, which is some bluesy Texas band. The bottoms of their bare feet are black. Chuck is running through the crowd, leaping as if to keep a ball in the air with his head, only there is no ball, and far across the room, there's Lewis, the crash of Lewis's voice, his head thrown back, his arm around a girl, his hand on the flesh between her upturned, tawny breast and her waistline. His hand is massive, and, beneath it, her rib cage just some pretty bones.

Denny takes me in his arms, I put my cheek to his, and we make a small space for ourselves in the press of other, drunker people. He holds our hands to his chest, and the music turns slow and familiar, a gentle Hank Williams redux. I lean back against his arm around my waist and touch his hair out of his eyes, tell him all about his cheating heart. He lets me, and I appreciate it. When the song is over, he kisses the top of my head, and I say I need a drink of water.

"Good night, Joanie," he says, as if he is tucking me into bed.

"Good night."

He is the first to turn away.

Someone has been bleeding in the kitchen. Dog biscuits scatter the floor, and two women sprawl against opposite walls, throwing them at each other. Their battle is wordless but intense, made difficult by the constant pass of caterers who seem oblivious, or at least well paid. I go into the refrigerator for a bottle of water and narrowly miss being struck. Lewis doesn't even have a dog.

Someone grabs me as I step back into the dining room, and for a moment I think it's Chuck again and I'm prepared. But it's Marshall; he has my face pressed into his shoulder, rocking me back and forth.

"Oh, God," he says. "You were lost and now I've found you. Hallelujah."

"There's dog food all over the floor in there. Lewis doesn't even have a dog."

"Joan, Joan, Joan. That's not dog food. It's a game of strategy."

"You've been in there?"

"I was there when it began."

He has, I imagine, found several Manhattans, and some of whatever else Lewis has to offer. His jacket smells as if he's been standing over a fire. His lips brush my ear.

"There's a camera in every single room of this house."

He points to a pinhole of light in the wall behind us. I think how funny we must look from the other side, to whoever must be watching, the party fishbowled around us. Marshall takes my hand and drags me to the next room, to another pinhole, through the crowd to another, and another. We press through conversations, couples, into bedrooms occupied and empty, stare into these tiny cameras for a moment before Marshall drags me on, room to room to room.

"Baby," I say finally. "Let's go home."

He opens a closet door, searching, finding. "Every single room."

"It's late. God, it's one o'clock. Come home with me."

He pulls my hand and we fall across a bed. He gathers me up against him to hide, maybe to hide the both of us.

He says, "I bet Lewis knows the dice before they even roll."

His eyes are glazy and bloodshot, as if they've been fired in a kiln.

The ceiling fan ticks above us to stir the heated house, the press of people like energy dividing, making more, and outside the bedroom, down the hallway, the music turns loud and bluesy again, people laughing, glass against glass. Marshall's breath comes shallow, as if he is being chased.

"Let's go home," I say. "Let's go home now."

I keep my voice as even as I can.

I drag Marshall inside and he collapses on the sofa, boneless and mostly asleep. I go back to the car for my purse and see that the lights are on in Gail's window. I let myself think Bannon is still there, that I could walk across the street and open the front door and he would meet me with a glass of something sweet, a plate, a bowl, a taste held out on his fingers. We would sit and talk, about the weather or the restaurant or the holiday rush, and the want I have for such a stupid conversation is near physical, nearly overwhelming.

I turn out all the lights and go to bed.

I'm not saying I would be happier, or that I would not be dragging Marshall from the car at such a late hour, but I would be different if Bannon were still alive. I would have made different bargains with myself. I would not want so much from everyone so on the spot because I could trust they'd be there in the morning, or some soon morning in the future, when I could ask again.

I spend a long time thinking of this before I fall asleep.

10

SUNDAY, THE WINDOWS are webbed with frost. Marshall finally did come to bed, but he slept balled up on the far side, far away. Now, he looks cold and alone in the tumble of sheets, as if he's fallen asleep in a snowdrift. I spread an extra quilt over him and close the door behind me.

In the kitchen, I want lunch. I go into an accordion file, get out Bannon's recipe for onion soup, and start chopping. My knives are sharp, but the onions make me cry, and I step away from the block, back and away, back and away. In Bannon's kitchen in the winter, he had a soup pot on the burner all the time. It was something he'd learned to do in Mendocino at a French place he worked, and he added to it every day, whatever was on hand, everything except meat, or wine, one common thing I can't remember.

I saute the onions in butter and realize I have not thought this lunch out, that we have no bread or cheese, that we're also out of milk and tissues and dog food. I cut the gas and leave a note for Marshall on the counter, just in case he wakes up and can't remember how he got home—at least he'll know why home is empty.

Luther is waiting in the front hall. I am learning there is nothing for him like a Sunday drive, so I leash him up. I pull my hat down low and dig my gloves out of the pockets of my coat, and when I open the front door my chest goes tight with the cold. Luther prances ahead of me on the frosted lawn. His feet don't make a sound in the grass.

Gail and I almost hit each other backing out of the driveway. I roll down my window to say hello, but she doesn't see me and pulls away. I follow her, all the way to the grocery store, all the way inside, before I can catch her sleeve.

"Oh, God, Joan. I'm just so distracted," she says. "Alice and Corinne get here next Tuesday."

I ask her what I can do.

"Are you still able to put one of them up? Alice, maybe?"

"Sure," I say. "Alice and I used to run around together."

Gail's eyes hang on my face blankly, and I push on, to get out of my own way.

"How old is Nick now?" I ask.

"I can't keep the two straight, honestly. Nick is eight and Gerald's ten, or the other way around. The last time I saw them, one of them was walking and one of them was still in blankets."

"It was Gerald. He was the baby then."

I'm doing it again, knowing too much. But Gerald is Bannon's namesake, and at the memorial service Corinne was beside herself, some sort of postpartum traumatic stress, and she wouldn't stop wailing or put the baby down. Someone finally called the doctor. After that, Gerald being the baby is not something you forget, but Gail wasn't there, and maybe that's come to be a sore point too.

The grocery store is warm, and I'm beginning to sweat beneath my layers.

"Have you got much of a list?" I ask.

I take a cart and push it along behind her as she gathers what she's come for: endive, arugula, radishes, a jar of mustard that costs six dollars, Port Salut cheese, frozen raspberries. She asks me to pick a bottle of wine, and I have no idea what she likes, but I can tell she does not want to hear this or to tell me her tastes, but only wants the task handled, so that is what I do. At the checkout, she pays with a card and gathers up her bags to wait for me. I tell her to go on home, that I've forgotten something. I tell her I'll come for Alice and Nick next Tuesday night and she gives me a grateful little nod and she's gone.

I go back into the aisles and try to remember what it is that brought me here.

In the car, Luther has fogged all the windows, and I have to wipe a space clean with my sleeve to drive home. He noses in the grocery bag and comes up disappointed. Perhaps Luther would have been a happier dog in France, where Bannon said plastic had yet to be trusted.

Marshall sits at the kitchen table when we get home, shame-faced and nursing a cup of coffee.

"Come on, Tex," I say. "It's not all that bad, is it?"

"No," he says.

"Want some soup?"

And that is all we say about it. We have never fallen into that thing of being married where I nag and shuffle, where he blows up about the credit cards. If he wants to get blind drunk at a Christmas party, it's his business.

I tell him I've offered to let Alice and Nick stay with us over the holidays. He doesn't know Alice, but this doesn't seem to register. He doesn't ask how long they'll be staying. I'm not even sure he's listening. I feel a flare of impatience, unexpected as a snapping rung beneath my step. When I set down our soup bowls, I take the place opposite him, and I keep my feet to myself.

Then he says, "I'm going out this afternoon. Should I get some flowers or something for the guest room?"

He looks up, and all the heat runs out of me.

"Yes," I say. "Flowers would be nice."

He thanks me for the soup before he goes.

In my office, I call up the archive and look for any accident in the Pendleton and Red Hill area during the late 1920s, something horrible enough to drive a young girl north. A young black girl. Enough to stay away for fifty years. I don't know anything about Mary Soomes, what kind of relationship she had with her family or the place she grew up, but from where I sit the possibilities for what I'm looking for seem few.

Klan activity was reported in the newspaper, as casually as Junior League activity or that of the First Baptist Church. As near as Greenville, the law was pretty much the same set of people under sheets. But there were also letters to the editors condemning lynching, and elected officials that took stands for moderation, and the politics of race were as complicated then as they are now. I just need a thread to follow, something at the right place and the right time, that might lead one thing to another and end up with Mary Soomes.

I run a dozen searches but can't find anything that suits. It's frustrating, as this is something that I'm good at. That spring afternoon at the hospital, Mr. Baulknight told me to keep those spoons in my purse and find out what I could about them. He said it would be a test.

When he called the next day, I knew those were spoons like the ones in the hospital kitchen during the forties. I knew there had been a young woman in the room above the spoons, above the hole in the floor, whose husband ran a mortuary out of their home, and that the woman had contracted pulmonary tuberculosis from a corpse in her husband's care. I knew the woman died in the state mental institution before she turned twenty-nine, and I have to confess, I still keep a picture in my head, a pale young woman, long black hair, digging a hole just big enough to drop herself into, as though the red clay were an elevator and it might take her somewhere else. That's not the story I found, but the one I made, and I think it holds up pretty well.

I think of Denny in his graveyard, his chips of bone and plate, the red-walled cellar dug out beneath his home. Part of me thinks Mr. Baulknight would be just the thing for Denny, that he's some version of Denny twenty years from now. I can see the two of them peering into holes, sifting through dirt, self-made gentleman anthropologists picking over the bones laid out on the sawhorse table, opera blaring on the Philco radio, glasses of bourbon in hand. They would make elaborate picnics of roast chicken and champagne out amongst the cemetery stones. They would talk endlessly about where to put their shovels next. The entire Junior League would leave their panties in the lane.

I call Denny and tell him I can't find anything untoward that might have sent Mary Soomes to Harlem and left a body in his yard, at least nothing that made the papers.

"That's all right," he says. "I'm going to make another pass at it. I called over there today and she invited me to tea."

"Tea?"

"I can do that," he says. "I can drink tea."

"There's not a doubt in my mind, Denny. You can drink anything you want."

But after we hang up, I go back and try another angle, and then another. I come out of the office for coffee, for dinner, and then back again to work, the search for racial violence drifting into other violence, then other topics altogether, and hours slip away from me. It's wasteful, I know. Marshall is home now, and this could wait until he's gone again, but then I'll only have to relearn how numbing it is to be alone, how much you rely on what keeps you busy.

He takes long naps in the afternoon, makes phone calls, to whom, I have no idea. It rains one day and I come across him standing on the front porch, watching the gutters overflow. He is talking, explaining something with his hand extended, about the gutters, the way they're flooding. I step closer to the sidelights; he's explaining himself to the dog.

The arrival of newspapers is a constant thudding at my doorstep, every dawn.

I read a story about two men jogging in Greenville, an old neighborhood with big oaks and bigger homes, where you can run to the quickie mart for brie and a bottle of beaujolais. It's afternoon. Traffic is light. Up ahead, a crew is doing tree work, thirty feet in the air, cutting a limb. They look up the street for oncoming cars. They do not see the joggers, and when the branch is cut, it's too late. One man stops, the other runs. The runner is struck dead before he even hits the ground, and the still man walks away.

I read this and my stomach tips. I push back from the desk and press the soft parts of my eyes. I see Bannon for the last, that day in the airport and how I kissed his cheek, a kiss I'd made a thousand times before, and I know he smelled like chestnuts and cut grass because he always smelled that way, but I can't lean close to him in my mind and smell him anymore. The way I can't make his voice anymore, only his words, only the picture of him speaking without sound.

And Marshall, how many times a day he chooses to run or stand still, how many times his day falls on that blade.

The newsprint blurs and I feel sick. Quickly it becomes more than that, and I rush to the bathroom, bring up everything in my stomach.

I run cold water on my wrists, rinse my mouth. Maybe it is morning enough to mean something other than worry, other than nerves. I look in the mirror, my face pale and beaded. Could I tell by looking? The idea dives through me, the chance that I am pregnant.

Late in the afternoon, Marshall comes into the office and sits with his book again, and I don't say anything about being sick. If it happens again, or if something else happens, enough of the same to make a pattern, I'll say something. I'm making deals with myself, my body too loud in my ears, everything a sign. But Marshall looks up at me from his book, and I think how much I would give for a baby of our own, how I would make any deal I can think of, with whoever's offering.

I'm sick again the next day, and the day after that I can't eat for the feeling it won't stay down. I stay in bed, and Marshall brings me the flat ginger ale and crackers left over from his flu. He smooths the hair from my forehead. His hands are cool and dry.

"How you feeling, Joanie?"

"Bad. Badly."

"I think I gave you what I got."

"Yeah?" My head goes light, as if the sun has just come up in there. "Promise?"

That stops him, his face closing down on a smile. "You think?"

I don't say anything, and he crawls underneath the covers with me, his head beneath the blankets, his boots still on, still saying, again and again, *you think, you think, you think*. He has me laughing, his mouth beneath my sweater on my skin, and I still feel filled with light, as if I might hit a wall and become a million different things at once. I don't say it, but all I am is yes.

The next afternoon, the chance is gone. I don't know how to tell Marshall. I can't remember the last time I was able to tell him face to face, and the not remembering makes it even worse.

He is in his chair, reading. I stand in front of him and just say it.

"Joanie," he says. "Oh, I'm sorry."

It's what he's said for nearly a year. I push my face into my palms until it hurts. We've got a better chance this month, I can plan it better, I can start right now and make it right, me, me, me.

"You know, maybe it's you." I laugh, but it's short, mean. "Maybe it's your body, something you're doing. Like at Lewis's? Because it can affect things."

He goes forward in the chair and scrubs his cheeks, the back of his neck.

"Yes," he says. "But I'm not."

And I believe him, but I push on anyway, because I feel alone in this, because he's there to push.

"It's not like I would know it if you were."

"Come on, Joanie."

"Come on, nothing. I feel so mean. God. I could just kick you, kick myself, kick something. Move it."

I make a drink in the kitchen, a big one, with lots of bourbon. Marshall's right behind me, taking a glass of his own from the cupboard.

There's nothing he can say, and he's smart not to try. I sink down the cabinets and sprawl my legs out on the floor. Marshall sits beside me, not touching but there, entirely there. I am trying not to cry.

"I'm sorry," I whisper.

"Me too."

I let my head onto his shoulder. What a gift he has, to let me be angry and not make it anything more than that, or less, either. I am not so good. He reaches up and takes the bottle of bourbon from the counter and tops off both our glasses. We let it grow dark outside like that, dark now so early in the day, and us on the kitchen floor, sullenly getting drunk in each other's company. He opens a drawer above his head and fishes out cards; we play double solitaire until the suits run together. Then we stretch out, head to toes.

"Remind me," Marshall says. "Tomorrow I will show you what a dust mop is."

"Yes. Do that. I have been waiting."

He lifts his head for another drink and then lets it smack against the tile. "Is this what you do when I'm not here?"

"Lay on the floor?"

"No. When you get your period, and I'm not here. Do you pour yourself a drink, and play cards, and skip dinner?"

"We did skip dinner, didn't we?"

"I'd like to know."

"Yes, then. Pretty much, this is it."

He is quiet for a long minute and I try to guess what he is thinking. I feel loose and silly and like I'm ungrateful for what I do have. I want to make him understand me differently, but I'm not sure where to start, how far back I'd have to go.

Then he says, "Now I can do this too," and there's nothing to explain.

We buy a tree and trim it. I hang a wreath on the front door, and Marshall helps me string all the lights he's bought in the crape myrtles. We go out, into Greenville to see music at the Handlebar and eat Vietnamese food, up to Asheville for a movie with subtitles. At home, we mull wine and drink it from thick glass mugs in front of the fire, and *Miracle on 34th Street* is always on TV. I cry when they dump the mail in the judge's lap. It's all that belief together in one place that gets me every time.

Tuesday night, I walk across the street to fetch Alice and Nick.

I ring the bell and shove my hands back in my pockets, cock my head up at the sky. The moon is full, and the night is blue with it, so bright I throw shadow back on the lawn, and I have the want to lay myself beneath this brightness the way you would lie down on a good sunny day. When the front door opens, I come up so quickly that I'm off-balance and into the house like a shot.

Gail is drunk. I've never seen her drunk before, but she is, and the house smells of burned food.

"Joan," she says. "Martini?"

"Absolutely."

And that's the only thing Gail says, the whole time I'm there.

Alice and Corinne are perched on the edge of the sofa, their empty cocktail glasses on their knees. I give hugs, tell each how well they look and ask after their flights down. I am good at this kind of conversation. Endless pleasant, time-filling questions are at my disposal, and I make all of us martinis with just a dip of the spoon into the vermouth, and three olives.

"Where are the boys?" I ask.

Alice makes a pillow of her hands and rests her cheek on it. "They've been up since four a.m."

Alice is a doll woman, fair-skinned and slender-limbed, like their mother. All of her expressions are in her hands, the hands of a pianist, which their mother was, full of beautiful gestures for sleep, for hunger, for bliss. She does not remind me one bit of Bannon. Corinne, however, could be his twin.

She is telling me a story about the airport in Boston, how airports are such strange public spaces, everyone with a purpose. Today, there was a woman and man, both weeping, the woman's shirt, a gray sweatshirt, streaked dark with tears. It was hard for Corinne not to stare, not to know what had made them so sad. She is going back to school to be a therapist.

"I had all the possibilities," she says. "Empathetically, I'm good. Death, loss, love, poor judgment."

She ticks them off on her fingers. She's cut her hair short and there's a lock of it that waves across her brow. I get a little want in my hands to tuck it back for her, so much her brother's. "Were they parting?" I ask.

"I don't know. They sat side by side, and they were both weeping, but they didn't look at each other, and they didn't get on our plane. And now, I just can't seem to shake them."

"Occupational hazard," I say.

"Without the occupation." She tells me she has another year of coursework yet, and maybe after that she'll just keep going. She says it like you might say you'll just keep going off the edge of the earth, and then she takes a big swallow of her drink, like she might need to start out tonight.

Gail hovers by the Christmas tree, a fat white pine decorated with only lights and bows. One of them is listing to the left, Gail or the tree; I can't tell which.

I look to Alice. "Should we go?" I'm already standing up.

"I'll get our things," she says.

She motions for me to follow her down the hall to the guest room. There, in bed, are the sleeping boys, sandy-haired and coltish little boys in plaid pajamas, one longer than the other.

"I can get the bags," she says. "You get Nicky."

"I don't want to wake him."

"Not a chance. He sleeps through fire alarms."

Their faces are so sweet and sleepful, their limbs flung wide, the covers tangled. These are the sheets, flannel and red, Bannon used to make up a bed for me when I was too lazy to walk back across the street. I rub a corner between my finger and thumb.

"You'd think these things would fade," I say to Alice, and she knows exactly what I mean.

"They were my mother's," she says. "How strange of Gail to use them still."

I gather Nick in my arms, even as he is probably too old to be carried, and he snugs his face into my neck. My heart breaks like fabric giving at its seams. The night is too heavy with the past and now this weight of a child in my arms on top of it. Alice tucks a quilt around us and we walk back into the living room.

Corinne is staring at a hook on the wall where Bannon used to hang his coat. Her face is guarded, but I am practiced at reading these expressions, like knowing another language I haven't used in years. She is biding her time.

She kisses her sister, her nephew, me. Gail comes in from the kitchen, drying her hands on a dishtowel, and there's the cluster of us by the door. She sighs. What a painful stretch of days lies ahead.

We go back into the night and across the street, my hand cradling Nick's head to my shoulder, his bare feet bucking at my thighs. He is solid, easy to carry. Marshall waits at the door in a wash of yellow light, and I make a quiet sound so he will know that Nick is sleeping. He puts his hand to Nick's head and it covers mine, an accident that has the feel of something more, something like words between us too complicated to say aloud. I pass through the house to the guest room, the bed already turned back, the lights already dimmed. I bend to kiss Nick's cheek, a kiss more for me than for the boy himself, and he doesn't even stir.

11

MARSHALL HAS LIT candles. He and Alice sit at the kitchen table with cups of coffee and the bottle of amaretto, what Marshall calls the slow way to the pillow. I get a cup for myself and join them.

Alice is twirling a lock of hair around her index finger. Apparently, the scene across the street started out as badly as I found it.

"I ran out of things to talk about very early on," Alice says. "Then Corinne—oh, God. Gail saw Corinne getting off the plane and turned white as a ghost. Every time she opened her mouth, Gail flinched. From there, where do you go?"

"She favors Bannon so much," I say.

"Yes." Alice sighs. "She plays with it some. But what can I say? Sometimes I think she's lucky to have that."

I rest my chin in my palm. "Gail's a tough one."

"Tough like what?" Marshall says. "She's never been over here, even to borrow the hedge clippers. I don't know anything about her."

"I just mean closed off. Tough." I make a fist on the table, knock on wood.

"She got lost," Alice says. "Driving from the airport, there was some construction or something and it was getting dark. She missed her exit. It was five o'clock traffic, and the boys were hungry. God, they could eat all day, the both of them. I guess it got loud in the car and it became apparent we were making a big circle. Corinne said something. Gail pulled over to the shoulder, got out, and sat on the hood of the car. For about two minutes."

"She got out a map?" Marshall says.

"It wasn't like that. I don't think she was really lost, just annoyed, or frazzled. She covered it. I mean, she tried to be polite, and she said she gets claustrophobic. But I kept my knees in Corinne's back after that."

"I don't think she has a lot of capacity, Alice. I think all that got used up for her. And you know she lives alone."

This comes out harder than I mean it to, as if people who live alone have rights she's treading on, but I have the want to defend Gail.

"Oh, I don't mean anything." Alice waves her hand as if to clear smoke.

"No. I don't either."

"We can make breakfast here in the morning," Marshall says, as if breakfast is the solution to everything. "We have breakfasty things, right?" He goes to the refrigerator and finds eggs, bacon, juice.

"Yeah," he says. "We'll be fine."

He kisses the back of my neck, tells Alice good night, and goes to bed.

She waits for him to close the bedroom door before she speaks again.

"I know I'm not fair," she says. She squints at me. "But what's fairness really worth?"

We laugh, but not in a funny way. She says she's wanted to tell me, and it's nothing against Marshall, but she always thought Bannon and I would be together. She seems embarrassed, apologetic, but I am not surprised.

"Those last years, you were always around, you two were always doing things. He loved you very much," she says.

I tell her I loved him too.

"I have to say, when he told us about Gail, I was put off. Really. The whole right-under-your-nose thing, and then it was too late."

I don't know if I can talk about this unless I have to, and so I will leave it up to her. She spins the bottle of amaretto on the tabletop, studies my face again, and I grow hot. She must have figured me out already.

"That's the thing," I tell her, "about Mexico."

It was March when we went down there. Gail flew in from California for the wedding arrangements and then Bannon was taking us on vacation. It was his idea; I was his friend, his neighbor, Gail to be his wife, and he wanted us to lie in the sun and drink tequila. It was like him, to think things like this were easy.

My mother was in a wheelchair, but her hair was growing back, steel gray and curly. Blessings seemed mixed, as opposed to nonexistent, and they were talking about a new stem-cell therapy, a drug trial at Duke. I went out behind the farmhouse one afternoon and planted six hundred zinnias from seed, right into the warming ground. It seemed a good time to get away, to think about getting on with things.

But that morning in Bannon's driveway, Gail was still in her bathrobe. They had decided she would come a few days behind us. The gardens they were using for their ceremony had doublebooked and apparently expected the brides to fight it out.

"Like you can know what's going on from California," she said, and she smiled at me. She smiled more then. I'm sure she was a different person.

"What are you going to do?" I said.

Gail chewed on a hangnail. "I dunno. Incriminating photographs?"

"That a girl."

Bannon touched his fist to her chin, first as a joke, then tipping her face up, and she turned to him and slipped her arms beneath his jacket.

"Do you have to go?" she said, and I was suddenly, completely, not there. She kissed his jaw, and I went around the car to put my bag in the trunk.

On the way to the airport, I have to confess, I was relieved. I knew his getting married was going to be the end of us in a dozen tiny ways, and I knew I needed to get to know Gail better, to be friends with both of them. But I wanted those last days with Bannon before everything was changed. We never talked about it, but I think he saw it coming too. I think I could feel it, on the way to the airport, I think I could feel his relief right in there with mine.

On the flight to Atlanta my skin started to burn underneath my tights. I couldn't figure it out, but when I went into the bathroom at Hartsfield, blisters were raised on the backs of my thighs.

I found Bannon in the bar. He handed me a beer.

"Poison ivy," I said, and he laughed.

I stuffed my tights into my carry-on bag. "Your sympathy kills me."

"Let me see it," he said.

"You're crazy."

He took a pencil from behind his ear and lifted the edge of my skirt, whistling. "Well, Christ, Joanie. You've torn up your legs."

"I can't help it."

"Here," he said.

He took my hand and reached into his pocket for a set of nail clippers. He cut every finger to the quick.

I had three bourbons on the way to Mexico City. The backs of my legs were on fire, but then I didn't care so much, and then I was asleep. I don't remember getting on the bus, but rather just a sort of transport and the sun setting in the dust as we wound the tight streets into the valley of San Miguel de Allende. My head was thick, and breakfast long ago.

"I bet you know where to get a good bite to eat around here, don't you," I said.

"Oh, Joanie. Do I ever."

On a corner of the square was a little place where the waiter knew Bannon, was glad to see him, and he led the two of us upstairs to a balcony overlooking the rest of the restaurant. He would not let us order. The ceiling fans spun overhead and hanging papier mâché angels threw shadows on the far walls, their faces wide and flat and Indian, and I was so hungry I thought I might have to put my head down. Sangria arrived, its thready float of wine atop the limeade, and it was good and tart, and then *queso fundido*, and a plate of mushrooms and garlic. We ate fast and well. We ate pinto beans and rice and *carne asada* rolled in tortillas with grilled spring onions, *enchiladas con mole*, and thick slices of avocado, which Bannon called *aguacate*. I kept saying that again and again to myself, a pretty green roll of sound in my head.

I won't pretend it was seamless. We had never traveled together before and had not planned to be alone. There were long silences we waited to fill, as if the things we wanted to talk about would materialize given the right amount of time.

"So," he said.

"Yes."

"I've only known her for six months."

"I know."

"I've never lived with her. I've only cooked for her twice. She has this big bare white kitchen, and no knives. God, it's awful."

"But when she's come to see you? You've taken her to the restaurant."

"Taken her. But Fideo's been back there, or James."

"Oh God, Bannon. She's a skinny girl. What if she doesn't like to eat?"

"Exactly," he said. "That's my point."

His eyes were wide, and I never took him to be serious anyway.

"You love her, though, don't you."

"Oh, yeah, Joanie. I do."

I got a snatching pain in my chest then, fast, like a failed breath, and I realized I was jealous. He looked so clear on loving her, so certain, and it suited him. His face was tan and lean, his shoulders thrown back, legs stretched out beside the table. I wanted to have his life then, to be heading off in the direction of a married person, a person in love and sure of it. I wanted it so badly, it hurt inside my chest.

"I'm not going to be called over for breakfast at three a.m. anymore, am I?"

"Joanie—"

"I am going to miss your omelets. And that thing you bake in the oven with the cherries?"

"Clafoutis."

"I'm going to miss your clafoutis, Bannon."

"I'm getting that from all the girls."

"Are there other girls? Ones that will miss you?"

"Christ." Bannon scrubbed at his face. "I don't know."

"You do too."

We hunkered down on the table now, our elbows splayed out, another pitcher of sangria on the way. He told me about a woman up in Spartanburg he'd been seeing before he met Gail, another one in Asheville that overlapped her. He'd spoken to them on the phone in the last six months, even gone to dinner with the girl in Asheville, but he hadn't told them he was getting married.

"So the next time they call, they get Gail on the line?" I said.

"Yeah. I know. It's the bastard's way out."

"I'm not saying you have to make announcements."

"Okay, so the dinner with the girl in Asheville kind of developed into a weekend."

"Oh. One of those."

In truth, it had been a while since I'd had one of those, had any of those at all. I was spending all my time with Mom, and Piper was not out of grade school, and so needed rides and lunches and help with her homework. I fell asleep on the sofa at the farmhouse by nine o'clock, and, if I was lucky, stayed asleep there.

The cancer was in her bones now, and she was crumbling at the joints, her hips, her knees. Denny would come up weekends from Atlanta and take the horses into the pastures with Piper, go to the grocery store or mow the lawn, but Sundays he'd go back to work and it was only me again, and Daddy. He would sit with her on the porch, the tears just running down his face, and he would tell her stories, tell her jokes, all the while tears falling from his chin into his lap. I'd have to make up reasons he had to leave her side, things he had to do, because I could not stand to watch him any longer. He began staying late at work; it was for the best.

I felt impossibly old and fragile, my life that of someone twice my age.

"The last one of those I had might have been in college," I said.

"College doesn't count, baby. Everybody's got it in college."

"I couldn't walk straight for two whole days."

"Well, then," Bannon said. "Let me tip my hat."

We drank more sangria, drank until I could not feel my legs to itch them, and when we left the restaurant, there were people crowded in the square and fireworks blooming in the sky above the cathedral, and I felt as if we were sneaking away from a party. Bannon left me at the door to my room, a kiss on my forehead, and then the sheets were cool beneath my cheek and I was in Mexico, very far away from everything else.

The phone rang, the middle of the night.

"You asleep?"

"If you want to call it that." My shoes were still on my feet underneath the covers.

"I have to ask you something."

"Hmm?"

"It's a favor."

"What time is it? Christ."

"I need some money. I'm in dutch, really. At the restaurant."

"Hey." I sat up. "What is it?"

"I just thought, maybe your dad?"

"Sure. Sure, Bannon. How much?"

"Ten. Fifteen."

"I'll call him tomorrow."

"No. When we get back is soon enough. I'll go with you. I just—"

"Bannon?"

"Yes?" I could hear him sigh.

"What the hell time is it, anyway?"

"Oh, Jesus. I don't know."

"We can talk about this in the morning."

"Yeah."

"Tell me something else," I said.

And we sat there on the phone, rooms apart, and he did tell me something else, a story about when he was a little boy and his father took him to the Kentucky Derby, where he had a share in a horse that was running. Bannon got to see her in the stables before the race, and she was tall and sleek and black with a blaze on her chest, and her jockey was as small as Bannon, himself just seven or eight. His father had been fifty then, and it was at the Derby parties that Bannon tasted his first bourbon, mint julep, his first oysters, raw, saw his first call girl, a long slender redhead with the jockey from his father's horse. She wore an enormous black straw hat that fluted at her shoulders, and his father had said of the evening, *Now that, boy, that is worth the price of the ticket.*

We fell asleep like that, the phones cradled against our faces. I could still hear him sleeping on the other end when I woke up.

Breakfast was a headache, and thick hot chocolate spiked with cinnamon. I had two, and bought one for a little girl who followed us into the restaurant, begging. When Bannon said no, we have no coins, she sat down with us at the table as if it had just been a way to start a conversation. She couldn't have been more than five, but she told Bannon she was nine and a half. She drank her chocolate and, when she was finished, thanked us and went back outside.

The air was warm and the restaurant open. In the square, more children swung from the balustrade of a small gazebo, not a school day in sight. A woman came by with flowers for sale, another with handmade dolls, a man with a basket of figs, fleshy and purple, and Bannon bought two of those. He asked the kitchen for chili and salt, carved the figs into wedges with his pocketknife, and in my mouth they were sweet and hot and soft. I ate every one he handed me.

"Watch it, there," he said. "It's the fruit that gets you into trouble."

"I thought it was the water."

"Yeah, and the knee bone's connected to the thigh bone. The thigh bone's connected to the —"

He was singing. I took another slice of fig off the end of his knife.

"Gail called," he said. "She won't fly into Mexico City until the end of the week."

"What's the holdup?"

Bannon waved a hand at me, like it was not worth going into. "I'll have to go back up there and meet her, is all. You could come too, and we could catch a flight someplace south. Chiapas, maybe. Or the Yucatán."

"Maybe."

"What, you have something better to do?"

But he seemed strange, and I couldn't figure out when Gail might have called, as we were on the phones all night. It seemed such a little thing to lie about, but I couldn't shake that feeling, that he was lying to me, that he was covering for something else. I thought of all those years that we didn't hear from Bannon, between high school and the night he walked across the street to my house. He was a man capable of disappearing for long stretches, of falling off the face of the earth and then surfacing right under your nose. I believed he was capable of anything.

We caught a taxi out of town to the *balnearios*, set in the bowl of the mountains off a dusty highway, the land lushing gold to green around us. We paid at the gate, and I'd brought a suit with me to change into at the bathhouse. Poison ivy chained the backs of my legs, red and weepy. There was an old woman with towels who kept staring. I tied a long scarf around my hips to cover myself.

I came out to sit in the shallows. The water was hot and sulfurous, and Bannon was already up to his waist.

"I look awful," I said.

"You're supposed to look awful. You have poison ivy."

"Yeah, but that woman kept staring at me, like maybe I was contagious."

"Come on. They've seen worse rashes down here."

I looked over to the bathhouse and the woman was in the doorway. She spoke to me in Spanish.

"She knows something that will take care of that," Bannon said. "If we give her some money, she'll go get it."

Her face was taut on her wide bones, her eyes black, her hair braided down her back, her dark dress and sensible shoes. She could have been an old woman in any sun-drenched country, anywhere but home. She kept talking to me, even though it was clear I didn't understand.

"Just give her the money, Bannon."

He went into his shorts pocket for some bills, folded and wet, and they got away from him, floating free in the water. The woman shook her head.

"She doesn't want us to leave before she gets back."

I nodded to her, and she went away.

I slipped off the side and under the water, my skirt rising to the surface like a tail. It was hot, a liquid version of the sun, and I swam as far as I could, to the other side of the pool where water rushed from a stonework wall. I let it pound my shoulders, the back of my neck. I cleared my eyes and there was Bannon at the other end, his money still floating around him, pretty bills marked with hummingbirds and butterflies. He wore sunglasses, but I could feel him watching me.

I dove, surfaced, and he was gone.

I dove again, and when I came up, he sat on the side of the pool with a tall glass rimmed with salt. He offered me a sip; beer on ice with a lot of lime. I was so hot in the water, the beer so cold. I could feel my thoughts jerking to the end of their reel.

"*Cerveza micheladas,*" he said, and I told him to get me two of those.

I lay back on the stones to catch my breath. When Bannon brought my beer I drank it down fast, and so was cold from the inside out, my body like some system of weather waiting to happen. Something was going to happen, was bound to, and I think I knew it even then.

"We could just stay here, you know," he said. "We could never leave."

He was standing over me where I'd stretched out on the stones. The sun was behind his head and the water coming off him was hot on my skin, still hot from its time in the earth. I felt as if we were running out of time, and he knelt down and I came up off the stones and there was something unfastened in his face and we kissed. His hands were in my hair. He tasted like limes and tequila and I was afraid to open my eyes and we kissed again and then he whispered that we should get out of the sun.

He helped me up, then dropped my hand. We walked out to the highway, apart, not touching, and Bannon flagged a taxi. We forgot to wait for the old woman, forgot to leave her money, and I never knew what she was bringing me or if it might have helped.

In the taxi, he pulled my legs across his lap. His hands were scarred and callused, fingertips long ago blunted with a slip of a knife, and now coming to my thigh and the blisters there, to my face and shoulders and to my thighs again, rough, fast. There was a smear of blood on his cheek. My lips had burned in the sun and split against his and were bleeding; now when we kissed, we tasted that too.

We went to my hotel room. I sat in a chair, Bannon on the edge of the bed, neither of us speaking or moving, one to the other. I could hear the clatter of children in the square, the maid singing in the next room, the breeze slipping through the open curtains, our breath, so loud in the room itself. This was not a good idea. I had that thought very clearly.

Then he knelt in front of me, and pulled aside my bathing suit. "Don't look away from me, Joan. Not once," he said.

And I didn't. There was nothing careful about what we did there, and, even then, I thought how we would not have another chance.

There was no way to talk about it, and so we did not talk. We went out into the street for food or air or something to drink and we did not hold hands or lean into each other's bodies. We'd get what we had come for, and then something would snap and Bannon would back me up against a wall, dragging his mouth over my neck, my cheek, finally my mouth and then he'd pull away from me as if I'd hurt him, as if I'd held something sharp against his skin. We would stand there, on the street, in a doorway, squared off, and it didn't matter for how long, because there was no time between us, all of this happening outside of those things like time and conversation and good sense. One of us would say, *let's go back to the room,* and then we would.

Like that, until the call came for me.

My mother was in the ICU at the medical center in Columbia. She had pneumonia, and her blood counts were down. It was very bad, and I should come home. I said I'd catch the first flight out in the morning.

Bannon took the bus with me back to Mexico City. I felt very thin inside, very wrong, and I stared out the window at the dawn whipping past us. I did not want to go back to her sickness, but I did not want to stay for what was coming either. Bannon told me to lay my head down in his lap, and he stroked my hair back from my face, his touch careful and sweet, the old Bannon, the old me. I told him I was scared.

"You're being punished," he said.

"You think?"

"I don't know. Somebody's going to be punished."

He laughed then, and I got that feeling in my stomach as if the ground had dropped away beneath us.

"What are you going to do?" I asked.

"I don't know," he said, which meant nothing to me.

I think I wanted to tell him then how much I loved him, but he knew, had always known. It was only a small thing that had changed between us. I did not expect him to leave Gail, had not thought of Gail, or going home, or what would happen then, until that very moment. I did not expect anything at all. I knew nothing for sure.

Out the window, coming into the DF, we could not even see the volcanoes, Popocatépetl, Iztaccíhuatl, for the thick, dark smog.

Alice is crying. I am telling this and she is crying, not like it bothers her to cry, but not like she can stop. I can't stop telling either, not now. I tell her how he walked me to my gate at the airport and how I kissed his cheek, a kiss I'd made a thousand times before, as common between us as borrowed sugar, a call across the street, and all I kept thinking was *what in God's name have I done*. I told Bannon I didn't think I'd make the wedding, to apologize to Gail for me, and he laughed at that, said he would, he would. He said he would see me when he got back, but I didn't know what that meant either, and so I nodded and passed on through security to the jetway.

"I felt his eyes on my back," I say. "I knew I'd fall apart if I turned around, so I didn't, and that was it."

Alice wipes at her face with the backs of her hands, makes a low, frustrated moan and reaches for a paper towel.

"I miss him, Alice. And it's different from how you'd miss a brother—I don't pretend to know what that's like, but I miss him how we were before Mexico, and the rest too."

"Well." She laughs. "I hate to say I told you so, but God, I did. I knew it."

Alice looks at me flatly, her eyes blood-rimmed. I would not say that she is angry, but I can't qualify what she is feeling either, a kind of curtness, maybe, and a kind of anger not entirely for me. I have not told this story about myself in so long; it's strange to see it sit with another person.

"Do you think it helped?" she says. "I mean, your mother lived what, another month or two? Did it help to be so broken up over him you couldn't see straight? Because I'm sure you were. I remember you were."

I shake my head; I don't know. I feel slow to her point, as though I am still trying to understand her first question, but she keeps coming, keeps talking.

"Once you're down there," she says, "it's so much easier to get around."

I trace a circle of water on the tabletop, try to make the drops hold together. I don't remember any ease about that time, don't remember much at all about it, really. There was a night at the farmhouse in the attic, after Bannon, and I was up in the boxes and trunks, the baby clothes my mother had packed away in lavender, and I don't remember what exactly happened, but they had to come and lead me down the narrow stairs. There was a prescription for Valium after that, and other days I've half forgotten, bottomless, scrambling days, then more Valium. I don't expect those have gone away entirely, don't expect they ever will. But it's different now; I have Marshall.

"There's what he said, about being punished," I say.

"Oh, please."

"No, not that. Not him." I gather myself, find her eyes to say this. "I didn't get pregnant then. I can't get pregnant now, at least not easily, and I'm starting to think there are bigger reasons for it."

"Well, that's stupid too. Have you been to a doctor?"

I shake my head.

"That's what they do, Joan, whole fleets of them, and they have drugs, and procedures, and blah, blah, blah." She puts a fist to her forehead. "You could have gotten pregnant in Mexico?"

"Yes."

I can still read the prints of tears on her cheeks, but she rights herself with this thought, this long-ago gamble not come due.

"Oh, what if," she says. "Oh, what if that?"

12

I STEAL INTO bed sometime after three. I pile my clothes by the door and, lifting the edge of the quilt, I find Marshall's back. I fit myself to him as tightly as I can.

"Your cheek," he says. "You're so hot."

I nod into his shoulder and he reaches around to haul me over his side to face him, and the covers get lost and I complain, but all he wants is to know what's wrong.

"Alice and I were talking. I guess I never told her what happened between Bannon and me in Mexico."

"You never told her?"

"Why would I? I never told anyone."

"Of course," he says, and he's got my head pulled in against his chest, his hands in my hair, and his voice is not bitter or difficult, not even a little.

It's not entirely true; I did tell my mother, or, rather, she knew. I went to the medical center in Columbia straight from the airport, and she was slipping in and out of morphine. She'd broken three ribs with her cough.

"Good Lord," she said. "Look at you."

"Shhh," I said. "They want you to stay quiet."

"So I can die quietly?"

"Mom—"

"What was she like?"

"Who?"

"The fiancée."

"She hadn't gotten down there yet when I left."

She closed her eyes then; it was a struggle to stay focused.

"That's no good for you, Joan. You know that."

I didn't make her go on. Her breathing was watery, shallow, her face expressionless, as if to show what she was feeling would take more effort than she had.

"I know," I said. It was the second to last thing we ever talked about.

In the morning, a blade of white winter sun bends across my face. The house is quiet. I make my way over Marshall, and by the time he wakes, I'm close to where I want to be.

We have always lived alone. There were never roommates to consider when we were dating; I had this house, and Marshall, a condo in Hartford, Connecticut, a very ascetic, neutral place with blond hardwood floors, a platform bed, and a great set of Turkish bath towels the size of billboards. And since he's been home, we've lapsed into this private-island way of thinking. We do not dress to make coffee. We step in and out of each other's showers and we hardly ever whisper.

Now I do remember, somewhere in the back of my mind, that we have houseguests, but it's different when I hear the running feet outside the bedroom door. I stop.

"What?" Marshall says.

I put my forehead to his and my hair drapes our faces. "They're out there."

His eyes close. He pretends to concentrate very hard. "What?"

"Let's get in the shower."

He groans and snatches at me, but I get up anyway and start the water hot. We have a chunky old ceramic tub that's deep and long; I lean against the back lip, letting the spray strike my knees. Marshall folds himself onto the bathmat to sit beside me. He slides the shower curtain open enough to see my face.

"You want me to wash your hair?" he says.

"Mmm. I want you to give me a baby."

He tucks his chin into the crook of his arm. "Tell me about that, Joan. Tell me again how you want it."

I start with his cock inside me, wanting that, which gets him in the shower. I put my mouth to his ear and tell him how it would change me to have a baby, how I would swell and go full, and that would be him, us, a third thing made of us inside me, and how it would start here, now, in our house, our life at the end of the year. I have my eyes closed against the water and just keep talking, as if the talk is part of how it happens, some fortunetelling, spell casting.

"There now," he says. "There now, Joan."

Marshall bridges up on his hands and knees, blocking the spray with his back.

"Now can I wash your hair?" he says.

In the kitchen, Alice, Corinne, and the boys ring the table. Their faces are moonish and blank, and I feel stupid now. I shuffle at the coffeemaker, calling stupid things over my shoulder, like how did you sleep, would you like some breakfast, when Marshall comes in and, very softly, says, *Jesus Christ.*

I turn. Corinne and Gerald are covered in some kind of rash.

"Oh my God," I say. "What happened?"

Corinne starts crying, and Alice puts a hand to her back. She picks up Corinne's wrist and holds her arm out for me to see. The welts are red and raised and knotted with pus.

"Do we have Calamine?" I say, and Marshall goes back to our bathroom for the medicine cabinet.

From where I'm standing, I can hear him perfectly. The bottles rattle on the shelf. Something falls in the sink. He mumbles. I think I can hear him scratching his head, and my neck flushes up red and hot.

Corinne and Alice are staring at me. "What happened?" I ask again.

This morning, Corinne and Gerald woke up to a bedfull of spiders. There were hundreds, a hatching, more in the hall, a trail of them. They were coming from the Christmas tree.

I ask if Gail called an exterminator and Corinne gives me a withering, slit-eyed look.

"I didn't wait around, you know?" she says.

Marshall comes back with the Calamine lotion and capsules of Benadryl, and I leave him to pass those around. I tell Corinne I'll get her luggage and we can wash everything out, that she and Gerald can stay over here, or I can get them a hotel room in town, it's up to her. Her nose is running and she swipes at it; now it's smeared with pink.

"Oh, Jesus," she says, and she's crying again.

Gerald, on the other hand, is scratching his bites until they bleed.

"Honey, don't do that," I say. "They'll get infected."

He looks at me from where he stands, chin high to the open drawer of kitchen utensils. He reaches in blindly and takes a corkscrew, starts digging at the back of his leg through his jeans.

"Nope," I say. "No way."

He puts the corkscrew back, and this time takes a swivel-blade vegetable peeler.

"You got to be kidding."

"I got it," Alice says, and she bumps the drawer closed on Gerald's fingers. He doesn't flinch but creeps his hand out, stuffing the vegetable peeler down in his back pocket.

Alice pours juice, shuffles pans on the stove. Corinne gets her face dry and clean, and Marshall rallies the boys for TV. I head across the street for Gail.

She does not answer the bell, but the door is unlocked and I let myself inside. The tree is gone in a trail of needles and cords, lights left broken on the floorboards. There's water running in every faucet, and the house is frigid, windows open to the cold. I call her room to room, the twisted, far-flung sheets, the spent cans of Raid. The phone cord stretches out the French doors to the patio, and I go back out the front to walk around.

Gail has her feet propped up on the wrought-iron table and she's smoking menthols. She is still in her nightclothes and slippers, an afghan across her lap. She hangs up the phone, lifts her chin and jets a long plume of smoke into the air.

"Joan," she says, and it's like she's calling roll.

"Hey. Did you get an exterminator?"

"No. But I did get some Zoloft."

I come around the patio and take the chair across from her.
"You want me to call an exterminator?"

"No."

Gail finishes her cigarette and lights another. The fallen
Christmas tree looks prankish, a smashed jack-o'-lantern, a wind-
shield dripped with eggs. I feel as if I should do something helpful
with a garbage bag or a hose, but I don't have a clue where Gail
might keep those things.

The patio is shaded by heavy hemlocks, and I'm freezing. I rub
my hands together and blow into their cup. I keep thinking whatever watch we're keeping will soon be over, but Gail flicks her
spent cigarette out into the lawn, lights another, and we sit some
more.

"What happened?" I ask finally.

Gail sighs. "I bought the fucking Christmas tree at one of
those cut-your-own lots in Pickens. It was cheap, and I was looking for the whole experience. Stopping by the woods on a snowy
evening."

"Right."

"Right. So. When you do that, it seems, you take home whatever else was calling the tree home. In this case, spider eggs."

"Are you bitten up too?"

"It seems I'm too rich for their blood."

"Come on, Gail. Let's call the exterminator and get this over
with."

She flashes a look at me, and I get the idea that's only the half
of it.

"Corinne," I say.

"You bet your boots, Corinne."

"What'd she say?" Gail just shakes her head, lets out another
spool of smoke into the winter air.

But I can guess it. I remember when Corinne was six and she
trimmed her eyelashes down to the lid with her mother's sewing
shears, as she was tired of hearing how long and pretty they were.

She was twelve and she sold the lawn mower to a neighbor boy across the street in exchange for his mowing the lawn every week, every summer, until he graduated high school, which, amazingly, he did. She was fifteen and she quit her first three waitressing jobs because the kitchens were filthy. She has always been the sort of person who decides the tenor of a given moment and then sticks with it, no matter what you say, no matter how she got it wrong. She returns later, to sort out, smooth over, but if she woke up this morning to a bed of spiders, I'm sure she did little to make the situation less uncomfortable for Gail.

And that's really how I think of it, not as something that was Gail's fault, or Gail's oversight, but only a situation to be made easy or hard depending on whom it crossed. I think I am alone in this. I think everyone else here has somebody to blame.

"We'll get them a hotel room," I say. "We'll get all of them a hotel room over in Greenville. They can stay at the Poinsett. I bet there's somebody over there who's making Christmas dinner, and I bet there's stuff for the boys to do. They can go to the zoo and feed the elephant."

"I just want them to go home."

I realize, right then, there will always be something in Gail that makes me nervous. I have long gone past wondering what she knows and does not know about me and Bannon, if she likes me or does not like me, or even if she cares about such things, but sitting there, cocked back in her deck chair, she sets her eyes cold on me and I feel inspected. I think, for the millionth time, *Why am I here? Why do I still come over here and pretend I'm welcome?*

I sigh. "Do you want me to call an exterminator?"

"No. I have to go to the drugstore. I can get some bombs while I'm out."

She laughs then, and I think it's the idea of bombs she's finding funny.

Across the street, the boys are propped up on the sofa, taking in a videotape of Marshall's, Mexican wrestling, which is surprisingly more theatrical than wrestling you can get here. Marshall is calling the plays, and Gerald is high on the Benadryl. His eyes are fixed and dozy and Nick has his arm in a lock, slicing the tops off his bites with the vegetable peeler.

"Good Lord, Marshall. He's bleeding on the sofa."

"Come on, guys," Marshall says. "Off the sofa."

I grab for the vegetable peeler but Nick is too fast. He slips out of my reach, Gerald slumping into the space he left as if his body has been made liquid. He stares up at me, laughing now, still bleeding, and pulls a little silver nutmeg grater from inside his shirt.

I call for Corinne.

She comes from the kitchen, wiping her hands on a dishtowel she's tucked into the waist of her jeans, and I am caught off-guard. There is another day, winters past, and Bannon is coming out of his kitchen, wiping his hands on a towel at his waist, and the air smells of cardamom and apples. I have quince for him, or pomegranates, or some fresh runny cheese, and he takes the paper bag from me, kisses my cheek, feeds me lunch and wine. It is a day that stretches long for us, this day passing into night and then into the next, and we have all of it, all to ourselves. We are not lovers. We have not even thought of it, and still the prospect of that day drops through me now like a dive from a high, high cliff in a dream, into nothing but rush.

Corinne touches my arm, and I'm embarrassed. I wonder what Alice might have told her, but not enough to ask.

"Your son is cutting himself with my kitchen gadgets," I say.

"Gerald." She whips the towel off her waist and pops it in the air. There's a flurry of finger-pointing, Marshall included, and Corinne gets her face down very close to Gerald's ear. He hands her the grater, a bottle opener, a lemon zester, and the top off an opened tin can. She does not even look at the things he's giving her, but keeps speaking into his ear.

Alice stands behind me. She holds a platter of deviled eggs. I take one. They're curried.

"He's been in trouble at school," she whispers. "Crawling through the shelves of the library. Forging her signature on homework papers."

"These eggs are delicious."

She gives a little bow of her head, then leans into my ear. "You know, she and Francis are separated."

"Oh, no. How long?"

"Six months. Gerald sees him Wednesday nights and every other weekend, but it's hard on him."

I remember when Corinne and Francis got married. Francis, never Franny or Frank. It was before Mom got really sick, and she and Daddy gave a big party at the farmhouse after the rehearsal, with bluegrass, barbecue from Bridge's over in Shelby. Denny and Bannon and I got drunk, probably too drunk for a wedding party, and Bannon stood up to make a speech that blew way out in front of him. He ended up throwing Corinne over his shoulder and pretending to run off with her into the woods. Francis leaned over to me and said how he thought that kind of thing had finally been banned in the South, as if incest jokes were funny. He grew up in Manhattan, the Upper West Side.

"I always thought Francis was a prick," I say.

Alice shrugs, as though maybe I have a point, maybe I don't, and I'm sure there's plenty I don't know. She offers another egg.

"There's ham and biscuits in the kitchen," she says, and passes into the dining room.

Marshall is standing six inches from the TV, remote in hand. He's watching these enormous men in makeup and panties throwing each other around, and he's concentrating, like he is trying to learn something.

He catches me watching him, and there's something in his face that I feel in the backs of my knees. I wish we were alone.

"I wish we were alone," he mouths.

"Marshall and I are going to the store," I call. "Who needs something?"

Alice is still talking from the dining room when I pull the front door shut behind us.

He drives my car. A dead end, an empty lot, and he cuts the engine, throws me in the back seat, and pulls my jeans off by their ankles. The back seat is full of papers, and I slide on top of them. He gets out, comes around, looks around, unbuckling his belt, which I am reaching for. He closes the door with his foot.

"I've never done this before," I whisper.

"Honey, we just did this before."

"I mean in the back of a car."

"Really?"

"Really."

"Well, it's an art form."

He lifts my hips to straddle his lap. I rest my forehead on his shoulder.

"Be gentle with me," he says.

We are covered with newsprint. When we get to the grocery store we take turns in the bathroom with paper towels, wiping the front page from our supporting parts.

I come out of the swinging doors from the stockroom and he's sitting on an orange crate, feeding himself from a dangling bunch of grapes. He stands, dangles the grapes for me until I take one; *No hands,* he says, *no hands.* I feel criminally happy.

"What are you making us for supper, Miss Joan?" He tucks three fingers in the back pocket of my jeans, as if we're in high school. "I do believe I'm starving."

When we get home, Alice says that Denny's called three times, which is the most he's called me in months. I'm flattered, and whatever squeamishness I had about the bones feels worn thin under his attention. A person can get used to anything.

He has been to see Mary Soomes, and so when I call him back I ask him how he takes his tea.

"Tea, yeah. After she had me blow all the leaves out of her backyard, hang her storm windows, and drive her to the post office, she gave me a cup of tea, and a potted meat sandwich."

"Oh. Old lady food."

"Extra pickles, extra mustard."

"Wow. She must really like you."

He's got something else he wants me to look up, a settlement back by the railroad tracks.

"Like a town?" I ask.

"No, more like a housing development. She was pretty vague about it, lots of backtracking. She knows a good bit about the railroad, though. Maybe it was railroad men, or a hobo camp? They had hobo camps, right? I mean, it was the Depression."

"Whose tracks?"

"Southern."

I tell him I'll see what I can find.

I run Southern Railway through the archive and get mostly acquisitions around the turn of the century, lines in eastern Virginia and Tennessee and northern Georgia that allowed people from here to go more places faster than ever before. I find schedules and price lists, several lovely advertisements for travel to Mardi Gras, and charges to look ahead, look Southern. But there's no mention of settlements or camps or black people or violence or anything that tells me anything about whose bones Denny might be keeping in his cellar.

Tomorrow I can go to the library. Lewis has access to the state's Department of Archives and History, and he can pull up census reports, population maps, vital records, and land conveyances, but I can't seem to say that's all right, that's enough, and let's shut out the lights. It seems wrong to me, to trust that the computer has it all. I get down on the floor and run a finger along the spines of the bound volumes I've borrowed from the vault; there's the *Greenville News* from May 1927, the *Anderson Independent Mail* from December of that year. I put my back to the wall and start turning pages.

There's a description of the new schoolhouse being built on the north side of Greenville, with desks for a hundred and fifty kids. The town of Traveler's Rest can have power if every homeowner will promise to use an appliance of some kind, and Durham's Store on the Pendleton Road now has a phone and a runner boy for messages. A doctor's nurse was found disoriented and throwing her clothes down a well in her backyard; her husband committed her to the hospital where she'd once worked, saying he was certain she was in good hands. Bales of white cotton lined Congress Avenue, wanting to be loaded on the rails, and the price of bread was seventeen cents a loaf.

Marshall knocks at the door hours later with a plate of blue cheese and walnuts, a glass of sweet wine.

"You missed dinner," he says.

"Oh, God. Really? I completely lost track of time."

"You missed dessert too."

"You should have come and gotten me."

He shrugs, holds out the plate of cheese, and I take a bite. I'm starving, tired, and he crouches beside me so I can sip the wine. I rest my head on his knee, chew, swallow. I turn another page of the volume that's open in my lap.

"Did you find it?" he whispers, stroking the back of my neck.

"Not yet."

"You will. Keep looking."

He sets the plate and glass beside me and closes the door on his way out. It's some hours before I give up entirely and make my way to bed.

In the night, I dream that I am under water, underground. It's a weight in my chest I cannot lift from, cold on my skin and pulling down. I dig and scramble, but whatever covers me is thick and stubborn and hard to fight.

When I wake, the bed is empty. The sheets are soaked, and Marshall's gone.

I panic quietly, uncertain how awake I am. There's a banging on the side of the house, regular and hard, the sound of a tree branch or a rock, hitting and hitting again.

In the hall, Luther runs impatient laps, as if to show me something basic I have overlooked, the stove in flames, the child in the well. I'm impressionable; the banging on the side of the house eases itself into a headache. I check the den for Marshall and the

TV is dark, his chair empty. I look out the sidelights at the front door. His car is in the drive.

Gerald stands in the kitchen. He wears pajamas with racecars on them, trails a pale blue blanket, the ends of it dark and ratted from wear. He is too old for blankets like this probably, but too young for much of what else is happening in his life: his father's absence, his mother's curt resolve.

He doesn't hear me behind him. He's watching out the back door.

Marshall has a first baseman's mitt and a tennis ball, and he's playing catch against the side of the house, diving in the rimy grass, rolling, coming up with the ball and throwing it again. He's commentating to himself, I think, his lips moving, and he's barefoot, wearing only his shorts and a field coat he took from the garage on his way into the backyard.

The field coat is wool, with wide red and black checks, a hunter's plaid. There is a game pocket in the back of it, loops for shells over the breast, a cigar burn on the sleeve near the wrist. It was my father's jacket. He used to hunt quail, and he used to take Denny with him on Saturdays into the pastures, the both of them with shotguns broken over their arms. I saved the jacket for Denny before the farmhouse was sold, and the first baseman's mitt was his as well.

I wonder what sent Marshall into those boxes in the garage, clearly my boxes, my things from my family, my childhood. I feel a twinge of ownership, and still the headache I woke with, the pounding like the pounding on the house. He must have been up for hours to find those things. He must be freezing out there.

"Gerald," Corinne says. She is standing in the kitchen doorway. "Go back to bed."

Gerald turns as if he has been sleepwalking, looks at me, and then his mother. He was not surprised to hear her voice, and maybe he has known of my company all the time. He takes one last look at the window and obeys.

Corinne comes to stand beside me, watching Marshall too.

"Does he do this frequently?" she asks.

"He's never been a good sleeper," I say.

"But he's conscious. He'll remember this in the morning?"

I think of the night he spent beside the bed, the sweat running off his shin. I think of the nights he's sat up watching old movies, or fallen asleep in the shower, the night he swept all the glasses from the kitchen cupboard to the floor.

"Sometimes yes, sometimes no."

"Has he ever hurt himself," she asks, "when he's like this? Or hurt you?"

I shift to face her. "That's not what this is about."

"Okay."

"No. He hasn't."

"Good," she says. "Okay."

I turn back to Marshall. I want to go outside and get him, take him back to bed with me, but I want Corinne to go away first. I feel her eyes on me, her education. I keep my arms folded against my chest until she runs herself a glass of water from the tap, says good night, and leaves me alone.

13

In the morning, Marshall is at the sink, brushing his teeth. He kisses me with toothpaste, and I tell him I'll put the coffee on. He is fine: a little dark beneath the eyes, but he smiles at me and I can tell he's fine.

Corinne is waiting at the kitchen table, leafing through the Oconee County weekly that arrived this morning. I tell her I have to go to the library but that I should be back midday. Marshall will watch the boys or take them anywhere they want to go, whatever she would like.

"How is he?" she asks.

I don't even turn around to answer. He is just fine, and thanks for her concern.

"Sleep deprivation can be crippling. Has he tried any medication?"

"Medication?"

"Even over-the-counter might help."

"Corinne," I say, "you'll have to talk to him about it."

I go back to the bedroom. Marshall is lying on top of the covers fully dressed, his arms crossed over his forehead. I touch his elbow.

"Corinne is up. I fear she wants to practice on you some."

"Practice what?"

"She's troubled by your sleep habits."

Marshall groans, reaches out and runs his hands down my sides, but he keeps his eyes closed. I kiss his mouth, his chin, tell him I'll be back soon and to play nice. He holds my sleeve until I pull away.

"Hurry," he says. "Please."

It's windy and cold, and campus is empty for the break, like a park closed down for winter. At the library, Lewis is in the stacks behind an overloaded cart, shelving books.

"What, you got busted down to manual labor?" I say.

"Long story." He looks tired. "Here, take the wheel."

Behind him runs a trail of what has not made the trip.

I push the cart for him and we wind through the stacks, Lewis nursing a tall cup of coffee and not saying much. He has not shaved, and his shirt, I think, is dirty. He does not seem to notice the books he's dropped or the ones I keep stopping to pick up, each hardback against the floor like a bullwhip in the silence. He hands me something, and I shelve it. The furnace powers on, its fan humming and tense, like the sound of blood in your ears when you plug them with your fingers. There's no one here but us.

Lewis walks for a time with his eyes closed, then half closed, then closed again. It's disturbing how quiet he is, how disheveled. I'm sure he has not slept in days.

Finally, it occurs to him that I do not belong here.

"I need your computer," I say. "Rather, Denny does."

"Oh, for God's sake. Still?"

"He's looking for something on a settlement out near Red Hill, something that would have been there in the twenties or thirties—"

"Okay."

"He's got this woman—"

"Enough."

"Lewis—"

He puts up his hand. For a moment he looks parental, exasperated, then on the edge of true concern. I think of the job he offered Denny, and how maybe it was the best Lewis could come up with, given his area of expertise. We are his friends, after all. He loves us. And, yes, to work for him shoves things off in a criminal direction, but for all my good intentions, I'm just aiding and abetting. I'm not sure which of us is worse, or which of us is wrong.

We take the elevator down to the reference desk, where Chuck sits with his face in his hands, weeping.

"Jesus," I say. "Chuck?"

I look at Lewis, who shrugs.

"Are you guys going to be okay?"

"It's the holidays," he says. "The holidays are hard all over."

We go back to his office and he slumps behind his desk, closing his eyes again. I reach across him and punch up the computer.

"Census?" I say.

"Here, let me."

I push back in my chair and look out the window, condensation running on the pane. It's as if we're inside a tank. Lewis asks what name, what year, still testy. He chuffs and sighs, and I begin to feel like a pain in the ass.

"What on earth brings you to work in such a state?" I say. "I mean, it's not like today of all days the place would fall apart without you."

"I had some people coming through," he says. "I have a life, you know."

I shut up until he turns the monitor my way.

In 1920, there were four houses between Red Hill and the train tracks, and four men lived there. They were of Swedish and Irish and Welsh descent, born in other parts of the country and moved here for jobs with the railroad. Also in the houses lived four women, Negroes, and seven children, also Negroes, all under the age of twelve. On the census sheets, the women's ancestries are listed as Trinidad, Dominica, West Indies, their names marked with X's, only one of them able to sign for herself.

Miss Bernadette Soomes has a perfect, flowery hand, one daughter, and two sons.

"What about 1930," I ask.

There was no one, nothing. In ten years, they were all gone.

"I'll be damned," I say.

"When you're done," Lewis says, "hit the lights."

He puts his feet up on his desk, leans back in his chair. His mouth hangs open as if he will eat sleep if it tries to get past him this time, as if he will swallow it down whole.

When I get to the cemetery, Denny and Mary Soomes sit on the porch, a large and elegant tea tray between them. Denny has cream in a creamer and sugar in a bowl, a small china plate of cookies, and each of them holds a cup and saucer. Denny makes a lovely introduction.

"How do you do," I say.

Mary Soomes sits in the rocking chair with a plaid wool blanket laid across her legs. Her face is lean and strong, the rest of her body sloping into itself with age, her lap shortened by the soft knolls of the rest of her. She must be close to ninety, if not beyond. She offers me a cup of tea as if this is her porch, and her hand is palsied when she pours.

I settle onto the steps at their feet, lean my back against a post. It's cold even with the tea, but Mary Soomes doesn't seem bothered by it, if bother is even something she allows herself. She scans the breadth of the cemetery to the highway with a gaze as clean and hard as glass. Her eyes are a lovely shade of dove gray.

"Well," she says, "this is all quite horrifying."

"I guess it is," Denny says. "I'm sorry."

"What are you sorry for? It's the nature of the thing, I'm sure. There are very few people who find something at the bottom of a hole and simply throw the dirt back over it."

"All the same. I appreciate your help."

"I wish I could say you're welcome, Mr. Patee. You'd be welcome in any other circumstance."

Mary Soomes turns to me.

"You've seen the archaeology project?"

I tell her I have, and she sighs. I remember Body speaking of her pride and I can see it in her face, in the set of her shoulders against the chair; this encounter with Denny's bones has put her pride on edge. I imagine she is someone accustomed to reviving the past on her own terms. The bones must have forced her hand.

That's the feeling left in the air on the porch, even amidst the tea service and pleasantries, one of resentment, resistance, and loss. I do what I do in these situations and change the subject, ask about Hedy and the chickens, the cold weather, anything to stem the unease. It's hard going. The two of them have finished with each other, and now seem worn out with conversation altogether.

From the other side of the cemetery, there's the sound of a high-octane engine approaching. It's Russell and Body, plowing out of the woods at high speed on some tricked-out ATV. Mary Soomes fixes her eye on Denny, and he looks at his shoes.

"My chariot, I believe," she says.

"Yeah," Denny says. "I called them."

Mary Soomes rests her teacup on the edge of the tray and readies herself to stand. Denny comes to her side, which she allows. He asks what she would have him do out there, and I'm not sure if he means the place her home once stood or the place he dug the bones, but he's asking if she would like a marker of some kind to name the spot.

She puts her hand to his sleeve and looks into his face. She smiles, but there's something lost in it.

"Honestly," she says. "What difference would it make to me?"

The ATV is so loud upon us now that the rest of what she says is lost, but her gesture is delicate and resigned, full of what looks to be a hard-earned peace. She is an old woman, after all. I'm sure she's earned everything she's got.

When Body cuts the engine, Russell looks confused and abashed, like something here is all his fault and he's waiting to be told what it might be. He looks from Denny to his mother and back again.

"What in God's name are you doing out here, Mama?" he says.

"I suppose I was waiting on you."

"But, Mama—"

"Russell. Don't talk back."

He drops his head, and that seems to be the end of it.

Body steps around from the driver's side and offers Mary Soomes his arm, which she takes in exchange for Denny's. Denny thanks her for her help, and she cuts him off with the snap of her hand.

"It was nothing," she says. "Nothing at all."

It's clear the subject is closed.

Den and I watch the ATV disappear into the woods at the edge of the stones, the smell of diesel clinging to the air. Denny puts his teacup on the tray and pushes it aside, slumps into a chair. Niceties are over.

"I think her father was a white man," I say.

"Yeah," Denny says. He lets out a long breath. "And I've got what's left of him in my cellar."

He lets his head fall back on his neck and talks at the ceiling of the porch, the bare light bulb dark in its socket. He tells me how the railroad men and the black women moved out here from town when Mary's brothers were babies, as their eyes were blue and talk was loud. Mary was born out here, and other children too. A drummer came from town once a week, and they had big gardens, raised chickens and rabbits and hogs. The men all worked for Southern; they had good jobs and were paid well and went back and forth between the Pendleton station and the settlement, but the women and the children never went anywhere they couldn't walk. For years, people left them alone and just the drummer came from town.

Then cotton prices dropped and the boll weevil rose up, people in town lost their jobs and their land, and the governor at the time said something about how lynchings were necessary and good. It was summer, and it did not rain for fifty-one days. On the fifty-second day, Mary's father's horse arrived back from his shift with her father tied into the saddle, his throat slit from ear to ear.

The women buried him. The men put the children on the trains.

Some went north, like Mary's brothers, to Detroit and Chicago, some to New York, some to Philadelphia. Some passed as white when they got where they were going, with their light eyes, their fair features. Most of them, Mary never saw again.

Her train went to Atlanta, on to New Orleans, where someone had an aunt who would keep the youngest children. She left in the dead of night; the tracks went right past her home, between Red Hill and the cemetery. The babies were sleeping against her, and she did not wake them for a last-glance goodbye, and she was glad for that, because when the train went by Mary could see her mother and the other women pulling furniture and books and china from the houses out into the yard. She could see her home, on fire.

"And so there's nothing left?" I say.

"We went out there this morning. You'd never know it to see the spot, but, I swear, Mary could tell one blade of grass from another."

"I bet it was hard," I say, "to come back here after all that time."

Denny doesn't say anything to this, just stares at the ceiling, his legs stretched out before him, his arms crossed beneath his head. He seems weighted with the day, and, like Mary Soomes, ready to be done with it all. Then he tells me how last winter he went back out to the farmhouse after it was sold.

The barn, he said, was full of steam engines and parts for steam engines, and a family of cats. He didn't know what he was doing out there; it was late and he was driving back from Lewis's and he'd gone by habit, pulled up to the barn and opened the doors, as if to feed the horses. The steam engines were huge and oily. He walked around the house, looking in the windows at the family's heavy antiques, their plasma TV. He walked out to the pastures. They were empty, overgrown.

It was cold. He was tired. He let himself in the back door of the house, which was unlocked, and spent the night on the family's sofa, leaving in the early hours, before anyone was up. He took a black cat from the barn. She's the one who lives here with him now.

I close my eyes against what he is telling me and try not to picture him out there alone, looking for his home in the cold, in the dark. It's no use, and my heart is broken all again.

I'm getting ready to go when I remember Christmas dinner is tomorrow night at our father's. I am not sure if Denny is planning to come this year, but I don't want to be the one who puts the idea in his head to back out. He always brings the ham. It's smoked, with a brown sugar crust, and I've asked him where he gets it, but all he'll tell me is the name of a strip club in Seneca.

I ask about the ham.

"Don't you be going over there by yourself, now," he says. "Those girls will scratch your eyes out, as soon as look at you."

"Come on, Denny. I bet you make that ham yourself."

You'd think I asked him to prove it.

In the distance, there's the bawling of an engine again. I think Mary has forgotten something and sent Body back on his ATV, but it's a motorcycle, coming fast from the highway up to Denny's, a sleek silver chopper bike with something sawed off so as to make plenty of sound. Denny excuses himself and trots out to meet the rider in the lane.

They shake hands and stand and talk, the bike still running. The rider is stocky and thick, wrapped in black leather and wide sunglasses, without a helmet, as that is not the law in South Carolina, and I can't hear what they are saying over the rumble of the bike. The rider laughs. Denny claps his shoulder. They finish talking, shake hands again, and Denny walks back to where I'm standing.

"That was Boyd Henderson," he says, like it's amazing but true. "You remember him? We bumped into each other at Lewis's the other day."

"What's he do now?" I ask.

"Blows things up, I think. Pretty exclusively."

Which explains why he was out at Lewis's but not, really, what he's doing here.

"What are you up to, Denny?" I say.

"Minding my own business," he says. "From now on."

I shrug and turn away, but I see his exhaustion from earlier differently, no longer what might clean him out, put him right again. I look at him, and he seems just the same ole Denny, but there is never any way of knowing what is going through his head. And I wonder how he seems to someone we grew up with, someone who knows only what they have heard about him since he's come back to town, the half-crazy things, amplified and amplified again.

He must seem like Boyd Henderson does now, as dangerous as hell.

At home, in bed, I tell Marshall all of this, about the settlement, the railroad men, about the murder and the burning. I tell him about Denny and the kid we grew up with, who now gets paid to play with explosives, and how Lewis offered Denny a job.

"What are they thinking," Marshall says, "some kind of French Connection?"

"I think he might be serious, now that the bones are put to rest."

Marshall strokes my hair. He tells me not to worry, that Denny can take care of himself.

It's very, very late when I realize that's exactly what Denny told me about Marshall the day at the cemetery with Leonard Lopey: not to worry, he'd be fine. It sounds so stupid now, that such a thing could bring relief, the equivalent of saying don't look at it and it will go away, don't feed it and it will find another home.

Considering the source, I worry all night long.

14

CHRISTMAS EVE, Corinne and Alice borrow my car. They have some errands, they say, and they put on skirts and nice shoes and ask if we would watch the boys for them. They'll be back in time for dinner. I offer directions to the mall, but Alice is painting her fingernails at the kitchen counter and she doesn't write anything down. I don't think they're going shopping.

It's Christmas Eve, though, and somebody has to go shopping, so Marshall and I take the boys with us into Greenville. They have rolls of money from their fathers, and Gerald wants to put it all together and buy a trampoline.

"How would you get it home?" I say. "They won't let you take a trampoline on the plane."

"You could use it," he says, as if this solves the problem.

"Think smaller, man," Marshall says. "Think electronics. Think power tools."

"A cordless drill?" Nick says.

"A Sawzall."

Gerald still wants the trampoline. He stares out the window, limp and sullen, like he's been since the spiders. "It's my money," he says.

"Come on, Gerald." Nick is strongly affected by the fistful of sugar cookies he grabbed on the way out the door. He seems to be vibrating. "We can build a birdhouse or something."

"Birdhouse?" Marshall draws back. "The thing looks like an M-16 rifle. You could cut a car in half with a Sawzall."

The tide turns; Gerald is very interested in halves of cars.

"Longways or shortways?" he asks.

Marshall wheels his seat and grins. "Either way you want."

And he's being genuine. I caught him this morning reading one of Gerald's wizard books after Gerald had put it down, and when Nicky broke his Stealth Viper Zoid, Marshall went out to the garage and used a soldering iron to fix it. He took Nicky with him, knew to let a boy watch anything that involved melting plastic, and it's hard to say who's talked about it more since.

I drop the three of them at the Home Depot, which is as close as Marshall gets to shopping. He'll drag the aisles and buy things we have no use for, the garage already full of D-cell batteries and belt sanders, calipers, hand planes, fittings and switches, hinges and screws. He likes having the stuff around, and maybe because he knows nothing about it.

I want to pick up some candy at Vaughn-Russell off Augusta Road to take to Daddy's for dinner, chocolate-dipped ginger and orange peel and almonds. Alice and Corinne felt obligated, and last night they made sweet potato pie (Daddy's favorite), cornbread dressing (Marshall's), and some kind of gratineed cauliflower with horseradish. Gail agreed to come as long as she doesn't have to ride in the same car with Corinne, which I thought was generous, considering, and Piper will be home from school. The house will be full, like it should be for a holiday.

But I feel how near this undertaking sits to disaster. There's a loosening in my guts when I think too long on it, but it's what we've always done Christmas Eve, since before Mom died, and it's hard to stop a thing in motion. So I pick up my candy, as if that might be what takes us safely through.

The woman at Vaughn-Russell is wearing reindeer antlers and an enormous, nearly chemical smile. She fills a pound box with chocolates and wishes me a Merry Christmas, but like she really means it. I buy Marshall's present a few stores down: an antique field desk I've had my eye on, marled walnut, inlaid with maple, heavy rag paper and a German fountain pen to fit inside. It's as much a present for myself, but that's the sort of thing we've always given, more allusions than gifts, like the ring he brought me for a baby. I find a Victorian pincushion for Alice and some silver candlesticks for Corinne and leave the antique store for my car. The sidewalks are glutted with shoppers, the shoppers piled with packages, Handel piped into the air. A red VW Beetle parks near me, the back seat full of poinsettias, and I have the feeling the scene is planned, that I'm passing through a set, that a song or a meaningful speech will be expected of me any moment. Then I'm stopped by a window full of baby clothes.

They are so tiny, these little blue and white and yellow things, slippers and gowns and crocheted blankets, lace bonnets with long satin ribbons. I'm drawn into the store, and there are smocked dresses and little overalls with appliques of fire engines and airplanes, giant grosgrain hair bows, cardigan sweaters embroidered with fly rods and trout, flowerpots and vegetables, pink radishes for pink rabbits the size of dimes.

I've always thought Marshall and I would have a boy, just a sense, a picture in my head of a blue-eyed, brush-cut boy in overalls, in summer, a boy child with Marshall's mouth. I have to go back to our father's grandmother on my side to find blue eyes, but that's what I picture, and there's no way to know about Marshall's biological family. I don't even think he's bothered to find the agency he came through.

The saleswoman tells me the snapsuits are all long-fiber combed cotton from Sweden, the very softest, and she has customers who dress their babies in nothing else. I nod, make a sound in my throat, smile. Her glance drops to my waist, quickly and back. She says how they make wonderful gifts.

"If you need any help," she says.

I wonder how many women she gets in here like me, if she can spot us, if we make ourselves obvious, an expression we can't imagine we share. And then I realize I'm clutching a fistful of baby things like a bouquet, pink and blue and ranging sizes, and I'm headed to the register to pay for them. I feel accelerated, like a wheel inside me has slipped its channel. I tell the woman to wrap it together, that I can sort it out later. She ties the box with a big yellow bow, as if that will solve the problem.

When I get back to the Home Depot, Gerald is carrying a huge red amaryllis. Marshall has a bag in each hand and wants me to pop the trunk so he can go back inside and carry out some things in secret.

"What you get me?" I ask.

"Not in front of the children, Joanie."

"It's Christmas, for God's sake." I'm calling to him now, out the window. "Don't I get a real present?"

Marshall fills the trunk so full with bags, he can barely latch it closed.

I make the call for ice cream and get cheers, even though it's cold, even though we have not eaten lunch. Even Gerald is pleased, and he asks for double scoops. We drive downtown to a place that adds whatever you want to your ice cream with a pastry blender. Marshall and I share, cinnamon with chocolate chips. Nick gets vanilla with gummy bears and bubblegum and pineapple, and he wants more, but the girl behind the counter tells him to relax. He is not yet old enough for this to be embarrassing.

The afternoon is gray and blustery, and the Christmas lights are blinking on, a wefting through the trees along Main Street. The wind kicks up and Marshall slides his arm around my shoulders, the boys running ahead, Nick's ice cream running down his wrist, our noses red with the cold. For a minute, it's easy to see all these boys as mine.

"That was fun today, with those guys," Marshall says. "They remind me what I liked when I was that age."

"I didn't realize you'd forgotten, what with what you've got in the trunk."

But Marshall is serious. "I just see it differently now, I guess."

He's not close to his parents and, for an only child, has no memories of being doted on or spoiled. His mother once told me that when Marshall was a baby, he threw up on his father and she was so embarrassed. We haven't spoken to them since Thanksgiving, and they've never been down here to visit, except for when we got married. It troubles him more than he says, and on a holiday especially. I press my cheek to his shoulder for a moment. We let it pass at that.

Nick leads us in dirty carols, all the way home.

It's getting late but Corinne and Alice are not back yet, and I tell the boys how they should get changed, their cords and nice sweaters already laid out on the guest bed. They groan and wheedle until Marshall promises Mexican wrestling again, which is enough for Nick. He practically tears the door from its hinges, but Gerald pulls me aside in the kitchen.

"Here." He puts the amaryllis in my hands.

"Oh, sweetie —"

"It's for my mom." His smile is polite, paling to business. "I want you to tell her my dad sent it."

"Yeah?"

I feel a hot pain in my chest, but he's looking up at me, resigned, his eyes the eyes of an old pet. I imagine he's sick of sympathy. He's been living with Corinne in this separation, and he's eight, not so young an age when it comes to gauging need and lack, high emotion. I get the idea that this is more about his mother than the fact she is not living with his dad.

"Don't let Nicky blow it," I say, and he nods his head, as if we have struck a fair deal.

I make a note on some card stock, then drop it in the sink. I'll say I was filling the pot and must have let the card slip out, now smeared beyond the point of reading. Marshall batters in with his Home Depot bags, and I roll my eyes.

"Gerald gave that to you?"

"No. It's for Corinne." I wave him away. "Just keep your mouth shut."

"An intrigue."

"Marshall."

"No problem. I love an intrigue."

"I am sure you do."

When Corinne and Alice get back, I am dressed for dinner, a slim tweed skirt and jacket, my hair pinned up. I'm pulling the casseroles and pie plates from the fridge to load into the car, and the noise is loud enough to tell them where I am. They wear measured smiles into the kitchen, prattling about the weather, the cold, but I can tell they've dropped their conversation in the hall.

Alice spots the flower right away.

"Wow," she says, leaning into the blossom, but there's no scent. "How beautiful."

"It came today," I say. "For Corinne."

Corinne gets a little flush to her cheeks but finishes slipping off her coat, draping it, folded, across the back of a kitchen chair. She studies the flower, drawing the backs of her fingers over the petals the way you'd stroke a cheek.

"Where's the card?" she says, and the look she turns on me is beamish and soft.

It's then I realize there's someone else who might send her flowers other than her husband, at least someone she'd rather receive flowers from. I lose my words, my feint, look over to the sink and pluck the air vaguely.

"I dropped it. Yes, I'm sorry. You know how florists are, with the holidays. It was dry when it got here, and I went to water it and I don't think I even saw who it was from."

Corinne takes the card out of the sink and snaps her wrist to clear the water from the ink. She looks to me, then back at the card, and Gerald comes to stand at her elbow. He shakes his head, as if I've failed him, have missed the point. And I guess I have.

I stare at my shoes. Like an act of God, there's a run in my stockings.

"Well, for chrissakes." I turn my ankle up for them to see, and I sound like a shiny new penny, too bright to be real. "These things don't last a minute."

"No," Corinne says. "They don't."

As I leave the kitchen, I hear Alice say, "We forgot to put gas in the car, Corinne. You were supposed to remind me," and even that seems weighted with what's been revealed, her words laid down like a called bluff.

I lie back on the bed and close my eyes with the crook of my elbow. Marshall wants to know if I'm okay. I take my arm from my face and he's standing in the closet, the file of shirtsleeves behind his head.

"I am," I say. "Barely."

"The intrigue failed?"

"Oh, yes."

"You have a run in your pantyhose."

"I know."

He's leaning over me, his hair still wet from his shower. "May I?" he says, and I have no idea what he is asking me.

"Yes," I say. "You may."

He reaches down and takes the shoe from my foot, tucking the sole against his ribs. He slips a finger into the tear in my stocking and pushes, the threads laddering all the way up to my hip. The sound is a fastening one, even as the action is the opposite.

I stretch out my other leg for him to do the same.

Then we're all dressed and polished and waiting by the car doors while Alice and Corinne load the food in the trunk. There is engineering involved, and Marshall looks over their shoulders to give suggestions. He holds up the box with the yellow bow.

"This fragile?"

"Oh," I say. "No, it's fine."

He wedges the box in between two casseroles, and I put my back to the whole thing, no longer the whim it was this afternoon. I feel a little stupid for buying baby clothes, and I hope to God no one opens up that box, so I don't have to feel stupid to anyone but myself.

Gail comes from across the street, her heels high and her skirt short. She has beautiful legs, something I'd not noticed before.

They are the kind of legs that make you wish you could see her run. She carries a cut-glass bowl covered with tinfoil.

"You didn't have to," I say.

She shrugs. "Ambrosia."

"With marshmallows?" Nick's sugar intake has reached critical mass. His pupils are dilated, and he reminds me of Chuck at the library, as if he might crash at any time.

Alice will have none of it. She herds the boys into the back seat and climbs in between them, Gail taking the passenger side. Marshall and Corinne follow in his car, and we head north of the city to the scenic highway that runs along the ridge of mountains. The heater comes up and we are warm in our coats, the sky a clear dark blue, no house lights, a waning moon out ahead of us, a single star beneath.

In the rearview mirror, I see Nick lick his hand and wipe it on his thigh.

"Smell this," he says, but no one is listening. "Smell this, Gerald."

"No." Gerald sounds mad.

"Smells like drool and pants."

"For God's sake, Nicky, keep your hands to yourself," Alice snaps. "For God's sake."

But then she seems to feel sorry for her shortness, and she reaches over to stroke the back of Nick's head. The boys must be entertained: there are knock-knock jokes that quickly turn lewd, then the carols from the afternoon, not so funny in front of Alice, requests for drinks and snacks, but all we have between the three of us is a half stick of gum from Gail's purse, which she seems loath to give up.

I offer what stories I know, how the Cherokee used to hunt these hills in summertime, how my father dug their flints from his backyard as a boy, how there are wonderful places to camp and fish and they will have to visit again when we can pick blackberries and buy fireworks and eat boiled peanuts from the roadside stands. I am not as good at this as Marshall, and the boys look politely bored. I wish I knew a little something about power tools.

"Well, goodness, Joan," Alice says. "You paint a kind of paradise."

She moved to Boston when she was eighteen. This is her first trip home in years, and I wonder if she still even calls it home, and what it was that made her leave, and why she's really come back now. It's sure not to spend Christmas with Gail.

Like to agree, Gail says, "I wouldn't know camping if it hit me in the face."

She's pushed against the door, her neck craned up to see the moon. Her home is California, and yet she's stayed here, all this time, and I can only think it's because of Bannon. I want to ask Gail how she sees it here, in terms of season and fruit, what keeps you outdoors or in. But we have never asked such intimate things of each other, and this hardly seems the place to start.

We stop at tracks to let a train go past, the cars printed with tall white letters: SOUTHERN. Mary Soomes's train.

I think of her strong face the other day at Denny's, her watch over the cemetery when we ran out of things to talk about. She lost everything she had here, her family, her home, her welcome, and yet when the time came to settle down, she came back. In the end, what you lose to a place might be as strong a tie as any.

We turn off the highway and the boys begin to catch glimpses of the lake, the marina lit up for the holidays. People decorate their boats, and every once in a while there is a Christmas tree impossibly afloat, a lighted sleigh and Santa Claus, a mastline full of stars. I crack my window and we can hear singing, liquored and off-key.

"That's how it goes, Nick," Gerald says, disgusted. "*God rest,* not hot breasts."

"Whatever." He's still licking the palm of his hand.

We pull up my father's driveway and Piper is home. The rear end of her car is pasted with stickers, for bands and butterflies and well-being, the back seat filled with laundry and books and kid toys. I realize I have not seen her since August, when she started school again. I feel a sudden sadness for that, my occupation with my own life such that phone calls were enough. I have missed her, more than I was aware.

Marshall pulls behind me and cuts his lights. When he gets out, he seems troubled with whatever he and Corinne have talked about. He doesn't have a natural fondness for revelation and would not want to hear the things with which Corinne might be forthcoming, her fractured marriage, her troubles with Gail. Plus, she's wanted to talk to him about stress management ever since she witnessed his night in the yard throwing ball, and that conversation could only try his patience. I take his hand.

"Yeah, but did you get to tell knock-knock jokes?" I whisper.

"Oh, you have a point."

I want him to smile so he does, but it's wired, tight. We file inside, two by two by two and Gail, her bowl of fruit balanced on an upturned hand.

Piper sits next to Daddy on the hearth with her arm slung around his shoulder, some sort of cocktail in her glass, and they are laughing, their heads together. They have been this way as long as I can remember, different with each other than they are with us. She is his baby, his youngest child, the last woman he shared his house with. The fire trembles behind them, and Daddy stands. He looks red-faced and windblown, as if he's been sailing, even as it is too cold for that, and I think it's just talking with Piper that's made the difference.

And she is a beauty queen. Tonight she wears tuxedo pants and a lacy red blouse, high-heeled sandals, fishnet stockings. She throws her arms around my neck, the most affectionate of all of us, a giver of hugs, a sender of cards, and genuine about it, genuine with everyone. Her dog, Sequoia, nudges at my knees, smelling Luther on my skirt. She's a wonderful dog, comes when she's called, sits, stays, listens, will save your life if it's put in danger, has saved Piper on more than one occasion. And Piper will always be a little bit of that girl she was when our mother died. This is to say, we are all grateful for the dog.

I pull back to look at her, and there are tears running from her left eye.

"Piper."

She pulls a tissue from her pocket. "Yes. I know. It droops."

"What happened?"

"Oh, jeez. The doctors say Bell's palsy. It's much better now, and it will probably go away completely."

"Palsy?"

"It's just what they call it. Temporary paralysis. One morning I woke up, and my eyelid was resting on my cheek."

She laughs, but I'm dumbfounded. I take her chin in my hand, turn her face to the light.

"Why didn't you tell me?" I say.

"Oh, Joan. What could you have done? And, see, I'm okay now. I'm fine."

She takes the bowl of ambrosia from Gail and I follow her to the kitchen. There're drinks to make and food to warm, and soon everyone is busy. I don't get to really talk to her. I watch her in the kitchen with Alice and Corinne; they talk about exam schedules and pilates classes as if they've always been friends, and she's right. The eye is barely noticeable. She looks wonderful, happy. In love? It's hard to tell. She's always some of that.

And Daddy has a sense about women who are not his own. He's sought out Gail and is telling her a joke about how he was a German shepherd in his last life. When the punch line hits, he'll scare her half to death, barking. The boys roll on the floor with Sequoia, and Marshall winks at me from the bar. He brings me a glass of ice water and I drink it down fast, as if that was the point of his bringing it.

"Watch this," he says.

He makes a show of handing my sister a twenty-dollar bill.

"What?" she says, but she's already smiling.

"Well, if you want to dance," he says, "you have to pay the piper."

She laughs, and he's proud of himself. Men always say this sort of thing to her, because she is blond and branchlike and has the posture of a pajama model. I've heard men tell her how her birthday should be a national holiday, that the light in her eyes outshines the stars, that she sure smells good. Once we were in a bar and some stranger slipped his hands up her knees, told her how he wanted to take her to a hotel room and drape her hair all over him, and that had scared her, had sounded like something to be done to her hair without her attached to it. But Marshall, tonight, with his money, she takes him up on it.

They sway a waltz, Ray Charles on the stereo, and he tries to get the twenty back until she tucks it inside her shirt. It's hard to get her to come together in my head; my sister, this beautiful woman, flirting with my husband. She asks about the baby-making, as if it's something the three of us can work out together.

"You know what the trick is," she says. "You have to do it like it's prayer. You both have to want it that bad."

Marshall rolls his eyes, spins Piper out along his arm fast, as if to shake her from this line of talk.

"So you think it's a cosmic problem?" I say.

"I'm just saying. Everybody I know who's gotten pregnant saw stars. Right afterward, like they'd been hit in the head."

"Everybody you know who's gotten pregnant did so by accident. Maybe then it's like getting hit in the head."

"True," she says. "Maybe that's it."

Marshall dips her back over his arm, and they laugh, finished. She goes inside her shirt to get his money and he says no, for her to keep it, buy herself something pretty. He takes his drink from the coffee table and raises it in our direction.

"To accidents," he says, and drains it to the ice. He leaves us for the kitchen and a refill.

"You don't think I upset him?" Piper says.

"No. I don't think so."

And he doesn't seem upset, just loose, unwinding. Piper lets out a heavy sigh, pulls the tissue from her pocket, and dabs her eye again. Maybe we look different to her, from the outside. I think of Lewis's party, the cameras in the walls, Marshall and I running from room to room, the other day in the grocery store, how giddy we were, and then Marshall in the backyard, throwing ball against the house. Without what happens in private, just between the two of us, maybe it does look as if something's going wrong.

Soon the table is set and the food is hot, but Denny and Hedy are still not here. Cocktails make their third round. Alice asks if she can make plates for the boys, who are now chasing Sequoia as opposed to playing with her, and I can see a pulse throbbing in my father's temple. He apologizes.

"Why don't we all sit down?" he says. "Denny can fend for himself."

"Oh, no." Alice is embarrassed. "I don't want to rush anyone."

"You're not rushing. It's nearly nine o'clock. Who eats after nine o'clock in this country?"

Piper puts a hand to his back. "Let's first finish our drinks then," she says, as if the plan is good and our own to start with, and he agrees to that.

She has always been able to soothe him, an ability that right now seems of nearly divine power. I am struck with a kind of grateful envy, like I would be if she'd calmed the seas, or drawn the sun from behind the clouds. I wonder what she'll be like at my age, when she can lay her hands on her own life, outside the structures of school and home and Daddy, myself and Denny still so under his thumb. Perhaps she will be the one he will let go, because he can.

People will follow her in the street.

Waiting does not suit my father once it's been brought to his attention that's what he's doing, and the throbbing in his temple ranges over his face; he blows a vein in his eye, grinds the ice in his glass. We find chairs, walls to lean against, but it's hard to keep from looking as though we're waiting. Corinne yawns against her hand. Piper says she has to feed the dog, and Marshall and I both offer help.

I go into the kitchen cabinet for a bowl while Piper gets the dog food from the car, and I find a stack of papers.

They are job notices copied from classifieds and online journals, each description close to the description of my father's job now, only for universities in Wisconsin and Delaware, in Texas and Toronto and upstate New York. Each one is dated. They were all printed in December.

"Daddy," I call.

He steps into the kitchen, his glass full again, but his face still unhappy.

"What are these?"

"A-ha," he says, and he takes the papers from my hand. "I meant to toss those out."

"Yes, but what are they?"

He looks into his glass, and I realize if it had been his first drink, this is as far as I'd have gotten. I wait. He is deciding. He grins at me.

"Schelling's been sending them for months," he says.

"What?"

"Yes. In my box at school. He does it to everybody sooner or later."

"Jesus Christ, Daddy."

"Now. Come on. Like I said, he does it to everybody sooner or later. He's a jerk. He has too much time on his hands, and he just digs up old dirt. Let's not worry about that now, on Christmas. Put those things away."

But I cannot be made to believe that they are nothing, that they mean nothing. There must be thirty notices here, more than one a day.

"This is ridiculous," I say, and the front door bursts open.

Denny is as white as paste, the foil-wrapped ham tucked under his arm, his breath fogging in the cold. He looks ten years older than yesterday and I know, in my bones, something is wrong.

"Denny?" Piper says, and she is reaching for his shoulders, but his face doesn't shift, doesn't come around.

I look to Hedy and she's his opposite, candent, sparkling. She draws all the light in the room.

"I'm pregnant," she says. And, I swear, she says it right to me.

15

ALL NIGHT, it's like I can't get a deep breath. Denny and I, on the sofa—I'm sure we look exactly the same: pale, dumbstruck, unhealthy, unoccupied. I think about our mother, so long ago, locking herself in someone's bathroom after such an announcement, and what she got for it was Denny. I could lock us both in a bathroom and see what happens, but I'm not even sure Denny knows the story.

I'm afraid he's lost. I press my leg against his, and I'm relieved to have him pressing back.

"Want to go to the bathroom with me?" I say.

"Can we stop off for a drink on the way?"

I look at him, his scruff of beard as much silver as not. He's not a boy anymore, and has maybe reached the point in his life where the idea of a sea change is tired. I hate to think of Denny as tired. I say what I shouldn't.

"What are you going to do?"

"What are you going to do, smarty pants?"

"Yeah." I sigh. "Okay."

He tips his glass at me, as if he's shot back well.

Dinner is forgotten. Somebody has set out the ham on a platter amongst the other dishes, but the tableware is salvage, leavings of knives and spoons and napkin rings across the cutwork cloth like bones at the end of a hunt. Marshall stands over a casserole of green beans, licking his fingers. Suddenly I'm so hungry I feel faint.

"You want a plate?" I ask Denny.

"If you can get it down the neck of that gin bottle, I do."

"A piece of pie, then. Corinne made it. You haven't seen them since they've been in town. She's cut her hair."

"I can see that from here."

"She's left her husband."

"It happens to the best of them."

"Yeah, but I think something's up."

I tell him about the flower and the note, and how she and Alice borrowed my car and were gone all day today. He nods along, barely listening, but I can't seem to quit talking now that I've started, even though I have nothing to say beyond hairstyles and pettiness. Again, I feel that pressing against what's coming down, that shoring up the hopeless thing, and maybe the fact is that I'm just more comfortable discussing somebody else's hopelessness than my own.

Denny gets a fix on me, one eye squinted shut. He's a little drunk.

"You know," he says, and he lets his hand splay out into the room. "I'd give all of this to you, if I could."

"Your kingdom?"

"I mean it."

"Don't, Denny," I say. "Don't mean anything you say just now."

"I would." He shrugs his shoulders, sucks the ice in his glass. "I do."

Marshall appears with a plate for me, and we slide over on the couch for him to sit with us.

"Hey, Denny," he says. "Congratulations."

They shake hands over me, and that's the end of it. I feed them bites of my ham, my cauliflower, alternating from my left to my right. Christmas seems to be going fine without us.

Nick has collapsed on his mother's lap, his legs trailing her hips as she rocks with him, a motion suited to a smaller child. Everything in him is given out, and I am envious: to be her, to be him. I miss my own mother, and even now, even all these years gone by, my first thought is how she must be here somewhere.

Her last Christmas was supple with painkillers and champagne. I carried her to and from her wheelchair and I held her much like Alice holds Nick now, her arms slung around my neck, her head to my shoulder. She weighed as much as a sack of groceries, a box of china, nothing, really, at all.

Now Alice hums, high and dulcet, her mouth against Nick's temple, and my thoughts double back on themselves, unfocused, unmatched but relative, children and mothers and children again.

I would like to think I'm pregnant, but I bet I'm not.

And somehow that's because Hedy is pregnant, as if it's a town not big enough for the both of us. She sits by the fire, flanked by Daddy and Piper, and she tucks her hair behind her ears, presses the back of her hand to her forehead as if to test the heat there. She drinks a glass of milk and there's a pillow for her feet, like in a movie from the forties, and I bet she'll get fussed at for trying to lift her purse on the way out the door. Daddy is good at making you feel like you always imagined you would feel, holding the things you imagined you would hold.

This will be his first grandchild, a Patee child, but I have not heard him say a word to Denny about it.

Denny shakes his head. "But look at him work on Hedy. By the time we get home, she'll be thinking he put the sun in the sky. Much like you yourself."

I let this ride. "Didn't she have a class with him?"

"Yep."

"I thought I remembered her not liking him much."

"Well, I guess that's water under the bridge now."

His voice loosens to a kind of distracted awe. He watches our father like one athlete watching another, better athlete, to catch what he can. Hedy smiles at something Daddy's said to her, and the barest echo of a smile comes to Denny's mouth too.

Marshall slips his arm around me, his fingers trailing the back of my neck. I tip my head to see his face and he blows a half kiss.

"I have something to tell you when we get home," he whispers.

"Yeah?"

"A real something. Then that."

"Okay. Animal or vegetable?"

He is smiling at me with his beautiful mouth, but I can tell this thing he has to say casts some shadow, and I want to know about it now instead of later. I take his hand, make to pull us off the couch and into the hallway, someplace private, someplace he can say what he has to say.

But then dishes are breaking in the kitchen. Voices rise, and there's more breaking. Gail slams out the French doors to the deck, and it's not long before Corinne follows.

"Ooh," Denny says. "Catfight."

Marshall leans over. "Corinne is, what? Strung tightly?"

"You seemed to get an earful in the car," I say.

He shakes his head and settles back, as if it's too much to go into and not worth the effort. A hot pulse thrums in my neck. If Corinne is having it out with Gail, Bannon and me in Mexico is the first thing she'll bring up.

Denny goes on talking, as if dishes break in his kitchen all the time.

"Corinne ought to spend some time with our man Lewis," he says. "Quality time."

"I don't think hers is a medicine cabinet issue," Marshall says.

He snorts. "I'll tell you what her issue is." But then he doesn't, and I guess I've heard enough anyway.

I can't let what's happening outside go ahead and happen but can't think how to stop it either. I stand, sit, excuse myself, and stand again.

Denny wants me to take the long way past the deck, see what I can see, and report back. And then he wants ice for his glass, another wedge of lime, maybe some of that sweet potato pie I was talking about, but I wave him off. I walk through the dining room to the kitchen and cup my hands to the dark glass of the French door, looking out.

All I see are the boats on the water through the trees, beats of light, red and green and blue, an unreadable code. I close my eyes and open them again, but there's no change. Gail and Corinne have slipped around the other side of the house, and it's just me at the windowpane, anxious, frazzled, hard at the end of my chain.

Hedy bursts into the bathroom.

"It's okay," I say, flushing. "I'm done."

She spits into the sink, shifting from foot to foot, spitting again.

"Are you okay? Are you sick?"

"Constantly. I get all worked up and I think I'll feel so much better when I throw up, and then I can't. I don't want to make myself, but, God."

She unbuttons her jeans, sits down on the toilet, leans over and spits into the sink.

"Marshall and I had the flu a couple of weeks ago. You don't think it's that?"

"No. I just spit a lot. Nothing ever comes of it."

"Have you seen the doctor?"

"The nurse practitioner at the health center. They say they'll hand me over to a doctor at the end. They do it all the time."

"How far along are you?"

"Weeks." She counts on her fingers. "Nine."

"So, since I've known you. Since you all got jumped in town."

"Yeah." She spits again. "I guess so."

She rests her face in her hands for a moment, her elbows on her knees, her jeans around her ankles, her long hair loose and spilling forward. I stand over her. I want to turn another way than jealous.

Her eyes lift up, wet, as if they have been painted on her face.

"You want to see something?" she says.

She unbuttons her shirt and slides it off her shoulders, tipping her chin back to catch the light. A fine course of veins laces her chest and belly, over her tattoo in the arch of her rib cage, like a map.

"Isn't that something?" she says. "I just woke up one day like this."

I reach a finger to her throat, tracing down, her blood traveling the surface of her skin like it is not shy, like there is plenty and more to come. It is something, all that life beneath my fingertip. And then I think how I have brought a gift.

"I have something for you, Hedy," I say. "In the car."

I go out to the driveway for the box of baby clothes, go thinking I was not so crazy earlier today, but rather clairvoyant. I have looped around on myself; I think of penitents and Catholics, the long-kept practice of shrines, and how this is what I can do with Hedy. I can make an offering. It's Christmas, after all, a birthday, a holy day. I take the box with its yellow ribbon from the trunk and start back toward the house.

But I hear them on the deck when I try to go inside.

I stop walking to better listen. Gail tells Corinne to grow up. Corinne curses someone, something. There's a gasp and a thud and a breaking, then silence.

When I reach them, Gail is perched up on the deck railing, her pretty ankles crossed, twirling the broken stem of a wineglass in her fingers like an unlit cigarette. Corinne is half hidden behind her, out of the house lights, leaning into her elbows, looking out at the water.

"What do you want, Joan?" Gail says.

Her voice is as flat and cool as tile, and she doesn't look at me. She is bleeding thinly from a gash in her palm, and it drips onto the deck boards. As she turns the wand of glass, I can see a tangle of hair like a spider web, short hair, Corinne's.

The French doors open, shoving light onto the deck boards. It's Alice, whispering.

"Leave them be, Joan," she says.

"I'm leaving."

She closes the door behind me. "They'll work it out."

"What?" I look out the glass. Blood trails Gail's little finger. "Work what out? They've cut each other up out there."

"Corinne has a lot of pent-up emotion. A lot she's dealing with just now."

Alice turns away as if this settles it, but I have had about enough of hearing only half the story.

"You told her about Bannon and me in Mexico," I say.

"Some."

Her chin is up, regal like a schoolmarm or a horse, as if she knows what's right and what's wrong, and it's true, I did not tell her not to tell Corinne. But she knows the landscape better than I do; she's handled Corinne all her life and could not have thought it might come out differently.

"I hadn't intended to have that conversation with Gail," I say. "And now I have no choice."

"Maybe that's not what they're talking about."

"What, then?" I say.

She weighs the cost of being honest with me. What I finally get is as much truth as exhaustion.

"Well, maybe they are," she says. "How would I know."

"What did Corinne say, when you told her?"

"Oh, goodness. I don't remember, Joan. She was surprised, I guess."

"Surprised?"

"Of course."

I'm pestering her; she does not see the point in worrying about it when it's already out of our hands, and she's right—there is nothing to be done now. The thought floods me and I lose my footing, as if the floor has buckled, the furniture afloat. There is nothing to be done.

She says Nicky needs a bed, and I should be helpful and point her toward the loft, but she'll find it for herself. Out in the living room, Marshall and Denny are still on the sofa, a whole sweet potato pie between them, Hedy and Piper still by the fireplace, their skin licked gold. Denny laughs. Hedy puts a hand to her hair, and Daddy passes through with drinks. Everyone, just as they were before.

Hedy's coat is draped across the kitchen table. I leave the box with the yellow ribbon where she can't miss it, scratch a note on a paper towel that says it's hers.

Gail comes inside to say we are wanted down on the dock, a boat full of carolers that will not be sent away. Daddy and Piper collect bottles of champagne, glasses, Denny staggering up from the couch, Marshall and Hedy close behind. I stay where I am; the idea of an empty house, even just for a moment or two, is a good one.

But Gail seems to be thinking the same thing. She goes to the sink, flips on the faucet. She looks surprised to find me still in the room when she shuts it off.

I feel enormous, and ugly.

"Is your hand okay?" I ask.

She prods the cut on her palm, reaching for a paper towel. It's deep, and still bleeds. She does not look at me.

"I'm fine," she says.

"Do you need a bandage?"

She lets her head drop back on her neck, waits a long minute, her words collecting in her throat, and then, "I don't need anything. For God's sake, go outside with the rest of them. Just go on."

And it's funny; the first and strongest thing I feel is relieved.

The boat at our dock is big, a cabin cruiser, close to thirty feet, which is more than this lake needs. An inflatable Santa Claus rides in the bow, roped down with strings of lights, and to that, attached like ornaments to a tree, is most of a lighted manger scene: a shepherd, a wise man, kneeling Mary, and the baby in his hay. I take the steppingstones through the yard, walk out to the end of the dock where everyone has gathered, and I know it's Lewis's boat I'm seeing, borrowed, bought, or stolen. I hear his voice, loud above the others.

There are no women tonight, but the boat is full and the men are drunk and otherwise out of sorts, hanging from the railings, swinging their feet over the side. I see an NBA forward from Pelzer, home for the holidays, a state representative who's been in the papers over his opposition to the Confederate flag. I see Boyd Henderson, his arm slung around another steel-faced man in black leather, the two of them laughing over whatever Boyd is saying. The tips of two of Boyd's fingers are wrapped in gauze, and he holds them out in front of their conversation, making an inching motion, the funny part of the story. When the man Boyd is talking to laughs, I get chills straight up my spine.

My father wants to make a toast to his new grandchild. Someone on the boat has a bottle of champagne and a Citadel cadet's sword; he holds the bottle over the bow and sabers the neck cleanly open, everyone cheering and clapping, the dock asway beneath our weight. I take a glass, raise it high like the others. We drink to the future of this one-day ballplayer, this native son, this joy of joys to his grandfather, this baby not yet born.

I drain my glass in one long swallow and hold it out for more.

When the caroling starts up again, Nicky's words are all that come to me, hot breasts and jingling balls, angels we have hard-ons high. The dumbness rises in my throat like nervous laughter and the champagne, the sweet, cold, stupid fear for what is coming next. I watch the roll of Lewis's boat against our dock, feel my stomach rolling with it. What in God's name has Boyd Henderson done to his fingers? The first ten things I think of leave someone else in pain.

16

I DRIVE IN THE darkness, the roads I know by heart, the rest of the car sleeping against each other like puppies. Marshall follows behind with Gail, and at home I know there are stockings to fill, presents to wrap, but the whole idea of a holiday has come apart for me. Alice and Corinne will be leaving in the late afternoon for Boston and their husbands and their snowbound houses in the suburbs. I don't know if they'll be back, and I don't think I care.

Gail, however, I will see every day. I am embarrassed for what she must think of me, the me in Mexico with Bannon. I don't know what to tell her; the truest part of an explanation has atrophied inside my head, eight years gone. But then there's how I'd feel if it were Marshall, and I know time doesn't pass the same for wives as it does for those who've gone against them.

Alice comes awake in the driveway with a start.

"I was really out," she says, and she gathers up Nick, Corinne behind her, fast into the house with their sleeping children on their shoulders.

Marshall, Gail, and I stand in the driveway, nothing to carry inside, and there seems no easy way to end this night. Marshall rattles the change in his pockets and tips his head back at the stars.

"It's freezing," he says, then, turning to Gail. "Let me get you that bandage." Gail follows him inside, where the lights have been turned on, and the heat has been running, and there's a kettle in the kitchen to make tea.

I just don't want to go in there. It would be better if Alice and Corinne were across the street with Gail, and I look over to Bannon's house, unlit, unwarm, impossible.

Gerald's amaryllis beacons from the kitchen table. I go straight past to the bedroom without saying good night, curl up under the covers to wait for Marshall, for him to tell me what he's been keeping to tell me all night long.

"Hey," he says, a finger to my chin.

"I just want this to be over with."

"I know."

He sits on the edge of the bed and takes the earrings from my ears, unbuttons the top of my blouse. His face is solemn, set; too late, I have the thought that this is a face he wears for the bad news he gives to strangers.

"Alice and Corinne went to Atlanta today," he says. "They met Bannon's body off a plane from Mexico."

He says more, but I stop hearing in any real way and rather watch the words leave his mouth; his beautiful mouth and these strange things he's saying, remains and flights and so much time gone past, too much to bring it all flying back on an airplane. I close my eyes, as if this will be easier to understand if I don't have to watch Marshall say it.

The body had been lost at first, then ransomed, then lost again. If he had to guess, he'd say Bannon's death made trouble for somebody with a good deal of money or influence, enough of either to make an American disappear. In the beginning, Bannon's father called whomever he could, sent dental records, paid fees, and when he died, Alice and Corinne made those calls, regularly at first, then once a year, a gesture. They had not expected anything to come of it and were surprised to have their call returned.

I open my eyes. Marshall's hands hang between his knees, broken at the wrists. He has a watch he is not wearing, a stainless steel watch from Switzerland with a blue face and a dial that lights in the dark. I try to picture the watch where he has left it, next to the sink in our bathroom, time gliding its track. I don't know how long we sit like that.

If I had a wineglass in my hand, I realize I would break it too.

"They wanted me to tell you," he says. "They wanted me to wait until they'd left, I think, but hey."

"How long have you known?"

"Corinne told me in the car, on the way to your dad's."

"For chrissakes."

"She wanted me to tell you," he says again. "She thought it would be easier to understand coming from me."

"Why?" I say. "Which part?"

"I guess the part about how they've already handled it."

"Yes, but why?"

"Well," Marshall says, and he says it slowly: "I guess because the two of you were lovers."

I never felt as if this fact had bearing on us, on him and me, not until now.

"Okay," he says. "So now you know."

I come forward to lean my head on his shoulder, but I feel cheap about it. I want him to say it's okay, he's okay, but he would have to mean it, I would have to know it. Our month has slipped away from us.

"I think I'll go for a walk," Marshall says, the way he'd say I think I'll have pancakes for breakfast, and I start to cry.

"Joanie," he says, but he does not stay either.

I feel sorry for myself, for us, for Marshall, out in the cold, thinking about the girl I was before I met him, and how maybe that girl was not somebody he would want to know. I wish I could say he was being unfair. None of this feels unfair, just unexpected and unwelcome, completely out of my control.

I see Mary Soomes again with her hand on Denny's sleeve, saying how it made no difference to her what he did with what he'd found. I mistook her soft way with him for peacefulness, for a sense of full circle with her past, as if the realization that we have run a circle with our lives could be a peaceful one. That hand was out for balance. That softness was not soft, but only empty, the way your chest goes soft when you've had the wind knocked out of you.

In the morning, Gail is on our sofa, her long limbs folded like a fawn's. The stockings hang over the fireplace, even a little one for Luther, filled with things Alice and Corinne have brought.

I try to be quiet, but Gail wakes, stretches. I haven't got anything for her but coffee, so I bring her a cup, sit next to her on the sofa, which is still warm from where she slept. I have that wish for what's coming to come on, swift and final and finally over with.

The Christmas tree lights are blinking, one strand off time from the rest.

Gail sighs. "You know, I never understood why you people associate with Lewis DuRant."

"We grew up with him," I say. "There was one summer, he and Denny and Bannon lived in the pasture behind our house in tents. It was like they had no homes except those, like permanent Boy Scouts."

"He's a drug dealer."

"Yeah."

"He was always around the house, that spring. The two of them always had their heads together."

She flexes her hand, studies the fresh red blood on the bandage.

"Bannon loved him," she says. Then, "He loved all of you."

"Gail—"

"He didn't die in a hospital."

We have not ever talked about Bannon's death, his last days as she remembers them. She never brought it up, and I never asked. I knew I wouldn't be able to help myself, that, in asking, I would tip my hand. Now that's beside the point.

She says, "He ended up in a hospital, and that's where I saw him, but I'm telling you, I don't think he died there, and not from anything they gave him."

"How do you know?"

She looks at me. She's the only one who was there to know at all.

He left the hotel on an errand. He wouldn't tell her what it was, but he said he'd be quick and back for dinner. Hours went by. Darkness fell. Some men in uniforms came to her door. Their English was lightweight, and her Spanish that of a child; they said to come, that the man had collapsed, and they drove her through the DF for nearly an hour before arriving at the hospital, all the time speaking into radios, all the time concerned with something other than Gail in the back seat. When she got to Bannon's bedside, he was dead.

The nurses said he'd just stopped breathing, *susto, susto,* and they brought an American from the lobby to translate. The American told her he was from Arizona, and that Bannon had been sick when he got to the hospital, that they'd given him medicine, he'd reacted badly, and he was dead.

The men in uniforms took her back to her hotel. It had seemed faster going back, but the city was crazy and she was lost inside herself; everything was fast. They waited while she packed her bags, while she settled the bill, and then they drove her to the airport to catch a flight back here.

"There were phone calls from the room," she says, "A dozen, each day you'd been back in South Carolina, and they were to a South Carolina number, and I was sure they were to you. I knew he'd been calling you—I was positive. But I got back and checked his phone book and I was wrong. The number was Lewis Du-Rant's."

I think how Bannon needed money, had asked me for money, had probably asked Lewis too.

"It was so long ago," I say.

"You ask Lewis about it, then. I bet your life that errand Bannon ran was for him. You ask."

"Okay," I say slowly. "I will."

"But I'll be damned if I tell those two in there anything," she says. "With their sense of closure, with their family privacy. I was his *wife,* for God's sake."

She turns to me, and her face is shining.

"But I guess I'm the only one who thought so," she says.

I drop my eyes. Gail's bandaged hand curls in her lap, still bleeding.

"I'm sorry," I say.

She dabs at her face with the back of the bandage, cursing softly: *fuck, fuck, fuck.*

"It was an accident," I say. "Unplanned."

"Yes. Inevitably, an accident."

"I'm sorry."

"Yes. You've said that. And I'm sure you are."

We sit there together, the house coming awake behind us, the pipes groaning, Marshall turning on the shower. Gail will have to break this thing between us; it seems her right, and I will take whatever she has to say until then. But she is quiet, and that is almost worse.

A door opens in the hallway, testing, closes again.

"Look," she says, "tell them I said Merry Christmas," and then she slips her shoes on and goes home.

Lewis and I have never talked about Bannon's death either. After Mom died, he started calling me for drinks more often, but Denny was in Atlanta, and it's almost as if Lewis was watching out for me in Denny's stead. We both worked in libraries then; we had a lot of other things to talk about. Only now does that seem evasive, and maybe just because Gail wants it to. She said how she has never liked him, and I'm sure she's spent years holding someone responsible, something, somewhere.

I should call Lewis now and tell him about Bannon's body, but I don't. I realize what I would have to ask him, and I don't know if I have the courage to do that, if our friendship could bear it. I think about what Gail said, how many ways it's possible, how many ways it's not. It is a lousy way to spend the Christmas morning.

Gerald and Nick are awake and running. Santa has brought them IOUs, and at home Nick will find some sort of game system, Gerald a trampoline. Marshall is in the kitchen, making French toast, and when I touch the back of his neck, he presses his ear to his shoulder and traps my hand, a sign in my direction.

I walk back toward the guest bedroom where Alice and Corinne are packing. I can hear them in low voices and want to make myself known before I'm eavesdropping.

"Orange juice?" I call out, and when I come around the doorjamb they are both looking up at me.

"Yes, please," Alice says, and I come back with two tall glasses. "Do you all want to open presents before breakfast?" I ask.

Corinne is downing her juice, but makes a motion with her hand, and Alice affects a smile.

"Yes, sure," she says. "However you do it. Or we could take them with us."

"Maybe that would be better."

She files her suitcases by the door, takes Corinne's off the bed, and smooths the quilts. She is ready to leave, as soon as we can get the day's formalities over with.

Beside the suitcases, there is a blue box they did not come with.

"When were you going to tell me?" I ask.

She looks blank for a moment, then sits back down on the bed. Corinne drains her glass entirely, puts the back of her hand to her mouth. I can see the old welt of a spider bite on her wrist, ringed with bruise.

They glance at each other; Corinne speaks.

"When we got here. We could have met a flight into Boston, but we thought Gail had a right, and you, Denny. Neither of us really knew Gail very well though, and then things went so badly."

She sounds as if she's talking about a failed dinner party, a missed appointment.

"And, really," she says, "it was Gail who left him down there in the first place."

I look at Alice, who is looking at her shoes.

"You could have told me," I say. "I could have gone with you."

"Yes. You could have," she says.

Her voice lifts, as if she's just seen the idea in clear light and it was in fact possible.

"But what?" I say.

"He's not any less dead now, Joan."

What she says sounds mean, even as I don't think she intends it to be, and it sounds true, but really just true for her and Corinne. This has put an end to something for them, the phone calls, the waiting, the recovery their father started years ago. This will be the last I see of them, I know that; and Bannon goes with them, I know that too. They can now move forward, as Corinne would say, with closure. I sigh, and turn to leave.

"If that's how you see it, Alice. Good for you."

When Marshall gets back from taking everyone to the airport, I am in my office.

"Do you want to go to church?" he asks.

"Church?"

"Tonight. Candlelight, hymns. Church."

"If you do, I will."

"I do," he says, and closes the door behind him.

In the paper, there are stories of the Christmas babies, born in stalled cars and elevators, makeshift deliveries all over the state, as if the hospitals were closed, as if there were no room at the inn. One man says, "I don't know what the shepherds did without cell phones," and this strikes me as sad, corny, and fake. It's as if he were thinking, the whole time he was helping his wife deliver their daughter, of something funny to say when he told the story later. What will his child think to read this one day, that her father was an ass?

Perhaps I don't have the temperament for this today.

The phone rings, and Marshall answers it. I can hear him laughing in the other room. I wait for him to bring the phone to me, someone calling to wish us Merry Christmas, but he doesn't, and after a time I realize he's hung up. It is silly to work on a holiday when I don't have to, to be distant from my husband who is seldom home.

And there is nothing here to fight about, but I have made him uncomfortable. As they were leaving for the airport, I asked Alice to consider burial down here, with their parents. She hedged. I kept my hand on the car door. Marshall ducked to see me through the passenger window, his face a concentrated blankness.

"You're freezing," he said. "Go inside."

But I asked her one more time.

In the den, he's watching football. I climb over the back of the couch, tuck my feet under his thigh. I say, "So what are we today, Baptists?"

He smiles. "Episcopalians."

"Oh, good. I have always liked to kneel."

The church is dark, and full with people shaking the cold from their coats. There is communion, which we take, passing a loaf of bread and a cup of wine, aisle to aisle, hand to hand. We sing "Joy to the World" and light our candles, raise them high. I cannot tell what Marshall is thinking, maybe of miracles and virgin births, maybe of a steady earth that does not crash against itself, maybe of peace, of joy, of me. I lean into him, just to feel his length against my side.

At home, I give him the writing desk and I can tell he loves it. He opens all the drawers and pigeonholes, and I've left something in every one, sheets of stamps, a lock of hair, a bottle of violet ink and a pen. He looks happy, and suddenly I feel clear-headed, straight-arrowed.

"I love you," I say. "Very much and always."

And he tells me the same, and I know he means it, but he doesn't feel the way I do right now, reborn to loving him, and maybe it is just the holiday. I don't care. He puts his arms around me, kisses my cheeks and forehead.

"Merry Christmas," he says.

"Yes," I say. "Merry Christmas."

"I bought you a circular saw."

"Really?"

"Yeah." He kisses my neck, where my throat beats.

"What in God's name am I going to do with a circular saw? I mean, thank you, honey. Are you going to teach me how to use it?"

"No."

"So it's a circular saw slash coffee table? Oh, wait. It's for you?"

"I'm building a workshop."

"Yeah?"

"And I'm going to build bookcases. Cabinets. Bedroom suites."

"Yeah?" I've never seen Marshall hold a ruler.

"And I'm going to retire to my homestead in the hills of South Carolina."

"When you're seventy." But I feel a little catch in my chest.

"When I turn in my notice. January first."

I sit up straight and shove at his shoulders, but he's got his face pressed into my neck. I can feel him smiling, though, can feel his teeth against my skin.

"You wouldn't tease me, Marshall Mackie. That would be cruel, and you know it."

He makes the Boy Scout sign, even though we both know he was never one. He's laughing, but he's telling me the truth.

He says, "Valentine's Day, I'll make you a fucking birdhouse if it kills me."

17

THE NEXT WEEK is like the end of war. I understand that Marshall will be going away again, but it all seems a formality, points on a map to be negotiated, and on impulse, I buy gallons of paint at the hardware store, robin's egg blue, and paint our bedroom. We lie on the dropcloths and admire the color, talk about the summer and a trip together, which we have never taken. Marshall says I should go to Italy with him, to Capri, which smells of lemons, Sorrento, the Aegean, which is the color of our walls. He knows some conversational Italian. He can say he has no communicable diseases, ask if you would like to hear him burp. We practice that one, *mi voui sentire ruttare*, over and over again.

He spends hours at the computer in my office, drafting an appropriate letter, but we both know it doesn't matter what he says, and there are moments we just look at each other and laugh, swept along, keyed too high. We make love, but there is something cursory, something wandering about it. The paint fumes are heavy around us. The dog begs at the door to come inside.

Lewis invites us for dinner New Year's Eve. He is a horrible cook but has excellent taste; he says he has help, which means a woman from the past. Regardless, I don't really feel like it and don't want to pick apart why. When Marshall hangs up the phone, I ask him if he really wants to go. He sounds distracted, something in his tone. He's rifling the yellow pages and nodding.

"So is this one of his big elaborate affairs?" I ask.

"It didn't sound like it."

"Haven't we had enough parties?"

"It's New Year's Eve, Joanie. Not really a party, anyway. Denny and Hedy, he said, and Barbara."

"I thought they broke up."

"Still friendly." He looks up at me. "You know Lewis."

"She threw a horseshoe at his head last summer. He has a scar."

He shrugs. "I'm sure he's recovered by now."

I have the meeting with the board in Charleston next week, and I need to organize my files, prepare a presentation. Now that Marshall is home for good, this job is what we'll live on, whether I feel like working or not. I've got a piece on mill towns through the century, several profiles on people who wrote regular letters to the editors, who took the paper as a daily challenge to their personal sensibilities. I've gotten releases from their families for interviews and even some promises of personal effects: one man's typewriter, one man's clipping scrapbook, with angry notations in the margins. I have a big file on technological change and it's effect on newspaper coverage: the first interview by telephone, the first bank robbery with a getaway car, the first bale of cotton shipped out on a train.

I think of Mary Soomes's train all those years ago, southbound to New Orleans, and the child that she would never see again nestled in her lap. Going to that station in Pendleton was the first time she'd set foot outside Red Hill, the first time she'd set foot on paved streets, wearing shoes in summer, this girl who'd never been anyplace before she couldn't walk. Her family was in shambles, her home on fire outside her window as her train pushed southward to the city, the first of several trains, several cities, before she would come back here again.

That train was full of other passengers, that fire behind a prominent church. Her father would have been missed on his shift the following day. I found nothing in the newspapers, but then, the news is like water, rushing in to fill whatever space allows.

Something else must have risen up to take its place, something the shape and size of what really happened.

I clutch at this idea, that what Mary Soomes kept secret can be fit around what was printed in the papers, the eggs and bread and school board meetings, so much who-shot-john. In the back of my mind is that blue box Alice and Corinne left here with and whatever fitting I need to make of it in my own life, but now I'm focused on Mary Soomes, on work, on making something right. Denny dug up her father's bones. There has to be some way to make them lie back down again.

I wonder if I could get her to consent to an interview.

I call Denny for Mary Soomes's number, but there's no answer. I try information, but she's unlisted. I leave a message with Mr. Baulknight's answering service that I need access to the newspaper vault as soon as possible, and then I sit there with the phone between my elbows, like if I don't watch it, it might get away.

Luther is whining at the front door. Marshall has gone on a walk without him. I whistle, and he runs to my office and back to the door, as if I might be able to fix this for him. He's frantic, and it's annoying. I don't know why Marshall wouldn't have taken him along.

I clear the trash from my desk into a black garbage bag, find my steno pad, find an old coffee cup roped with rubber bands two inches thick. I trim my nails too close with a pair of scissors. The day is useless until somebody calls me back.

At the grocery, there's a boy with an armful of sunflowers, a basket of fruit, a lattice-topped tart. He's choosing fish out of the case, and I like how careful he is about it, as if the difference between salmon and char is significant in the course of his evening. I buy cream and gorgonzola cheese, a London broil, and a nice bottle of wine. I think how maybe I will light some candles at the table, linger awhile, as if Marshall and I have time to spare, because now we do.

I walk back past the fish case on my way to the checkout and there's a little girl there with her father, maybe three years old, pigtails and knee socks, her jacket unzipped and shoved down on her shoulders. She tugs her father's hand, pointing, but he's talking to the fishmonger. She leans over and, very delicately, licks the glass right above the whole trout.

It hits me again, how Denny is going to be a father.

Driving home, I take the turn for our neighborhood and there's Marshall, coming out of the door of the vestry of the Methodist church, a church we have never been inside of in our lives. Nonetheless, it's him.

His head is down and he doesn't see me for his thoughts, his hands to pockets of his jacket, his strides long and measured. His hair blows against his part in the wind. I begin to get the idea this decision to quit his job was not all about me and having a baby, but something more troubling, perhaps more troubling for both of us. I don't think lingering over dinner is going to make a difference.

He comes into the kitchen as I'm boiling water, breaking the cheese with a fork in the bottom of a large speckled bowl.

"You got me this," I say, lifting the edge of the bowl.

"In Vermont."

"Vermont."

"Vermont this time of year is an awfully lonesome place. All that snow."

"And nobody to warm your cockles."

He smiles. "Cockles. Exactly."

He takes the cordless phone with him into the other room.

Suddenly, I don't know what to do with myself, this distance I feel from him. There is no halfway around the world to it, and if he left me now it wouldn't be some horrible accident; it would just be leaving. The thought shivers through me, too horrible to hold, and I want to ask him what he's going through, but I've never had to do that, don't know how. It doesn't seem like he would answer, or should have to answer, to me.

And I believe there are things we feel that we do not need the help of others with, that we are better sometimes for being alone, and that Marshall and I are better because we do not flay ourselves before each other on a regular basis. There is such a thing as privacy.

But I'm dying to know whom he's talking to on the phone.

I go into the other room and he's watching TV, a silent movie into which new music has been spliced. I watch for a moment, leaning over the back of the sofa.

"Lon Chaney," he says. "He's the one without arms."

Lon Chaney lights a cigarette with his feet, drinks a glass of wine he holds with his toes. He has a sidekick who's a midget, and they both wear long black cloaks.

"But Lon Chaney really had arms, right?" I ask.

"Yes. In fact, he has arms in this movie for a time, but then he cuts them off again, to get the girl."

"The girl being?"

Marshall shoots me a grin. "Joan Crawford."

"And I guess you'd cut your arms off for her."

"Boy would I. But then, no more wire hangers."

"It would probably be easier just to stick with me."

"What's for dinner?"

I swat him on the back of the head, leaning over to pick up the cordless phone beside him. I feel like I'm being transparent and we both know the phone is the reason I came in here, which makes all this flirting just pretense. It's awkward.

"There's a message for you on the machine," he says.

Mr. Baulknight called while I was at the store. I get his service again, but it's after hours and now just a recording. I leave my name, but it seems less reliable than speaking to an actual woman. Knowing Mr. Baulknight, he only takes messages from her anyhow.

"Why don't you just go over there?" Marshall says.

"To the hospital?"

"It's where you work, technically."

"Yes."

"I'm sure there's somebody there."

"You want to come?"

"Oh." He glances up from his movie, Lon Chaney pulling the levers of disaster with his feet. "Maybe. When?"

He doesn't mean it. I pretend I don't hear him, don't answer, go back to the kitchen to open the wine, and pour myself half a glass.

I leave Marshall to dinner and take the interstate. When I get to the gates at Piney Mountain, it's after nine o'clock.

The workers are gone, the hospital sealed back into itself, the lawn trimmed and green, even in this wintertime. There are no cars in the drive or in the strip around the back of the building, but it's too late for that. I'm not sure what I expected. I think of Marshall back at home, bent over his plate of food. If it were me there, alone, I'd have the paper folded open at my plate. If it were Marshall here, at the hospital, I wonder what he'd do. The radio station out of Spindale cuts in and out with the wind. I chew the cuticle of my left thumb until it bleeds.

I go to the front doors and put my nose up against the sidelight glass. I can see the hulking, clawfooted furniture shrouded in the foyer, the fringe of Persian rugs. Someone has kept the grass neat, the doors locked, has paid the workers to finish their jobs and go away. The same people who are paying me, and have never missed a check, but this is not a place that's open for business.

I walk around the back, jimmy the lock on a minor-looking window, and boost myself inside.

The place is spotlessly clean. There are no exhibits in the cases. There are no portraits on the walls, just the gracious furnishings of a high-priced lawyer's office, still covered in sheets, not even arranged. It's eerie, and it occurs to me that I don't know enough about this foundation to have the faintest idea who should be here, and when, and doing what, and I don't know how I've let it go this way so long.

But in the basement, the vaults are filled with papers.

Mr. Baulknight has more than fifty thousand volumes here, all of them carefully shelved and under temperature-controlled protection, all of them previously scanned into computers so that they will never be lost to water or heat or time. And in each volume are thirty issues, each issue in sections, each section in articles, each article holding dozens of small pieces of dozens of people's lives. All of this, kept here, kept now, for always.

I take ten volumes from 1927, enough to get me started, and once I get Mary Soomes to give me the exact date she left home, I can narrow my search. I'll leave Mr. Baulknight another message on his service, and I'm sure he won't mind, but still, I've broken in here, and I'm taking things that don't belong to me, and my heart scuds in my chest. I catch the reflection of the portico in the window getting back into my car, the red bricks, the white stab of column against the blue sky. I feel myself made small, very small. If I duck down, I disappear entirely.

I'm almost to Denny's house, and it would be nothing to drop by. I could get Mary Soomes's phone number, and I need to tell him about Bannon's body being sent back to Alice and Corinne, but I sit in my car with the engine idling. It's so very late. I open one of the volumes I've taken, and like that, another hour disappears.

I'll come back in the morning, when Denny will be home alone. And it's not that I don't want to see Hedy, but don't want to realize what I see when I am seeing her, what's ahead of her and how I want it for myself. I feel that tight-fisted panic again like on Christmas Eve, as if there's only so much expectancy in the world and I have lost my share.

I need to realize this is all changing, that Marshall is staying home and we will figure this out, but he has been so strange. I've tried to leave him to his own devices, to trust and accept and hope for the better, but springtime is just around the corner. Hedy's belly will be big soon with that child. I doubt any simple faith will be enough to hold me then.

18

THE NEXT MORNING, Denny wants to make burgoo, which he cooks outside for three or four days in an iron pot over a low fire. We go to the grocery store and buy pound after pound of pork, of sausage, of beef round, four roasting chickens, the grocery cart creaking along, a ten-pound sack of potatoes, another of onions, can after can of crushed tomatoes and quart bottles of Texas Pete. He is worried he doesn't have enough salt at home and buys a bag of that.

"Who's eating this?" I ask.

"You're welcome, of course. But I owe Body and Russell and those guys. They've been doing some work for me."

"At the cemetery?"

"Around, yeah."

"You still digging?"

"No."

But he's studying too hard at the brands of salt available in bulk, and I don't know what he's hiding. I ask if Bannon ever worked for Lewis. I honestly don't know.

"He catered all that shit, remember. What year was that?"

"No. I mean, worked for Lewis. Like maybe down in Mexico?"

"Jesus. I don't know. He did go down there a lot. I always thought it was for the food stuff."

"Gail says he called Lewis from down there before he died. A bunch of times, not just to say hello."

"I don't know, Joan. What difference does it make?"

I tell him about Bannon's body, and what else Gail said, and he's quiet for a long, long time. I can't tell if he's piecing things together or if he doesn't know what to say to me about it. The last years Bannon was alive, Denny was in Atlanta. He didn't see as much of Bannon as I did, and maybe he doesn't know if there's something to be suspicious about or not. He begins to act as if the conversation is over or perhaps never happened at all. He pays for the groceries and we haul them to the car, filling his trunk as if we'll feed an army on meat and potatoes. He takes two beers from the twelve he's bought, opens them for us on the edge of the steering wheel.

"*Salud,*" he says, and drinks down half the bottle.

We sit in the parking space for a long time, Denny staring out in front of us, people coming and going to the grocery store. He starts the engine, but just to run the heat.

"When we were in high school," he says, "Lewis's father was shithouse crazy. Seriously. He'd get home from work some days and buy us all a case of beer, but other days he'd start yelling for Lewis to get up here, get over there, and I don't know. There was something not right about it. It was more than temper, or different. You remember, Lewis dislocated his shoulder playing baseball?"

I nod, and Denny snorts out a laugh.

"Yeah. Well, that was the summer we all moved out to the back pasture, the three of us, because if Lewis stayed at home, his father was going to kill him. I don't even know what it was about. But Lewis got his first personal script for Lortab with that arm, and that was, as they say, the beginning of the end."

"I don't remember his father," I say. "He must be enormous."

"A hundred sixty-five pounds, soaking wet. But he can still swing a bat like nobody's business. So you know where Lewis gets it from."

"I always assumed those were his people. Hired."

"Sure," Denny says. "He's got those. But sometimes it's just ole Lewis and his daddy's baseball bat. I suppose it depends on how bad you've crossed him."

Denny drains his beer and I look away from him, out the window. We are quiet. There is a swelling apprehension in the car, the owning up to blind loyalties from the both of us. I remember how Bannon asked me for money that night on the phone in Mexico, how he was in trouble at the restaurant, and how Gail said he'd been calling Lewis every day. I hear the sound of another beer opening against the steering wheel, the rub of Denny's hand against his jeans. When I look back at him, he's studying the space between the gas and the brake pedals.

"I can guarantee you, Joan. There are two people I know who've always got cash lying around, two people I can think I'd go to if I needed money fast."

He looks at me. His eyes are wet.

"Who do you suppose Bannon went to first?"

Hedy's car is in the lane when we get back, even as she ought to be in class. Denny coasts up behind, lets his bumper kiss on hers. He says something under his breath but then won't repeat it for me.

"Help me get this started," he says, and throws his empty bottle out the window.

We take the groceries under the bare limbs of a poplar where he's got a block set up, a pit, and a cast-iron kettle on a stand. He doesn't even go inside the house to ice down the beer, but opens two more for us and sets the rest under the tree, as though we'll drink them fast enough. I don't guess he and Hedy are going to get married over this baby coming, but I don't bring it up. He seems agitated enough on his own. I don't even want to give him the hard time he's got coming.

I chop onions while he lays the fire. It's cold and my nose runs, but I chop the whole bag and start in on the potatoes, mounding the food in front of me until there's no more room to work.

"Should've had you chop meat first," Denny says. "We don't have any bowls out here." He looks back toward the house as though it's impossibly far away.

I sigh. "I'll go," I say. "I need to blow my nose anyway."

"Yeah, okay. And grab the spice rack while you're in there."

I tromp the front steps as if knocking mud from my shoes so Hedy will know I'm coming. The house seems empty; maybe she is napping. I take a paper towel from the kitchen and blow my nose once I get back outside.

Body and Russell are under the poplar with Denny and Russell's son Eamon, who must be in high school. They have some sort of golf cart idling in the lane, and Russell says the thing will go ninety miles an hour. He wants Denny to clock him.

"How come Eamon won't clock you? Or Junebug?"

"Come on, man. All I'm asking is for you to look at your watch a couple times."

"I'm just saying, you've got perfectly good people to do that yourself."

"Lawd, Body. Listen to him. I had no idea our friend Denny was such a poor example of a friend."

"Maybe it ain't that," Body says, spitting over his right shoulder. "Maybe he scared. Maybe he just a pantywaist. All we done for him lately, he must got a good reason. Maybe he got a date with the lady there, 'cause we know the man is all about his ladies."

"That's my sister," Denny says. "You all have met before."

Body nods to me, Russell and Eamon turning to do the same. Denny fans at his fire with a folded newspaper.

"I can keep this fire here," Eamon says.

Denny tosses the newspaper into the flames. He really doesn't want to do this, and yet he's going to. He must owe Body and Russell something big.

"I have to get home, anyway," I say. "I was out late last night, and Marshall's there."

Denny sighs. "If this thing blows up, Russell—"

"What do you mean, blow up? What car I've ever worked on blows up? You lie, Denny Patee—you lie like a dog."

"Like a snake in the grass," Body sings out.

"I can keep your fire here just fine," Eamon says.

Denny looks at me. "She say anything to you, in the house?"

"I didn't even see her. I think she was asleep."

He sighs again. "Just tell me where you want me to stand, Russell."

The course is set in Red Hill. The three of them load into the golf cart, Denny taking the bench facing backwards. He looks forlorn, shanghaied. He tips his beer bottle at me as they pull away.

Eamon sets to balling up newspaper for a stockpile. The fire is too high to cook on now, but who knows when Denny will be back. I go inside again to get some foil for what food is set out on the block, even though I wonder if any of this will be finished, today or after that. So often with Denny, the workings are worth more than the end result.

The house is quiet. I call out for Hedy and get no answer, wander toward the bedroom and listen in the hall. I crack the door to see the bed, unmade on one side, as if only one person has been sleeping there.

I go out onto the screen porch and lift the door to the root cellar.

"I don't think I want to talk to you just now," she says. "Even if you want to say you're sorry, I don't think I want to hear it, or that you've opened your mind, or even that you'll think about my—"

She turns and sees that it's not Denny after all. She sits at the sawhorse table on a high stool, and she wears glasses that have slipped down her nose, her hair kept back with a red bandanna. Bones are piled at the table's edge like so much kindling, forgotten, and before her, Hedy has hundreds of pieces of china. There are peach baskets of china on the floor around her feet, and the room smells strongly of solvents and glue. She holds a tube in one hand, a fine brush in the other. She's putting these plates back together.

"Joan," she says, and she starts to cry.

I go to her and rub her back and she makes little moaning explanations I don't listen to, Denny this, Denny that. I imagine that we should talk about what's really going on, how Denny isn't ready to be a father, how Hedy must be scared that she will be alone with this baby, alone in Denny's house or even farther away than that, but we don't. I just rub her back.

The plate she's working on is bone china, translucent even in this sallow, swinging light, rimmed with emerald green and almost whole. She's left the clay in the fractures and so now the plate is red-veined, like a plate aware of what it was made from, a plate with a sense of self. I take it from her, turn it over. The back is stamped with SOUTHERN RAILWAY, 1925.

There are small piles of pieces sorted in front of her, a stack of finished plates separated by leaves of newspaper, nearly twenty high.

"How pretty," I say. "You'll sell them?"

She wipes her nose with the back of her hand, nodding. "For a lot of money."

She hands me a piece of paper: the history of the cemetery, the custom of breaking the plates over the grave, the exacting process of restoration, *singular, significant, art, culture,* repeated enough times to make a needful kind of rhythm. She does not mention Mary Soomes's story, and I'm not sure she knows it. She has made her own.

"You write well," I say.

"I got ahold of a dealer in Atlanta who says I can name my price per dozen."

I make a gesture toward her belly. "You'll send that kid to college."

"I'll send myself to somewhere," she says, turning back to her plates. "I will."

Before I go, I ask her for one. I tell her it's not for me, but for someone who'd appreciate it. I offer her money, which she waves away, embarrassed.

"Take it, Hedy," I say, stuffing the bills in the front pocket of her jeans. "Put it in the cookie jar for a rainy day."

When I go back outside, it's falling colder, and Eamon is breaking branches over his knee to throw on the fire, now roaring out of the pit and licking at the grass around it.

When I ask, he tells me Hedy pays by the basket. Body and Russell sort pieces for her down at the shop, and they've told her stories about funerals they attended as boys in the Depression, spoonfuls of hoodoo and foot track magic, just how Body came by that mayonnaise jar full of mercury dimes. Eamon says she keeps a little tape recorder in her pocket for those stories, and that she's talking about writing a book someday.

"They full of shit about seeing them funerals themselves, not unless my daddy made me when he was older than he is now, but they good stories. They like telling them to her."

"She pays for those too?"

"Nah." He grins. "But she stays and drinks a beer with them, and you know, she's a real pretty white girl. They tell her anything she wants to hear."

I smooth a piece of his crumpled newspaper on my skirt and wrap up Hedy's plate. I have that high-keyed feeling in my chest, nervous and thrumming, as if I need to bear down hard on something so as not to shatter.

"Eamon," I say. "Where's your grandma live?"

From Mary Soomes's front yard, you can see the football stadium at the university. Her house is angular and glassy, the windows well shaded by the trees in her woody yard. When she answers the bell, she insists that I come in, but it's hard to say if I'm truly welcome. It doesn't matter; I can't stop myself now. I hold Hedy's plate in front of me, flat and careful, as though it bears a cake. My palms sweat against the newsprint; I wipe their blackness on my pants and step inside.

Mary Soomes has no Christmas tree, no television, no computer anywhere I see, but most of the furniture looks straight out of a design museum. We sit in leather sling chairs before a blazing fire. She has a neighbor that lays it for her; she tells me she doesn't get down on the ground anymore, hasn't since Eamon was a baby and she chased after him. The strain of getting up again would probably put her in the cemetery.

"I just came from there," I say. "And I've brought you something."

I give her the plate. I watch her face as she unwraps it and her recognition is immediate, the green rim, the small logo at the top edge with the slogan. She doesn't even turn it over.

"Why," she says, "thank you so much."

She puts it back in the paper and sets it aside.

I'd thought this would garner more of a response, more of a foot into a conversation, but we just sit before the fire, Mary's hands folded in her lap. The quiet between us is a weight on my back. I can feel my cheeks flush with heat. I push ahead, because there's no place else to go.

"My brother's girlfriend is collecting these pieces and gluing them back together."

"Yes," she says. "Lovely."

"The pieces were found out by your father's grave. She thinks it was part of a death custom, to break—"

"Yes, I know. Quite something. Really."

"I'm here on business, really. I work for a museum that collects newspapers."

"Oh?" she says. "To what ends?"

"Posterity. Research. Conventional libraries are in the process of throwing them away in favor of microfilm, which is difficult to read, and really not the same. The loss to our cultural record will be enormous."

I tell her about the hospital, the vaults, and she runs a finger around the edge of Hedy's plate, still tucked in its paper on the table to her side. I talk on, but I become certain she's not listening, and my voice begins to drift toward strident, my words empty and academic. I tell her about the quotidian dramas. I tell her who-shot-john. I sound, I'm sure, quite crazy.

Then she says, "If I left this paper in the rain, it would disintegrate. If I threw it in the fire, it would burn. If I laid it on the ground, it would keep the weeds out of my garden. It's useful stuff."

She lets her gaze settle on me.

"Perhaps convention has a point."

"Yes. Well. That's possible."

"I'm sure you know more about it than I do."

I do, actually, and I'd go on, but she's stopped listening. The heat in the room is overwhelming, sapping, and I feel the sweat begin to run along my ribs, but Mary Soomes seems unaffected. Any minute now, she will find something else she needs to do. I go ahead and ask what she will tell me of her childhood.

"We were poor," she says, like she's just told me she's black.

"What did your family do for money?" I ask.

"What everyone did, I suppose. Farmed. Raised our own."

"What neighbors in Red Hill might you remember?"

"None close."

"Far, then. Someone else I could talk to, someone who might remember something of the area in that time?"

She rolls her head along the chairback and levels her eyes on me again, gray, bottomless eyes, so many years smarter than my own. Her irritation is clear.

"I am an old woman, Ms. Mackie," she says. "And it was a relentless life. They are all most likely dead."

"Ms. Soomes—"

"Have you had supper?" she asks. "I believe I could make an omelet. Some tomato soup? And then I'm afraid I must be going down the road. My neighbor is ill and needs company, someone to read the paper." She laughs. "Oh, I see there, the paper. What did you call it? The cultural record."

"I wish you would answer my question."

She stops her preparations to stand, lets out a melodramatic sigh, and gives me a look I remember from my mother, near amazement, near offense at how stubborn I can be. She keeps herself on the edge of her chair, like this will only take a moment.

"What would make you think I want to talk about something

now, with you, that I've managed to go seventy-five years without mentioning to a single soul?"

"I don't know—"

"Precisely, you don't know. The answer is, nothing. I don't. It's mine, and I will not share it. The end."

Her tone is absolute, and I stand scolded, exhausted, and, worse, deserving of it. Mary Soomes has no need to reconcile her past; she does not need to use it for anything. This fight, it seems, is only mine.

"I'm sorry," I say. "I've intruded." Which is an understatement, but Mary Soomes is somehow gracious.

"You have. Your brother has. Now I say, let it be done."

She asks me to take the plate with me when I go. It's not worth anything to her, so old and broken up. She does not think it would even make it through the wash.

There's a light on in the garage when I pull into our driveway. Marshall is out there; I can hear the whine of a fast blade, the solid thwack of wood hitting the concrete slab. I raise the garage door to find him at his new compound miter saw with a long piece of two-by-four. He's got a pile of cuts at his feet, shavings in his hair. He hasn't showered or put on clean clothes. He feeds the wood through carefully, measures, and feeds it through again.

"What are you making?" I say, but he can't hear me for the cutting.

I yell it again, and he turns off the saw. "You're late," he says.

"Am I?"

"I'm playing with myself here."

"Well, let's put a stop to that right now."

He laughs but turns the saw back on, cuts, cuts again.

In the corner, under a pile of boxes for drills and routers, are the things I saved from the farmhouse, the desk for Denny, the wingback chairs, the boxes of my mother's china. I think of Corinne asking if Marshall ever hurt himself at night, and how that was before Christmas, before he bought all his new tools, with their sharp teeth and cutting arms. His back is bent over his work; he seems serious, cautious, as if he knows what he has could hurt him.

I lower the garage door and go into the house.

He's got my day's papers spread out on the dining room table, all of them open and leafed through, scattered amongst different editions from different towns, too much for the table to hold. I pick up what's fallen and refold it, try to shuffle each with what it belongs, but I give up quickly. I can't imagine going back to all that now, not after what has happened with Mary Soomes.

Marshall's been reading all day. Like I would have, if I'd been here alone.

He does not come in for dinner, and I go to bed without asking for him, without mentioning the dining room. The whine of the saw comes through the walls of the house from the garage; it's the last thing I hear before I fall asleep.

19

NEW YEAR'S EVE, we go to Lewis's. We are the first to arrive, excepting Barbara, who knows her way around the kitchen and seems as comfortable with Lewis as ever, which is to say she has hung her clothes in his closets and gives over to periodic sulking when things aren't going in her favor. With Lewis, it has always seemed silly to have expectations of undivided attention.

He looks, of course, as sharp as a pin, a high-necked sweater and jeans, tooled oxblood boots that make him stand even taller. He meets us in the kitchen with a box of fireworks, an unlit cigar clenched in his teeth. He presses his cheek against mine and makes a smacking sound.

"Marshall. You're a man with matches, aren't you?"

Marshall pats his pockets. "I could be."

"Well, get on it. Grab yourself a beer and meet me on the slab out there."

The slab he's speaking of is a slate terrace overlooking his pool, the woods beyond. Lewis owns fifteen acres, not a neighbor in sight. He could set off a box of fireworks every night and nobody would know the difference, but this is a New Year's custom all across the state. It's legal to buy fireworks here, but not to set them off, which doesn't seem to bother anyone until the day after, when somebody's lost a finger or an eye. It will be in all the papers tomorrow.

Barbara has her hip cocked against the counter and a boning knife in her fist. She looks not happy, but not willing to do anything about it either, not yet. She rolls her eyes at me, and then we are alone.

"How did you get roped into this?" I ask. "Dinner for six."

"Eight." She makes a put-upon face, tucks a wisp of yellow hair behind her ear.

"Who else?"

"Denny and Hedy, you and Marshall, and Joel."

"Joel Jonath?"

"Yes. And his boyfriend."

"I thought he moved out west, Santa Fe or something."

"Me fucking too, is what I say, but this morning Lewis comes down and he's all torqued up because Joel called, and — open the champagne already — he's coming to dinner."

I know why Barbara is upset, and it's not because she's cooking for two more people. Joel Jonath and Lewis were very tight when he lived here. Some of it was work; Joel is a chiropractor who finished medical school, and he's generous with prescriptions. But some of it was private and makes for difficult competition, even for Barbara.

She's trimming artichokes for their hearts, rubbing the cuts with lemons as she goes, and I ask if I can help her. She hands me the knife and the lemons and turns her attention toward the refrigerator and its clutter of champagne. Fresh sheets of pasta rest on dishtowels by the sink, and she's melting butter for bechamel, grating Parmesan, lighting a joint and smoking it like a cigarette, as though she needs just a little off it for now and can let it burn in the ashtray. And she probably can, as there is always plenty at Lewis's, and so I think maybe she has more than one reason for being here herself.

The boys trundle in from outside, smelling of the cold and wood smoke, and the four of us talk about nude beaches because Barbara wants to. She has recently returned from a trip to the South Pacific, where the beaches were wonderful, and she has a tan she's anxious to show us. She wears no bra, so it's pretty all over. Marshall stares into the neck of his beer bottle as she talks, and I am trying to remember what else I know of Tahiti but can only, for some reason, think of dried fruit, which seems less interesting by half.

Lewis scrapes the pith of a lemon with his thumbnail and does not bite when she sets a hook, not once, not even when it's her bare breasts before his friends, pretty as they are. Barbara teaches high school, I remember; she must be used to plenty of attention.

"And the boys," she says, as if to tell a story, and Lewis checks his watch.

I excuse myself just to get away from it.

In the bathroom, I open Lewis's medicine cabinet. He keeps razors and toothpaste and Lubriderm and dental floss and bubblebath and a woman's brand of deodorant, one that smells like baby powder. There are tweezers and nail scissors and a jar of cuticle cream, and on the bottom shelf, a big bottle of NyQuil. That's it. And I know the house is filled with pharmaceuticals, but that's all Lewis keeps in his medicine cabinet, some cough syrup anyone could buy over the counter.

It's not like he sells drugs to children; even at the university, these are consenting adults, or at least near adults, and he doesn't sell needle drugs, and this is just what Lewis does, what Lewis has always done. But there is always the possibility that he will have to pay for what he's doing, that anyone involved with him will have to pay for what he's doing, even us, tonight. I think again of what Bannon said that morning on the bus back to Mexico City, how somebody has to be punished, and maybe he was talking as much about himself as what he and I had done. What good does it do to know what really happened when you cannot change it, but only play it over in your mind: his hands in my hair as I lay in his lap, those hulking volcanoes out the window that we knew were there but could not see for the dark, thick air. Five days later, he was dead.

Back in the kitchen, Hedy is taking off her coat and asking for a handful of crackers. She looks shaken, and Denny not much better. They have seen a wreck on the highway coming over, a car that jumped a guardrail to hit a tree. They were the first upon it, and Denny stopped, ran back.

"I don't think I've ever seen anything like that," he says. He stands at the sink washing his hands with dish soap, his skin a boiled red.

"The driver?" Lewis says.

"Oh, no. No airbags, nothing. It was a mess." He puts his back to Hedy. "The steering column went right—"

"Let's not talk about it anymore," Hedy says. "Christ."

"I stopped and called the cops," Denny says. "But there was a crowd by that point. We didn't wait."

"For goodness' sake," Hedy says, a hand to her throat.

Marshall stares at her. She's not looking at him and so doesn't know he's staring, but his face is unkept and sad. I'm embarrassed to have caught him so exposed. He looks embarrassed too, and I turn away so as to let him finish whatever he's doing without my help.

Denny leans up against the countertop, watching Barbara with her boning knife. I think there has been something passed between them too, as now Barbara has a wicked smile on her face and is going very fast and hard with that knife on a whole fish. Maybe Denny knew her from before, or between Lewis and now, or maybe he just can't help himself any more than that.

Hedy watches her peel the backbone from the flesh and passes out.

It's sudden and dramatic; she crumples down and back, her head ringing on the hardwood floor, all of us within arm's reach and yet unable to catch her. Marshall is fastest; he picks her up in his arms and takes her to the couch in the living room.

Denny asks Lewis for a washcloth, which he runs under the cool water in the sink.

"Here," he says, handing the washcloth to me. "Could you do this?"

"Jesus Christ, Denny. Do what?"

"Just make her feel better—I don't know. I'm no good to her these days."

I take the cloth, and he leans back again against the countertop. His skin is wintry, near gray, and I think he looks sorry for himself, which is close to sorry.

"Are you serious?" I say.

"Why don't you talk to her about it, if you think I'm not."

"Fine."

Barbara lets out a little sigh. She never dropped her knife.

On the couch, Hedy is sitting up with her head between her knees. Marshall stands over her, whispering to breathe, breathe, and I can see him rolling back into himself, like film in reverse. He returns to the kitchen as soon as I sit down.

We don't talk. Hedy keeps her head between her knees until she stops crying, and I wring the wet cloth, one way and then the other. She leans back, patting her cheeks.

"I seem to have a real strong response to dead animals lately. In my gut, like I have feelings for them, or something. Do you think that could be the baby?"

"Sure."

"Maybe all of this is the baby, then. I mean, if a fish affects me so, maybe I am a little worse off than I realize."

"Denny sent me in here," I say. "He wanted me to give you this washcloth."

"And all his love?"

"Oh, probably."

She puts her hand on my knee, palm up and fingers curled, as though I'm the arm of a chair. Her tears leave a mark on my jeans.

"He'd feel better if I said me or else, wouldn't he."

"I think he's more used to that, yes."

"Well, I'm not going to do it. I'm not sure I'd mean it if I did."

"Really?"

"I'm twenty-two years old and I cry when the wind changes. Maybe I don't have any business being a mother either."

I sit back. I realize what she's saying.

I think how this could be the thing I finish for her.

It's a fast thought, and goes at my head like a blunt instrument.

I have to concentrate to put the right words together, to sound un-affected, sympathetic, calm.

"You should talk to Denny," I say. "Tell him what you've told me."

"Yeah. Maybe."

She sounds more resigned than sad, and I spin with that too. I don't know if she's thinking of giving this baby up or giving the pregnancy up altogether, and I don't trust myself to ask. I shouldn't be alone with her right now. I am the farthest thing from a shoulder to cry on.

"You want me to get Denny?" I say.

She sighs, returning her hand to her own lap. "No. Not partic-ularly, I don't."

So we sit there for the better part of an hour. We can hear eve-rybody talking in the kitchen, getting drunk, stoned, laughing. I stay with Hedy like she's got a grocery sack too heavy that she might just turn and offer me. My thoughts continue fast and down toward desperate, gathering speed at the bottom, and I think she must hear them grinding through their changes. I feel as if I'm naked at an inconvenient, unrequited time, but I keep myself on the sofa beside her, to prove I can. I cannot say the all of what is keeping Hedy.

Lewis comes to fetch us for dinner. Joel Jonath and his boy-friend haven't arrived, but it's nine-thirty and he says everyone in the kitchen is starving. He stands in the backlight from the other room, rattling a glass of ice. There is nothing to him that's not blackness.

"Something probably happened with their flight," he says. "I would have thought they'd call."

"We can wait," I say.

"Well, Barbara can't."

"Oh, come on, Lewis. It's Barbara. What's she going to do, throw a horseshoe at you?"

He laughs. "I don't think she'll make that mistake again."

He hangs in the doorway, though, not moving until we do.

The first course is a salad of watercress and apricots, thin-sliced onions, and a rosemary vinaigrette. For a long stretch, there is only the sound of eating. Lewis keeps his eye on the door, takes his cell phone from his pocket and puts it beside his plate.

"So?" Barbara says, and she's talking to him.

"It's delicious," Marshall says, and everyone chimes in.

But Barbara is fixed on Lewis. I wonder what Hedy and I missed while we were in the living room, because there's something she wants from him that she's not getting, and Denny and Marshall are keeping their heads down, as though they have seen this blowing in on the horizon.

"Yeah," she says. "Great."

She throws her fork at her plate, clattering, and drains her glass of wine, shoves back from the table for the kitchen.

I'm not sure why we're here, why we were invited at all, if Barbara wants to be with Lewis who wants to be with Joel. Denny eats like he's digging a hole. He watches as Lewis checks his phone again and shakes his head, like he's watching a man ignore advice that even he would take.

"How do you get a nun pregnant?" he says.

"Jesus, Denny." This is his joke, his way to say he's had enough, he is not responsible for what happens next. The answer is, you fuck her.

"Denny's been starting his days with that one lately," Hedy says. "That and a beer."

"Shot and a beer," Denny says. "So? How do you get a nun pregnant?"

He's laughing, and I wonder how this makes Hedy feel, for this to be so funny.

"You fuck her?" Marshall says.

His voice cracks like a boy's and I look over to see he's sweating, his eyes as glossy as yolks. He puts his hand in my lap beneath the tablecloth. It is on fire.

"Marshall?" I say.

He wipes a palm across his forehead and studies it, the wetness, as if he's not sure how it got there, what to do with it. "Jesus."

"Let's go outside," I say, and he follows me to the terrace.

The cold air hits him and he can't breathe. He splays his hands on the railing and leans down low, his head through his arms, taking big lungfuls of air. I want to touch him but I'm scared to at the same time, the way you'd be scared to touch an overheated engine. The pines shoot into the sky, into the darkness, as far as I can see around Lewis's house. We are in the middle of nowhere.

"Something happened to you, Marshall," I say. "I can tell something happened."

I'm not sure he hears me.

"Do you want to go home?" I ask, but he doesn't answer, just keeps taking in those big gulps of air, as though he's been too long under water.

"Marshall?"

The face he turns to me is not one I know, hard and white like a plate. I see the sweat still running on his forehead. He tells me to go get Lewis for him, but it's not necessary, as Lewis is already at the door.

He has a coat for Marshall tucked beneath his arm, and his hands hang at his sides, the long, articulated hands of an ape. I don't know how I would get past him if he decided not to let me go.

"He wants you," I say.

I make a motion toward the railing and Lewis follows it, as if I have offered a seat, an invitation.

"Go on, Joan," he says. "Dinner's on the table."

He has been drinking. I haven't seen him drink in years, and now can only smell it, gin, medicinal and weedy. He tells me again that dinner's on the table, and I am sent inside.

Denny looks up from his lasagna, surprised to see me back so soon.

"Is he okay?"

"I don't know. It's like he can't catch his breath."

"Should we call the hospital?" Hedy says.

"I don't know. I don't know."

I'm rubbing my hands together to get the blood back to them, my teeth jerking in my head, even as it's warm inside the house. I look behind me, as though I could trace myself backwards into the evening and figure it out. How far back would I go?

"Lewis sent me away," I say.

I sound like I'm about to cry, even as I can't feel it for myself, my voice knowing more of how to handle this than I do. Denny is way out ahead of me, standing up, knocking his chair over, his mouth working over his words, spitting them out.

"For chrissakes. He's not a fucking doctor."

For a moment I think he's angry with me, for my clattering teeth and wringing hands, then that he's angry in my stead, and then it has nothing to do with me or now, but just an old simmering anger he's always had in him coursing to the surface, more than he can hold.

"Denny—" Hedy says, but he's already slamming out of the room, his open hand smacking the plaster by the door.

I right his chair, and take it.

Barbara has brought the fish out on a platter and set it in front of herself, it's poached eye filmy and fixed at the ceiling. She hands me a fork, and Hedy lets her forehead down on her folded arms.

I hold the fork in my fist, and Barbara turns back the skin of the fish, the flesh milky pink beneath.

"What's Lewis giving him?" she asks.

"I don't know."

"Does he get panic attacks a lot?"

"I don't know. I don't have any idea."

"You don't?"

"What are we talking about?" I say, and I mean it from the beginning.

I can hear Denny yelling on the terrace, and it's like a buzzer going in the next room, urgent, remote. Barbara spears a bite of salmon and hands it to me on her fork.

"Eat," she says. "You'll need your strength."

I believe Hedy is asleep. I think about her passing out earlier, how understandable it was, even in its drama, because she's pregnant. Something is going on inside her that will resolve itself. I know it's the same for Marshall and maybe it shouldn't be any more disturbing than a pregnant woman's faints or fragile stomach. And maybe not any more medicated, either.

Lewis comes inside and I follow him into the kitchen.

He's got the Bombay Sapphire out of the freezer and he's drinking it straight out of a tall glass, the phone book open to the airlines, the receiver tucked between his shoulder and his cheek. He's telling the ticket agent that he needs to know the location of two passengers, spelling out their names, sounding as cool as milk.

"Yes," he says. "Absolutely."

"You're trying to find Joel?" I say.

He turns, impatient. "Yes, I'm trying to find Joel. They were supposed to be here three hours ago, and their flight was on time—"

"Now?"

"For God's sake, Joan, I've got a pile of business wrapped up in this guy and if he's not where he said he was going to be, I need to know why. You want to be helpful? Figure out what got into your brother."

"What's he say?"

"It's all goddamn Greek to me."

He sets down the phone and braces himself on the countertop in front of his drink, not unlike Marshall on the terrace, trying to settle, to calm.

"I was wondering about Mexico," I say.

He looks up.

"Was Bannon down there for you, or to get away from you?"

He shakes his head, and I want him to tell me it's not true, that he loved Bannon, that he loves me, that he'd never do anything to hurt any of us, because it's only now I realize how that might not be the case. For the first time in my life, Lewis scares me.

"What kind of question is that, Joan?"

"I know he needed money. I think what happened in Mexico had something to do with that. Am I right?"

"Are you right?"

His voice lilts with this, mocking, and my face goes hot. Lewis leans even closer.

"I'll tell you about Mexico," he says. "Our boy was going to call it off when he got back. He said something happened down there, and he just wasn't going to marry Gail anymore."

He's almost smiling.

"Imagine that," he says.

He studies my face, my eyes, as though he means great intimacy, and I guess that's what has passed between us, the knowing all about the other. I feel tears in my throat and bite my lips against them, but I do not drop his gaze.

"Happy New Year, Joanie," he says, and he steps around me, back outside.

It's then I realize this whole night has been caught on film, and even if no one is watching now, someone can come back later, as often as they'd like, and see him tell me this again. Nothing I've ever done is as private as I thought it was.

I watch Lewis from the kitchen window on the lawn, his match flaring up, the slow drip of fire when he drops it, then another, then another. I see him light the whole book of matches; he holds the edge of it out to burn, then lets it fall into the box of fireworks at his feet. He shoves his hands in his pockets, walking backwards, as they start to explode.

If what he says is true, Bannon would have come home from Mexico to me.

And then I'm shuffling the past eight years, adding Bannon here and here and here again, to my bed where we never slept, to Christmas dinner that we never shared, to my mother's funeral, the pictures in my head like the pages of a book turned so fast they come to life. They nearly move.

Then I think how even if what Lewis says is true, Bannon never came home from Mexico, not to anybody.

But still: What if that?

Denny helps me gather Marshall into the car. He is floppy and semiconscious, mumbling and swearing. The coat he wears is Lewis's felted ulster, and it's more of a cloak than a coat on him, his fingertips lost in the sleeves, the hem tailing behind him. Fireworks burst in the air above us, without arrangement in this middle of nowhere, as if they are happening in the wild.

Marshall's cell phone falls out of his pants pocket, the car keys, change. Denny gets him into the passenger seat and I walk back along the driveway, picking up what he's lost.

"Mind if I make a call?" Denny says.

I hand him the phone and he fishes a business card out of his wallet.

"Hey, Stewart. Denny Patee," he says, and he launches into a long explanation about this evening, how he and his girlfriend witnessed the accident on Highway 28 where that Camry hit a tree, only they couldn't stop because his girlfriend is pregnant and the whole thing really upset her. Anyway, he has a license number, he says, a car that was speeding away from the wreck when he got there. He walks over to Lewis's Land Cruiser and reads off the plate.

"Jesus, Denny," I say when he hangs up.

"Well. It won't last long, if they even get over here. Stewart knows Lewis and I ran around together in school and he'll figure something is up. But man, Lewis hates to see the cops at his door, even selling Christmas cookies."

"It amounts to asking him if the refrigerator's running."

Denny grins. "If it is, he ought to catch it."

He hands the cell phone back and I study the smooth green face of it. Marshall never carries his cell phone, and it's a holiday. Who does he need to talk to that's so important? I hit the menu and check the received calls. The numbers are all from New York

City, and I think how long he was up there after September 11, months and months and months, and now I wonder who he was with. All that time we're not together, I wonder who he could have been with.

We all must have something we think we can keep to ourselves.

Denny is talking to me, saying how we're never going to know what happened, and he's talking about Mexico and Bannon and how he died, but he's right in the largest sense: there is no way to ever know any of these things, who loves you, how they love you, what happens when you turn your back, and Denny's made a life out of this. He's asking, *What do you expect, evidence?* and I'm shaking my head no, no evidence, that's the last thing I want, something colder and harder to carry in my head, a date, a time, a woman in a red coat running back to town.

He leans over and kisses my cheek through the open window of the car.

"Drive careful," he says, and I tell him I will.

Backing down the driveway, Denny raises his hand in a wave, Lewis's fireworks petaling above the tree line, so close and loud, so pretty, and Denny like he is headed off to a last and happy skirmish before the truce is made.

I have a long drive home in darkness, with nothing good to keep me company.

20

MARSHALL'S BREATH is deep and even in the passenger seat, and to wake him would be pointless. I leave him in the drive when I go inside the house, turning off the porch light, turning the bolt behind me. I feel shut out and wish to hand back the same, would like to hear him rattling the door at four in the morning and just roll over in the sheets, not let him in and see how he takes it. I get a pen and an old receipt from my purse and write down the number from New York, leave the cell phone on the dining room table where he can find it later, when he finally gets inside.

I take off my clothes and climb into bed. I try to think whom he could be calling, some personnel office or human resources, but my mind won't move in that direction. Instead I think of all those months he spent there and how few questions I asked; the letters he wrote me were heavy-hearted and sentimental, and I still have them in the nightstand, but I don't even know what hotel he stayed at. They must have been comfortless days, perhaps too much to stand, and now he's sorry, and now he's coming home, and now some woman is desperate for him to return to New York one last time, so desperate that she'd call on New Year's Eve. I come to see it all, just that fast.

I can't sleep. I can't read a book. I want a drink, a shower, a hand at the base of my spine, Marshall, but like I know him to be, not this. I put on a bathrobe and let Luther out into the backyard; he runs around to the front, whining at the car door. It's freezing, and I think maybe Marshall won't wake when he is too cold. I see him on Lewis's terrace, bent to fetch his breaths. Regret pours over me like water from a pail: mine, his, ours. I go back inside the house for a blanket.

I get in the driver's seat and start the engine, run the heat. He does not wake, his face ashen in the darkness, not a face I know and yet still somehow beautiful to me, the way sickness can make somebody beautiful, or tiredness, or fear. I see him for a moment with unfamiliar eyes, see how someone else would see him, even at this worst, as beautiful. It seems a thousand years ago now, but I remember the gallery in Washington where we met, how he knelt beside the model of some ancient Roman dome. I should have something honest to say to him about that, about us, something we can both pretend he didn't hear in the morning, but I don't. I recline my seat, put my bare heels on the dash, the steering column under my hips, and I think of the accident Denny and Hedy came across, what must have sliced that driver in half.

Marshall turns in his seat to face me, his eyes drawing open for a moment, focusing and letting go. He sighs, says my name, but I don't reply. My robe parts across my lap and I push it open, inspect myself in the pearling light, my legs fitting into my hips, my hips to my belly, my belly to the arch of my ribs. I reach over to Marshall, unzipping, and he stirs and shifts under my hand, but nothing more.

I tell myself it's all I want from him. I shut the car off, leave the blanket on the seat, and go back inside the house, get back in bed, put my hand to myself, what is left, but I'm no good there either. I want to sleep. I want never to remember this night, never to think of it again, but I can already tell, I am out of luck.

Early in the morning, it's his shower that wakes me. I go into the bathroom and sit on the back of the toilet in the steam and listen to the water sheeting against the tile.

He pulls back the curtain, and there I am.

"Jesus," he says. "I'm embarrassed."

"Come on," I say and roll my eyes. "I've seen you naked before."

"Really, Joan. I'm sorry."

"I'm sure you are," and I sound like Gail.

I get off the toilet tank and take a blue bath towel from the stack in the linen chest. I turn him like a child, dry his back, kneel down and dry his feet. I feel lost in my allegiances. I could kiss him now, make this all pass as far as words are concerned. He would still be going through the same thing, have done whatever he has done, but I would be sweet, supportive, a good wife in the bargain.

"I'm going to Charleston," I say.

"Now?"

"This afternoon. I meet with Mr. Baulknight tomorrow, and I need time to get myself together."

Marshall takes the towel from my hands, looks at the ceiling, his body arching backward, like to fall.

"I have to go to Hartford," he says. "I'll be gone when you get back."

"I know."

His head strikes the tile behind him, and he pulls the blue towel up to cover his face.

And that is it. I pack my bags, a few books, my laptop and presentation files. I think for a moment how I might stay away for a time. Marshall will be up north for a week, ten days. I wouldn't even have to tell him. It's the first thing I think, and so simple: *I wouldn't even have to tell him. He wouldn't even have to know.*

For all the time we've spent apart, for everything we've not known about each other, not witnessed, I've never had that thought, that I could keep something from him on purpose. But now there's his cell phone, the New York numbers, whatever is behind his strange, pitching nights, and everything seems connected, different, bigger than it was before.

He sits, naked, on the edge of the tub, watching me gather my toothbrush, my lip-gloss. There's a small meanness in my head thinking he should see what this is like, after all this time, to be left alone in this house with his desperateness and the dog.

When I am ready, I go into the bathroom with my bags in hand, bend to kiss his cheek.

"Please, Joanie," he says, but nothing else. He takes my hand and laces his fingers into mine, holds tight, as though he can hold me there.

"You want me to stay?"

If he says so, I will, but he doesn't say anything. After a time, he reaches back and turns the taps again, stands, the blue towel falling to the floor. He brushes the backs of our linked hands against his cheeks, first mine and then his own. He lets me go and steps back into the shower.

I cry all the way to Columbia.

I feel like I would not be able to stand if I tried, but just pleat on my joints like a fan. I get the hiccups and have to pull off the interstate until I can get ahold of myself.

I stare out the window at the afternoon, the wet front of my shirt chilling on my skin. I think about being alone, in a real way, not just in between Marshall being home. I think about thinking of myself as alone. I am in a gas station parking lot in the middle of South Carolina; I can buy gas here, a Coke, a bag of peanuts, a pack of cigarettes, a beer.

There's an ATM, and I withdraw the limit on our account in cash, then get twice that from our credit line. I stuff the roll of bills into the back pocket of my jeans and walk the aisles of sugared orange slices and potted meat. I don't buy anything but know I can the next time I stop, or the time after that, anything I can think of, anything I want.

I get back in the car and pull on my jacket, zipping it to my chin. I drive the rest of the way to Charleston with all my windows rolled down, my hair tangling, my ears numb and red and filled with wind. I am done crying and now just want to feel cold.

I check into an inn on Meeting Street near the Battery. The bed is a rice bed, the bathtub clawfooted, the ceiling painted pale, pale blue. I call Mr. Baulknight's service and sit on the floor with the phone in my lap until he calls me back.

"Joan," he says. "Let me take you to dinner."

I say I was hoping he would, and I realize that might well be the truth.

It's four o'clock; he says he'll pick me up at seven, and I take my roll of cash up to King Street to the boutiques. I buy a black lace dress lined with fleshy silk, shirred and fitted at the waist, flaring to the knee, a red leather trench coat, Italian stockings, strappy sandals, a long strand of jet beads to wrap around my neck. I buy lingerie too, everything new and wrapped in tissue, packed in bags. I walk back to the inn, climb into the clawfoot tub and run the water as hot as I can stand. I lie back and then slide down, flush to the bottom and letting the water rise around me, filling my ears so that all I hear is its fall from the tap, my own breath. I stay down there as long as I can.

I cut the faucet and wash. I pin my hair up, get dressed, and wait downstairs for Mr. Baulknight.

He takes both my hands and kisses my cheek. "It's lovely to see you," he says, and I answer in kind.

"I thought we could get a drink before dinner," I say. "There's no rush, is there?"

"None, none at all."

He offers his arm, and I hold it. He opens his car door and I swivel myself inside, crossing my legs, smoothing my skirt. There is opera on the stereo; when I ask, Mr. Baulknight tells me it's Ravel, *L'Enfant et les Sortilèges,* and I ask him to say it again just for the sound, the ease he has with another language. I reach over to the controls and make the music loud, make it fill the necessary space in my head to the brim until we can get that drink, that dinner, get on with something else.

The bar he chooses is paneled and rich, in the lobby of the Mills House hotel. We drink Irish whiskey of names I'm not familiar with, and Mr. Baulknight tells me I will be ruined for anything else when I go home. I tell him that's well possible; I laugh at his jokes and ask him questions about his life and when his knee comes to rest against my own I let my hand drop down onto it, as if it has arrived just in time to hold me up. He does not move away, I do not lift my hand, and when the waitress comes around we order two more whiskeys, straight up.

His face is lean and handsome, patrician, suited to his element. His shoulders are broad and square, his thigh, where my hand is resting, tight. I don't think about what I'm doing, or whom I'm doing it to, but only feel that thing in me turning over like a palm.

"How long will you be staying?" he asks.

"How long do you need me here?"

"What if we put all that business off for a day and you came sailing?"

"You have a boat?"

"I can get one."

"You sound like you would steal it."

"If I needed to, I guess I would."

It doesn't seem as though we're acting on anything necessary between us, but only that the possibility is there and we've taken it. I feel a peacefulness letting down inside me, a curtain, weighted and smooth, and I think this might be what it feels like to give up and let go, to drown, to be Denny.

"How old are you, Mr. Baulknight?"

"I am celebrating a significant birthday."

"Well, then." I smile. "We should celebrate."

He pays the tab and we walk around the block to a brick-walled restaurant, where he orders mussels for us both, a bottle of Marsanne. We talk of dessert, of late-vintage port, his children who live in Seattle with his ex-wife.

"How many years have you been divorced?"

"Oh." He laughs. "Probably since you were a very small girl."

"Do you see your children often?"

"It's funny," he says. "They are about to go to college, and I have always encouraged the reading of books, appreciation of beauty and travel, so I feel like their custody is shifting to me, in a way. But, no, my divorce was bitter, and my wife moved as far from me as possible, and most of our contact was orchestrated over distance."

"Was that hard?"

"It was not hard or easy. It seemed her right, at the time, and for the best of the children. You don't have children, do you, Joan?"

"No." I smile. It seems funny that he would not know that, but maybe only funny to me now.

I go to the bar and buy a pack of cigarettes off the bartender. I smoke fast, not to be long from the table or alone with myself, but then there's Mr. Baulknight's hand at the small of my back, taking the stool next to me.

"So you have nasty habits," he says.

"A few."

"I quit ten years ago," he says. "If you would, just lean over here and blow that in my face."

And I do.

Walking to his car, I take his arm. It's late, and couples like us spill onto the street, steadying each other home. We have no business driving, but I want to ride in the lap of that big car with the opera, the downtown streets shutting off their lights, the winter air whisking salt off the ocean.

He opens my door for me, hands me inside, and I reach across to lift the lock for him, but it's been done automatically.

"Don't take me home just yet," I say.

"What should we do?"

"Drive, I think. Just drive."

"Doesn't that sound lovely."

We take the old bridge over the Ashley River out of the city and along the plantation road, past Drayton Hall, Magnolia Gardens, Middleton Place, and Mr. Baulknight explains the intricacies of rice planting, the manipulation of tides, numbers of acres, numbers of slaves. Most of this is stuff I know from when I used to research for the radio. Nine of the ten richest men in the British colonies were planters in the lowcountry, and I can name them all.

The road is dark and draped with Spanish moss, spattered with subdivisions to one side, historic preservations to the other, and I keep my face turned to the undeveloped land, the marshy woods whipping past, a produce stand, a cemetery, and then the darkness all again, all the way out to the Ashley. Mr. Baulknight tells of the butterfly-shaped lakes, the beautiful azaleas in springtime, the yellow fever months of August and September. I wonder if he will stop and make love to me somewhere along this road, or if that's me again, already thinking what he's about to say.

My thoughts feel pickled, old. I press my eyes with the heels of my hands, but I don't see anything differently afterward, just the darkness sliding past.

We turn at Cook's Corners onto another highway and Mr. Baulknight keeps driving, south to Beaufort because I have never been there. He wants to show me the house where he grew up, the school he went to, the shotgun in the country where his Cherie lived, the woman who took care of him and all his brothers, with the bottle tree in the front yard. He loved the sound of that bottle tree, would hitch out to Cherie's house as a boy to hear it rattle in a storm.

I reach up and unpin my hair, comb my fingers through it, unlatch my seat belt and slide my feet in his direction.

"Do you mind?" I say, stretching out. "A catnap, until we get there."

He does not answer, but gently, and without looking down, unties the laces of my sandals and slips them off my feet, pulling my legs across his lap. I fold my arms beneath my head and fall asleep in seconds.

I come awake in stillness, the car parked and empty.

I sit up and Mr. Baulknight is leaning against the hood, a beer in his hand beside him, another empty beside that. We face into a tangled lot: the blackened piers of a porch, a trampled nest of ash and rubble in what night light filters through the live oaks. It's a house long burned to the ground, but it's like he is watching something taking place there on that porch, before that fire. I see the bottle tree he spoke of, its bare limbs tipped with glass, blue and green.

I slip my shoes back on and join him.

"They're for luck, right?"

He nods, offers me a beer. We lean against the car and the wind picks up, blowing the bottles against each other. He smiles like a boy, is a boy in truth for just a moment. I laugh. He looks at me.

"Where is your husband, darling Joan?"

"Home, I think. He leaves in short for distant lands, but tonight he is at home."

"Will he wonder where you are, and why you have not called?"

"I don't know," I say. "Would you?"

I catch up his empty bottles between two fingers and tip the dregs onto the ground. I slide back into the front seat of the car and wait for him to finish whatever we are doing here. I have lost the will to push it anymore, and only want to ride.

On the way back to Charleston, he tells me he has phone calls to make, some plans to shuffle to get us free for the day. I should take some rest. At the inn, he walks me to my door, says he will call for me again at two for our sail.

"Thank you for the evening," I say.

"Yes," he says. "Thank you."

He leans over and kisses me lightly on the lips but does not linger over it, as though it's just politeness. I go inside and stretch out crosswise on the rice bed in all my clothes, and this time sleep till noon.

I get the New York number from my purse and sit with it and the phone for long, long minutes. There is what I want to know and what I don't, and to call this number is to lose my choices. I pick up the handset and call home instead, where I can ask questions and get answers as opposed to information, let it ring, but Marshall is already gone, and maybe since I left.

I get out of bed and fold back the shutters. The day is eggshell blue, the water in the bay spangled with the sunlight, a day for sailing. I take another bath, pull on some wide-legged canvas pants and a heavy sweater, gather my things back into my bags. I go downstairs to the street, and it's warm enough to tie my sweater around my waist. I remember that Hedy is from here; I can see her disposition in the day, springlike in January. I walk around the corner for coffee, and by the time I get back, Mr. Baulknight is waiting.

"You look fresh," he says.

"And you, did you get some sleep?"

He holds up his finger and thumb and a sliver of space between. But he has packed us a beautiful meal, he says, and it is a beautiful day, and he has brought his telescope for watching the stars on a night like this promises to be. We just have to drop by his friend's and get the pass to the slip.

"Where are we sailing?" I ask.

"When did you say you had to be home?" He smiles. "Leighton's boat could get us to Jekyll in two days, or there's the Outer Banks."

"And the board meeting?"

"Let me worry about that," he says.

And so I do.

We wind downtown in the big car, doubling back to navigate the one-way streets, and a church bell somewhere striking the hour. The houses are slender and porched to face the ocean breezes, the gardens gated, the palms feathered overhead. I know of no other place like this, where beauty is crafted and cut to sparkle, and it seems as though we've slipped away already without a boat to take us.

At the house on Orange Street, a girl answers the door, fifteen or so, in a long white dress and elbow-length gloves. She squeals and tears away.

"George." Mr. Baulknight catches her at the waist. "Aren't you a picture."

"Oh, don't look, don't look, Sanger. I'm not really ready yet."

But she turns and puts her hands to the flat of her stomach, gazing down over herself. Compliments suit her, and he goes on.

"It's a beautiful dress."

"It's a wedding dress," she whispers, like she has pulled something over on us.

"You'll be perfect," he says.

"For goodness' sake, George," a woman calls from upstairs. "Get up here and let me pin you."

The foyer is high-ceilinged, with a bowl of red camellias and huge gilt-framed portraits of men in breeches and cravats. I watch George up the staircase with her long silk dress balled in her hand, her heels flashing cracked and dirty behind her, and again have the feeling that we have slipped into another time.

We pass through panel doors to the library, where Leighton reclines on a chesterfield sofa, the newspaper spread over his chest. He comes to his feet, and Mr. Baulknight makes the introductions.

Leighton is an architect. He bought this house from the original family who built it, and he shows me a musket ball still lodged in the frame of the front door, the Carolopolis stamp that certifies the authenticity of his preservation, inside and out. Mr. Baulknight has already had this tour, and he sits on the end of the chesterfield sofa. I feel awkward under his gaze.

Leighton is telling me about the initials etched with a diamond ring in the glass of the third-story bedroom window that date back to the women who lived here during Reconstruction when George glides back down the stairs.

Her dress has been fitted to her with pins and no longer trails the floor, and she's brushed her hair off her face, tucked a red camellia into the slender ribbon at her waist. Her father stops midsentence.

"*Bijou*," he says. "You look like Greta Garbo."

She laughs and spins for him, and Leighton is transformed, delighted by the real and present thing before him: his daughter, her affection. If I had to guess, I'd say the difference between them is the difference between Mr. Baulknight and myself, myself and my own father.

"Could I use your restroom?" I say.

"Of course," Leighton says. "George?"

George leads me down another flight of stairs to the powder room that's tucked beneath. Her dress shimmers in the lowlights, elegant even for a woman twice her age. She flips on the switch and walks in ahead of me, the close coral-colored walls, no bigger than a closet and tight around her. She's just a girl in a bridal dress, pretty as a picture; she has yet to do anything with her life she can't undo in the morning. For a moment, it's impossible to believe anyone has ever been that young, that fresh, or ever worn a dress so white.

She's checking the toilet.

"Our maid," she whispers, "dribbles."

I lock the door behind her, think again of my mother and that locked door in that strange house, so many years ago. I hear Leighton and Mr. Baulknight above me, the privy laughter of men in an empty room, and I wonder what she must have heard that day from where she was. We all have stupid, reckless thoughts when we are left alone. Perhaps I have been alone with Mr. Baulknight long enough.

When I'm finished, I turn out the light and take another flight downstairs instead of up, out the side door to the garden, its still-dormant wisteria, plumeria, its slated walks and arbors. I leave by the outside gate, nearly overgrown with the canes of a Lady Banks rose, a pale yellow flower that will be breathtaking come one day this spring, the day when all the Lady Banks roses in this pretty town decide to bloom.

There's a warm breeze on Orange Street. I walk back to the inn, get in my car, and take the beach road out to Folly. I sit in the sand next to the pier and watch the waves, the diving gulls, the shrimpers setting their nets offshore. There are blankets of people with the same idea, and it's warm enough to roll your sleeves up, to lie back in the sand and get the sun. I watch two children, a boy and a girl, ferry water back to their sandcastle, their mothers in lawn chairs, eating wedges of orange out of a plastic bag.

When the fog comes, it's low to the ground and gathers across the beach, lufting and thick, like batting, and I lose the children at the water's edge. They completely disappear in whiteness, even though I know there are right there, right off their mothers' hands.

I stand. The fog is only as tall as they are, and above it, the sky is as blue and wide and beautiful as before.

I get back in my car, collect my things, and go home.

21

THERE IS A letter on the dining room table from Marshall, a sheet torn from the stack of steno pads in my office, not the fine heavy paper I gave him for Christmas. He will be away longer than he thought. He tells me he left the dog with Gail and dropped the dry cleaning, tells me again that he's sorry for the other night at Lewis's, that he wished he could explain it, but he can't. It's more like a list than a letter. He will be longer than he thought, and Connecticut is a short drive from New York.

I imagine Mr. Baulknight is still at Leighton's on that chesterfield sofa, trying to explain what's happened to me. They've broken out the finer scotch, the Irish whiskey, and he has told of our evening drive in the big long car, the way I touched his leg, the way I put my feet in his lap. It was all my doing, all without thought for the after, and the after that, and I believe I would be sailing with him now if it had not been for Leighton's house, for George, her long white dress. But in the telling, I will seem a tease. It will be easy to fire me, when he gets around to it.

In my office, I have to step over the rolls and rolls of newspapers, stacked like cords of wood. I dig the number in New York out of my purse and call it.

I get a recording: *You've reached the offices of Craven and Wilkes.* She's a lawyer.

I get that feeling again that my bones are not to be trusted to hold me up, that they have been soaked in vinegar, eighth-grade science. I think of Denny and how it must have happened for him like this, one thing streaming into the next: a lost farm, a left job, a strange bed, sneaking out the back door and letting what was already in motion make its way to the ground. It's so much easier than I thought, so much more fluid and graceful and fast, to pass from one life to a lesser one. I could keep on going until there was nothing left of me at all.

The phone rings in my hand and the sound passes through me electrically, as if I've been shocked. I don't answer it. When the machine picks up in the other room, all that's left is a dial tone.

I whistle for the dog, but he doesn't come. I go from room to room, flipping switches and calling, faster as I can't remember the last time I saw him, the last time I let him out, or if I let him back inside. I am pulling on a coat to go out into the streets when I see the lights come on at Gail's house, the door opening, Luther bounding off her steps.

She has him on a retractable leash that is not ours, and I can tell it's cold as she skips a few strides, her knees high, and Luther prances as though the asphalt bites his feet. They take off up the sidewalk, and I watch from the sidelights of the front door until I can no longer see them, another woman walking my dog, my husband's dog, when I am perfectly able to do it myself.

The coat I've grabbed is not mine, but Lewis's that Marshall wore home the other night. I slip my hand into the pocket, and there's his pillbox. I recognize nothing inside, in truth have no idea what I'm looking at, but most of the pills are white like aspirin, shaped in the shapes you'd expect. Nothing looks too dangerous if taken on its own.

I swallow something with a glass of water and lie down on the sofa.

The answering machine blinks its messages, and I don't play them. The phone rings, and I don't pick it up. I don't take a shower; I don't unpack the car. There's nothing in the kitchen I want to eat, and I pass the evening like that in emptiness.

Mr. Baulknight's service calls. The woman sounds slender and efficient; she asks me to call Mr. Baulknight at his home number at my earliest convenience. I've never had his home number before, and I should write it down. I owe him an apology, if not an explanation, but then it comes to be night, too late, and I take something else. I sleep.

In the morning, the doorbell rings. I push up just enough to see down the hall out the sidelights; it's Gail, with Luther. I lie back down, and soon she goes away.

I drift in and out, the phone keeps ringing, becoming like the television or the radio, something that makes noise enough to listen to every so often, but with half attention. The doorbell rings again, and I push myself up to answer it. The dog is no trouble to me in this condition. Nothing seems to be a trouble in this condition.

I open the door, apologizing, but it's Dianne Schelling.

She wears a parka and jeans, her hair pulled back, large black sunglasses covering most of her face. And my father is right; her teeth are impossibly small when she smiles.

"I am sorry to bother you at home," she says.

"Well, it must be important."

I put enough bite in my voice for her to understand that I hate her, but it's not just her, but her shadow in my life. I lean against the doorframe. I do not ask her in.

Her car is pulled up to the curb in front of my house, loaded down with boxes and clothes and houseplants. She has left it running.

She sighs, pushes her glasses to the top of her head. "I was wondering if you'd give this to your brother for me."

She pulls a manila envelope from inside her parka and holds it out between two manicured fingers.

"Mail it," I say.

"I can't."

"Look, this is not my business."

"I know. But it's important. I think it might be important to him."

"Then you take it to him."

"I'm not going to. I'm leaving him alone, which is what he wants, but I thought he should have this, and if you care anything—"

"Oh, for chrissakes."

I snatch the envelope from her and slam the door behind me.

Inside, there are photos you would not frame, of her and Denny, an impossible amount of skin between them. There's a letter, not in Denny's handwriting, that begins with *Darling*, a police blotter clipping about Denny getting pulled through the window of his car, and stapled to the top corner, a list of names, men's names, seven of them, ready-made revenge. There's a wooden matchbox, and inside that, four tiny glass animals: a deer, a fish, a bird, and a dog.

Everything that linked the two of them fits in one manila envelope, and she has handed it over to me.

I wonder if Denny knew she was this sort of woman when they first went to bed together, if she even knew it for herself, how manipulative, how desperate she could turn. I watch her put the car in gear and pull away from the curb, as if she's been selling cookies door to door. She does not seem any more concerned over what she's handed me than that.

I drag the metal garbage can from the garage, a can of gasoline, and set the whole mess on fire in the driveway. And I'm sorry to Mr. Baulknight, but I have no care for her fine penmanship or what of her and Denny is being lost to history, in fact feel connected to history in this moment, to all the lovers, all through time, who have lied and cheated and paid for what they've done.

I go to the newspapers piled on my porch, pitch the rolls of them one by one into the garbage can, just to keep the flames high at the sides.

Across the street, Gail is at her dining room window. She has been watching me this whole time. I lift a hand to her, and she waves back, then lets the curtain fall.

When she opens her front door, I'm waiting on the steps. The dog noses through the screen to circle my feet, excited, his nails snicking on the concrete. I reach down to scratch his ears.

"Joan," she says. "You look horrible."

"I came for the dog."

"Come inside."

"I can't. I've been, well, I had a presentation to make in Charleston and I've been pulling straight shifts at the computer." I run a hand through my hair, dirty and flat. "I just meant to get the dog, and get back."

Her eyes comb my face, flick to the garbage can in my driveway, still burning.

"Okay, then," she says.

"Thanks for keeping him."

"Sure."

She lets the screen door close, but I can feel her gaze still on me as I cross the street. Then she calls my name.

I think for a second to act occupied with the dog, as if I don't hear her, but her voice carries and the street is empty but for me. I turn. She does not seem to remember what she was going to say. We have never had a way between us.

"It's going to snow," she says finally. "If you've been busy, you might not have heard."

"I hadn't." I tip my head up to the low-slung sky, nearly suspended by the treetops. It looks like snow. It smells like snow, but I have only noticed now that she points it out.

"Well," she says. "If you need anything, then."

"Thank you."

I go back inside my house, to still the ringing phone.

It's Marshall, leaving a message. He sounds tired, and I feel tired too, worn out. I want to hear his explanations, to give my own, and I let my hand go to the receiver, but then he says he has to catch the train to New York for an appointment, and I stop. He leaves his cell phone number, the name of the hotel where he'll be staying. He says to please call him back, he needs to talk to me, but as soon as he hangs up, I push the button to erase it all.

In the early-morning darkness, I get into the car. I let the dog come with me, and on the radio, they are calling for three to five inches of snow, which is a blizzard for South Carolina. There is not a loaf of bread to be bought anywhere across the upstate. The storm is due to hit at dawn.

I think of Dianne Schelling, down in Greenville at her sister's, or maybe farther on, past this weather, farther south. Maybe she pulled her car onto the interstate yesterday and now she is deep in Texas, or Florida, the orange groves in bloom, the swamp streaming past her open window. I have the want to tell Denny, not what she left for me to tell him, this revenge he never sought, but that it's over, that she's gone. And then I have the want to tell him everything.

I head out into the empty highways, the rest of South Carolina huddled in their warm houses, their quilted beds, waiting for daybreak and the snow. I strike the heel of my hand against the steering wheel in time to nothing, and I think of Denny's thumb beating time on his doorframe, of change jingling in pockets, of Alice, painting her fingernails at my kitchen counter on Christmas Eve, the red strips of polish butted to each other, her fine, steady hands. Most of all, I think of Marshall, and how our nerves show against us like shadows or like x-rays, dark or light against how we ought to be, and how they make us sweat and gasp for breath, make us sleepless, make us do things we would never dream of doing in a million years.

When I get to Denny's house, the sun is coming up, and I let Luther out of the car without a leash. He pauses, waiting until I send him on. His fidelity is absolute, enough to make me want to cry.

Hedy is standing on the porch. She wears a rag wool toboggan pulled low over her ears and does not seem surprised to see me. She hugs and kisses, hands me the cordless phone. It's Daddy.

"What in God's name did you do to Sanger Baulknight," he says.

I tell him I'm not sure.

"Well, he wants to talk to you. He says you skipped town on a meeting and you don't answer your phone. He thinks something's wrong with you, and I'm inclined to think so myself, if you're driving to your brother's in this weather—"

"What weather?"

"Kitten, have you not listened to a weatherman?"

Hedy sits on the porch steps at my feet. Her egg basket rests on her knees and she stares into the cemetery. I come to stand behind her, to see what she sees, the turns of path and long-limbed trees, the stones like teeth scattered in the grass. I know what looks so solid now will turn soft in spring, and green in summer, will bare itself again this time next year, and knowing such has never seemed to leave me so off-balance.

Hedy tips her head back and whispers that she's going to the chicken coop, but I can tell she is only trying to give me privacy for my phone call, my excuses. I watch her walk away, her basket swinging from her fingertips.

"Joan?" Daddy says. "You hear me?"

"Just tell Mr. Baulknight there was a family emergency. Tell him I'll call in a couple of days, I promise."

"Joan, this man's an old friend—"

"I know, Daddy. Please."

"You'll call him. Monday. I can tell him you will call on Monday and smooth this out."

"Yes."

He sighs as though he does not believe me, and I don't blame him. I don't sound convincing.

"Joan," he says. "When is Marshall coming home?"

I tell him I don't know, and we pass that back and forth for a while. I hang up before he can tell me again how concerned he is, how he doesn't quite believe what I am saying.

The sky is a facetless white that seems to be closing down on us. I haven't seen snow since last winter and that night with Denny on my front porch from Atlanta, his life parked in my driveway, and now everything seems flipped on itself. I close my eyes, make the wish for tons of snow, piles and feet and great drifts of it, enough to close the interstates and the grocery stores, enough to make everything clean and white and featureless and plain.

Denny lies on the kitchen floor. He has a fistful of wires and a socket wrench, his head inside the stove.

"Since when do you know about electrical things?" I ask.

"It's gas, anyway."

"Your specialty."

"Hedy wants to bake something, she says. She also wants to hang curtains, if you've got advice there."

There's coffee up on the hot plate, and the counters are wiped clean, a folded dishtowel by the sink. It's not seven in the morning.

"How's she feeling?" I ask.

He shrugs, slides himself back inside the oven. "What brings you out so bright and early?"

"I just felt like a drive, I guess."

"Well," he says. "Aren't you a daredevil. Have you recovered from your New Year's Eve?"

He's twisted around to see me through the space between his armpit and his chest. He has grease on the bridge of his nose. He is serious about what he's doing, which is fixing something, a whole new line of work for Den.

I reach into my coat pocket and toss him Lewis's pillbox.

"I could've taken these."

"You could've stuck your head in the oven."

"Right. Less mess."

"Less waste."

He slides out and sits up, wiping his fingers on a leaf of newspaper. He studies my face, and for a moment he seems what he should be: older, more tested of himself than me, someone to come to with all I've got. Then, he grins.

"You do look like hell," he says.

"Yeah. Thanks."

"I'm just saying, you'll want to think about a shower."

I drop my face into my hands, and we sit like that for I don't know how long.

Denny's fingers brush my shoulder, then squeeze. "Hey," he says.

"I'm fine."

"I know. I need you to move your car. I got to go to the hardware store."

"In this weather?"

"I'll put the chains on."

We walk out onto the porch, jingling keys.

In the far distance, Hedy is coming out of the woods. She swings her egg basket in one hand, and two hens in the other, their necks slack. She's weaving the headstones, her chin up, her hair loose under her hat and down the back of her jacket, and she's got breakfast in that basket, supper in her hand, and she's raised and killed it all herself. She is a resourceful woman. In this moment, I covet her very steps across the ground.

Denny steps off the porch to meet her. I catch the edge of his face, and something is changed in him, not just for a moment, but the whole time he watches her. I think that they will have this baby, and maybe somewhere down the line, they'll have another one, a son for Denny to raise how he sees fit to raise a boy. Maybe they'll buy a farm in the country where Hedy can keep her chickens, someplace that reminds Denny of the farm where he grew up, not the same, but likeness enough to make him happy, to straighten him out. I watch his face as she comes across that graveyard to him, carrying their food, carrying their child, and I know there's no need to tell him about Dianne Schelling leaving and her list of names. There has been Hedy to do that, to make it all beside the point.

They stand together in the yard, and Denny's hand goes up to the sky. She leans her head into his shoulder to see what he is talking about; the first snowflake, spinning through the trees to the ground.

Then it's like the sky splits open, a feather pillow, and the flakes are huge and clinging to each other, and Luther is running across the cemetery like he has seen a ghost, hellbent for the porch, for me. I crouch down, and I can feel the tack of new blood between my thighs, the beginning all again of it, that last thing snapping in my chest like the threads of a rope gone to fray. For once, it's not a bad feeling. It's like coming to decision, to rest. It's like coming when I'm called.

I put my face to Luther's muzzle. He licks at my ear, my throat. I think how much I love this dog, this true family of Marshall's. I go inside, take the phone from the table, and call him in New York.

He answers right away.

He has been worried about me, tried the house all hours, even got Gail to check on me, something he has never done before. But the day I left was so strange, and he felt so bad, so beside himself.

"I have been so worried," he says.

I have too.

I tell him I've most likely lost my job, and he says he doesn't care.

I tell him I'm not pregnant again, and he says he doesn't care.

He tells me to trust him, that he has a plan, that he is coming home. He saw his parents in Hartford and he's been making some calls. He's learned quite a bit about adopting babies. Maybe I would like to hear it sometime.

I tell him maybe so.

Denny comes back from the hardware store empty-handed, and Hedy sits with me at the kitchen table, plucking chickens, their speckled feathers dusting her lap, sifting to the floor. Denny bangs around inside the stove, cusses and spits and finally flips the gas, lights the pilot, and the burner flares up blue. It's soothing, the heat of it, the smell. Hedy fills a pot of water and puts it on to boil. Outside, the snow whitens everything, and Luther runs tracks through the stones.

Marshall and I stay on the phone all morning, while he showers and packs his things in his hotel room, while he takes a cab to the airport, checks in at the gate. His flight is delayed, and we stay on the phone until he finally boards the plane for Atlanta, where he will have to wait until the weather passes.

"I'll call you from Hartsfield," he says.

I tell him I'll be there when he lands.